THE LAST LAWYER BOOK

By

Steven A. Beckelman

ISBN: 1477452885
ISBN-13: 9781477452882

DEDICATION

This book is dedicated to my lovely wife Irene, who encouraged me to publish.

CHAPTER I.

Judge Harry Weiss would not have been Paul Sageman's first choice to hear any case. While most judges only reached the Probate bench somewhere between the onset of hemorrhoids and senility, Weiss was younger and meaner than the usual white haired, jowly specimen. You couldn't be sure you'd outlive him and he never forgot a mistake or a lie, so appearing before him was a professional hazard.

There was nothing more important than getting the right judge, which explained why assignment clerks lived so well. In this case, however, there was nothing a friendly clerk could do, even for a new Rolex. Robert Lufkin had died at his home in Claremont and Weiss was the only Probate Judge in Essex County.

The client, Theresa Stephens, had been Lufkin's mistress. She had been named as a major beneficiary of a prior version of Lufkin's will but did not appear in Lufkin's last will, which left his entire estate to his two children Fred and Anne.

Paul had been instructed by Joe Rose, the senior partner he worked for at Berry & French, to ask the Court for an order denying probate of the offending last will. Judge Weiss's reaction to the request would give Joe an early reading on how Weiss felt about the claim of an ex-girlfriend to a sixty million dollar estate. Then, if need be, work could begin on finding a way to disqualify him.

Weiss was known to have an eye, and possibly more, for talent. Well informed male law students didn't even bother to interview for judicial clerkships.

Frank Mairone, Lufkin's executor, had told Joe that Theresa Stephens, though in her forties, was worth a look, so Joe had told Terry to get on a plane and sent Paul scurrying to put together papers for the next day.

After filing the papers in chambers, Paul watched Weiss chop his way through the probate call in the courtroom.

By the time the Lufkin case was called, most of the motion day crowd had cleared out. Weiss asked for appearances. Paul squeaked that Berry and French was there for the plaintiff and Joe Rose was out in the hall.

"Tell Mr. Rose that some of the Court's business is actually conducted in the courtroom and before lunch, Mr. Sageman. And don't trip over his bag on the way out."

Out in the hall, Joe had cornered Lufkin's children, Fred and Anne, and their lawyer, Jay Ritzer and was holding forth on the one consuming subject of all his informal conversations - Joe Rose. Paul pulled him aside to tell him that the Judge was waiting.

"Are his pants down or up?" Joe asked. "I'll take another look around for Terry while you hold the fort." Fred Lufkin took the opportunity to subject Ritzer to a final whispering conference before going into the courtroom. Anne Lufkin, not knowing what to do, followed Paul, who hurried back into the courtroom.

The bench was empty. The court clerk told Paul that counsel would be seen in chambers. A few minutes later Joe Rose came into the courtroom with his arm around a fairly good looking blonde, who had to be Terry Stephens. She shook hands with Paul, seeming a bit nervous. Paul told Joe counsel would be seen in chambers, which Joe assured Terry was a good sign. Paul couldn't see why. Hadn't the whole idea been for Weiss to get a look at Terry?

Joe didn't want to leave Terry alone in the courtroom with the Lufkins, but at that moment Frank Mairone walked in with his lawyer, David Radin, a well known bankruptcy court fixer who had made Frank rich with receiverships and trustee appointments. A long court fight over the Lufkin estate would allow Frank to pay Radin back.

Joe brought Paul with him into chambers. The law clerk, Lisa LeMieux, tall, raven haired and very hot looking even for a Weiss law clerk, conducted the lawyers into the Judge's office, where Weiss was seated behind his desk.

"Thank you Miss LeMieux." Weiss motioned that the law clerk could stay and Lisa perched on a credenza to the right of Weiss's desk, making it difficult for Paul to take notes while he tried not to be caught staring at her exposed legs.

"Sit down gentlemen. I thought we could chat about this for a minute and perhaps give the court reporter a rest."

Weiss turned to Joe Rose. "Why do you need an emergency order Mr. Rose? From what I hear Mr. Lufkin is going to be dead a long time."

"You obviously never met Mr. Lufkin, Judge." Rose hadn't either, but Weiss didn't know that.

"But your client, I gather did have that pleasure Mr. Rose."

"For fourteen years, Judge."

"Well, what's the going rate, Mr. Rose, $250.00 a night? That could add up over fourteen years."

"I'm not that cheap Judge."

"Mr. Rose, I can remember when you were. But, knowing what little I do about Mr. Lufkin, I'm quite certain he didn't give it all to charity before he passed and I understand why you're here today."

The Judge turned to the children's lawyer.

"Mr. Ritzer, I don't imagine an estate like this could be distributed for quite some time anyway, at least if Mr. Radin has anything to say about it. Why shouldn't I enter Mr. Rose's order?"

Ritzer was prepared. He stroked his silver beard, which Paul thought must have been grown to conceal as much of an ugly face as possible or distract clients from his substantial nose, and began, rather formally for chambers.

"Your honor, Ms. Stephens, whatever her meretricious relationship with Mr. Lufkin may have been, had nothing to do with him for years before he died. Mr. Lufkin may have made provision for her in a prior will, but the will we seek to probate, made some eight months ago, makes no provision for her. She simply has no standing." Standing, the right to make a claim was, Paul knew, a problem.

"Standing, Mr. Ritzer, apparently had very little to do with Ms. Stephen's relationship with the decedent." Ritzer ignored the Judge's raillery and continued.

"Now under the laws of the state of New York where, as you know I also maintain an active estate practice before, among others, my dear friend Surrogate Lambert, there is a provision for a challenge by a pretermitted beneficiary, that is, someone who didn't make it into the last will, but not here. In fact Your Honor..."

Joe Rose interrupted Ritzer, which, Paul noticed, didn't seem to bother Weiss.

"If Mr. Ritzer would pause for a moment in his journeys between our fair state and that den of iniquity where he feels most at home, to read some law, he would know that there is no such thing as not having standing. The birds and the bees have standing, the trees have standing. You're not going to tell me someone who's been with a man for fourteen years, fourteen years Judge, doesn't have standing."

Ritzer refused to give up.

"Your honor, if everyone a rich man ever indulged himself with had the right to challenge a will we would need class action rules for the probate court. Mr. Rose knows better. Moreover your honor, under any state's laws you need a basis for a challenge. I don't know if Mr. Rose bothered to read the papers he signed, but they fail to allege any promise by Mr. Lufkin whatsoever not to alter his testamentary arrangements."

Paul began to worry about the papers he had drafted, which Joe Rose had indeed signed that morning without a glance, as Ritzer continued, adjusting his delivery to the setting,

"Mr. Lufkin was a very rich man, as Ms. Stephens undoubtedly knew. If Ms. Stephens didn't get it while the getting was good, she'll just have to look elsewhere."

"My, my, Mr. Ritzer, such oratory. Save it for when we go on the record, if you feel the need to oblige me to rule against you in front of your clients," said the Judge.

Even Ritzer knew better than to continue the fight. "I assume, Your Honor, that any order you enter would provide that it was not, in any fashion, a determination that there was any merit, any merit whatsoever to the claim Mr. Rose is trying to stake? Because, your honor, I am prepared to bring a motion to dismiss Miss Stephen's complaint at once, at once for failure to state a claim and I don't want to hear Mr. Rose taking the position that your entry of this order implied otherwise."

"Mr. Ritzer, I hardly think an argument of that ilk from Mr. Rose would persuade me and I'm sure Mr. Rose knows better, but if it will help you to convince your clients that you weren't manhandled in chambers, I will certainly add something to the order to protect your seat on the gravy train. Now gentlemen, if you hurry, you can each take your clients to lunch and explain your glorious victory." Weiss rose, signaling the end of the conference.

Joe Rose told Paul to wait for a signed order and left to find Terry. Terry was chatting with Frank Mairone. Fred and Anne sat in silence a few pews away. Fred was trying to overhear the conversation while appearing to examine the skylight in the ceiling of the courtroom. Joe, noticing Fred, motioned to Radin and they had a brief conference in the hall after which Radin came back and quickly collected Frank.

It had occurred to Joe Rose that the last thing he wanted was any appearance of a close friendship, or worse, between Frank and Terry. As the executor under both wills and a confidante of Lufkin, Mairone's value could be compromised by the charge that he had a particular interest in Terry. Once this was pointed out, Radin could be counted on to give Frank the appropriate advice about cold showers and how much more pleasant Terry's company would be after she won the case.

Paul was making unfortunate, and hopeless, comparisons between Lisa LeMieux and his wife while he waited in the anteroom of chambers for a conformed order. Marriage, he found, had only increased his interest in women he couldn't have. Lisa came out and handed him a copy of the signed order. She smiled momentarily and impersonally, reminding Paul he was only dreaming and he couldn't think of words clever enough to detain her before she went back into Weiss's inner office. Paul tried, unsuccessfully, not to imagine what Weiss did with her, or where.

When Paul got back to the Courtroom, he was surprised to find that Joe and Terry were still waiting for him. It struck Paul that Terry was quite attractive for her age and more refined than Paul had expected. Paul was even more surprised to be invited to lunch.

Still thinking of Weiss and Lisa, Paul wondered briefly if Joe Rose, all three hundred something pounds of him, would try anything with Terry.

Joe wanted Terry to have confidence in Paul, so that if she turned out to be an ear leech, like most female clients, Paul's blood could be drawn instead of Joe's.

Joe took them lunch at the Essex Club, where the bowing and scraping of the ancient waiters and the antique furniture, if not the food, could be counted on to impress a new client and, as an added bonus, Ritzer wasn't a member.

"You know, I don't think I've ever been here Mr. Rose, its quite nice." Terry said as Joe, brushing aside the waiter, pulled out her chair.

"Consider yourself fortunate, Ms. Stephens. Nothing but lawyers as far as the eye can see."

"Robert's lawyers were mostly in New York, I think. I remember going with Bob and Jeannine to see Mr. Weinberg on Madison Avenue, years ago, about a will."

"Jeannine?"

"Mrs. Lufkin."

"Whose will?" Paul asked.

"Don't answer that here," Joe said in his best attempt at a whisper, "Ritzer will be deposing all the help and we'll never get dessert. If you can come back to the office, I'll let Paul torture you until you confess."

Terry smiled at Paul "I'll be happy to tell you anything you want to know, but I don't remember business things so well. My sister Mary might remember."

Frank Mairone had his first lunch on the Estate with Radin, who deftly relayed the cold shower message and proceeded to consider how Frank could best take charge of Lufkin's properties. Rose had guessed correctly that Frank's interest in Terry was not entirely fiduciary, and Radin had to explain the substantial amounts Frank could expect to earn on corpus and income commissions twice before he had Frank's full attention.

Since a number of Lufkin's apartment projects were held in his individual name, Radin explained, there was a good argument that Frank would be the only person with the authority to run the business. Without a probated will, though, Frank was not yet the executor, a minor difficulty that Radin was confident he could overcome.

Frank had been unaware of the new will that cut Terry out until it was lodged after Lufkin's death. Lufkin had not mentioned it and they'd seen each other, Frank thought, at least three times over the last eight months. He had certainly been told about Lufkin's old will, even before it was written.

Frank first met Lufkin about five years before his death at a Republican function for some now convicted County politician. Lufkin, normally rather distant, had initiated the acquaintance after learning that Frank was on the City Council in Nutley, where Lufkin was trying to assemble a site and get zoning approval for a new strip shopping center.

After the approval for the center and a lot of insurance business from Lufkin Realty for Frank's brother Anthony both came through, Lufkin, impressed by Frank's success, had stayed in touch and actually become friendly in a way. He took Frank's advice on the art of strategic political contributions and, in turn, put Frank in a few development deals. There was no real socializing, but Frank hadn't expected it. After all, Lufkin lived in a mansion large even for Claremont, golfed at the Claremont Country Club and spent the summers on Shelter Island, and Frank was an Italian boy from Nutley.

Lufkin had called Frank at home one Saturday morning in July and asked him to come over. Frank was a bit surprised but didn't ask why. Frank assumed it was a further political favor that Lufkin didn't want to discuss on the telephone. Frank could still remember driving up the steep cobblestone driveway and seeing the huge cut stone Tudor style house. Lufkin had told him to park around back. The steep hill continued up beyond the house and turned into an almost sheer cliff running up to the ridge line of First Mountain after rising through several terraces formed by retaining walls. Around back was a circular driveway and entrance portico, where Lufkin was waiting for him. Frank had almost expected a footman.

Lufkin shook hands, and then put his index finger to his lips to indicate that Frank shouldn't say a word. Instead of inviting him in, Lufkin led Frank up the hill. When they'd passed a circular slate patio hidden among the trees and ascended two more levels, Lufkin stopped and turned to Frank, "Bugs" he whispered. Frank thought he meant the cicadas, which were deafening, echoing off the hill, until Robert explained: "You never know when Fred's listening in." Frank didn't know what to say.

Lufkin came to the point, looking down at his house while he spoke. "I was with my lawyer in the City yesterday about my estate. No one else knows that. Weinberg said I need an executor I can trust, who can stand up to Fred."

Robert's wife, Frank knew, was an institutionalized alcoholic, so he wasn't surprised that Lufkin didn't mention her. Frank didn't know why Lufkin would need an outsider to stand up to his son.

"I have a close friend who I want taken care of if something happens to me. How is your health?"

"Fine, I think."

"Good. After it's signed, Weinberg will send you a copy and I'll let you know where the original is. But you won't tell anyone else." Lufkin started walking down the hill. Frank followed him to his car, then drove away and didn't hear from Lufkin until after he got the will.

Frank didn't know whether he was supposed to open the envelope, but he did. He was named as executor and trustee and two-thirds of the estate was bequeathed to one Theresa Stephens. Terry was apparently a very close friend.

Frank first met Terry at Jeannine's funeral. She was introduced to him by Robert as an employee of Lufkin Realty. Watching the family, Frank got the feeling that Fred was more upset over Terry's presence than his mother's passing. Not that Lufkin was particularly broken up either. Fred spent most of the service whispering in Anne's ear and stealing glances at Terry. He undoubtedly knew about the relationship, if not the will.

Terry rode from the church to the cemetery in a limousine with Frank and Weinberg, while Lufkin rode with his children. There were only a dozen or so other mourners, which had surprised Frank. Frank remembered that Terry had seemed genuinely saddened about Jeannine and quite attractive. Frank assumed Lufkin would marry Terry and end Frank's role as protector but it hadn't happened.

Ritzer's lunch with Fred and Anne after court was hardly celebratory. Fred wouldn't accept Ritzer's optimistic generalities about what had gone on in chambers.

"What do you mean the Judge doesn't think she has a case? If she doesn't have a case, why isn't my father's will being probated?"

"You must understand, Mr. Lufkin, these things take time. The wheels of justice..."

Fred cut him off "How much time?"

"Well, I've already had my people begin a motion to dismiss her complaint, but I would counsel you to be ready for the possibility that the judge will want to give her some time to take discovery. Probably about four months."

"Will she get anything in the meantime?" Fred asked.

Ritzer was confident. "I think not. The new will cut Ms. Stephens off and there is a presumption that your father had capacity when he signed. No, Mr. Lufkin, I'm quite certain Ms. Stephens won't be in your pocket."

"Do I have to pay her fat lawyer's fees? I won't. My father was done with her and the new will is clear as day."

"For the time being, I don't certainly don't think you'll need to feed Joe Rose. The Radin firm may be another matter, however. An executor's counsel..."

Fred interrupted again. "I want Mairone out as an executor. He's already sniffing around Terry. How did she know to hire Berry & French if Mairone didn't tell her to?"

Ritzer stroked his beard and feigned concern. Getting rid of Mairone would be a major campaign in itself, and Radin, he knew, would fight like a drunk Indian for commissions on an estate the size of Lufkin's. There was nothing wrong with an unreasonable client, provided it was a rich and unreasonable client. “If you believe Mairone should be removed, we'll need to do some investigating.”

“Do it.” Actually, Ritzer thought Fred had stumbled on a good idea. A motion to remove the executor would be a good way to forestall Radin's inevitable move to have Mairone appointed as a temporary administrator of the Estate and sit him in Lufkin's office.

“Who will run the business in the meantime, Mr. Ritzer?” Anne asked.

“I'll run the business.” Fred answered for Ritzer, “or we'll have a new lawyer. My father wanted me to run Lufkin Realty when he was gone.” Anne doubted that, but didn’t say so. While he was alive, Lufkin had run everything.

After Combaf, Fred's commodities trading business had gone under, he'd come back to Lufkin for a job. Robert, after punishing Fred for six months, had made up some special projects for Fred to be in charge of, but hadn't loosened his grip until the day he died. In fact, Anne had signatory power on some Lufkin Realty accounts but Fred didn't. That was a condition Robert had insisted on but Anne was sure Fred would soon try to change. She suspected that Fred had already spoken to Ritzer about it. Anne didn't exactly miss her father, but Fred was like a new man since the funeral, full of plans and ideas, barking orders. She was worried about what he was up to. Still, for the moment she would have to sign Fred's payroll check, and as Fred could never hold onto money for more than a week, Anne thought that gave her some protection. She hadn't thought through what would happen if they did get rid of Mairone and for the moment it seemed like a good idea.

Fred hadn't actually squandered the money. He was a secret collector of Graeco Roman antiquities - mostly gold coins- and was well known at certain coin shops and galleries in the City back when Combaf was doing well. Even in his reduced circumstances at Lufkin Realty he continued to accumulate. The collection was kept in a series of safe deposit boxes.

CHAPTER II.

Paul had largely become inured to the subtle condescension of the Wasps who still dominated Berry & French. He imagined them sniggering, in their chinny conclaves, over the latest Joe Rose representation. Any client without the word Insurance in its name was of course suspect, but a jilted mistress would undoubtedly be seen as a new low.

Joe Rose had been, as he liked to say, the Jackie Robinson of Berry & French but only a trickle of Jewish blood had followed in the succeeding years, a situation that Rose secretly preferred. He had built a large practice on representing members of a segment of the local business community that he liked to refer to as the "morally challenged" but were more commonly known at the firm as scumbags. They were usually desperadoes who fleeced their partners and business associates. When the typical Joe Rose client got caught with wool in his teeth, Joe offered, along with his considerable skills, the unique combination of tolerance for the foibles of the unfortunate and the patina of respectability bestowed by the name of Berry & French.

Paul didn't think Terry fit the mold of the typical Joe Rose client and worried about whether to deliver The Speech or not. The Speech was usually delivered before any questions were asked of the client. Paul had heard Joe deliver it a few times.

"I am your attorney, and what you tell me is normally privileged and confidential. That confidentiality is sacred. More importantly, my license depends on my maintaining it. But I am also an officer of the Court. As a result, there are certain limits to the privileged and confidential nature of our communications. If you were tell me one set of facts and testify to a different set of facts, I could not continue to represent you. If you tell me that you are continuing or planning to continue an illegal course of conduct, I am obligated to disclose that fact and you still have to pay me. Now, understanding how the privilege protects us, tell me why your partners are calling you a three legged gonif."

The morally challenged client generally understood the message and the reasons for The Speech and was not offended. There were just certain things your lawyer shouldn't be told, and the client was glad the lawyer was smart enough to let him know it.

After lunch at the club Terry returned to Berry & French with Paul and Joe. Paul wasn't certain Terry would understand the Speech and he didn't want to offend her. On the other hand he could imagine that there were facts he wouldn't want to hear. Paul was also a bit unsure what questions to ask. Wills and personal relationships weren't his usual line, but he certainly couldn't ask any of the fossils from the Estates department to sit in on the meeting. Joe Rose had managed to excuse himself from the conference room right after lunch and Paul knew he wasn't coming back. Paul decided to give a polite version of The Speech and then let Terry give a narrative of everything in her relationship with Lufkin except wills and promises about wills.

Paul began the interview. "When did you meet Mr. Lufkin?" "I met Bob a year after my husband ran away, in 1973." Terry's ex husband John had been a detective with the Paterson Police Department. He was about twelve years older than her. Paul was surprised to hear that he ran away, but it seemed he couldn't handle the changes that came with the birth of their son, had taken to staying out late and eventually split entirely.

"I had to support Tommy, so I answered an advertisement at Lufkin Realty and became a bookkeeper. Bob hired me. He was very nice, and it was so sad about Jeannine. We needed each other." Paul was relieved by the delicacy, and it occurred to him that it was probably rehearsed. Paul wondered how the other people in the Lufkin office felt about the situation. The women, he thought, probably won't be very sympathetic witnesses. He made a note to ask about who in the office might know anything important.

"As time went on I became sort of a part of Bob's family. I handled some of his personal business. I went to the house and ran errands for him. When Fred and Anne weren't home I sometimes stayed for dinner. Jeannine would be home sometimes, but she normally stayed in her room. Actually we were friendly when we happened to meet. She knew I was from the office. I don't suppose she knew about Bob and me."

"What about Anne and Fred?"

"Well, Anne was always cold but polite. We had to work together in the office. She was too afraid of Bob to say anything."

"And Fred?"

"Well at first Fred was a little too friendly, if you know what I mean. Once he figured out how Bob and I felt about each other, he almost never talked to me again. I knew from other girls in the office that he was furious and called me the usual names you'd expect in the circumstances."

"Fred was also jealous that Bob talked to me about his business and his other investments."

"How do you know that?"

"Oh, from things Doris said."

"Doris?"

"Bob's secretary, Doris Ryan. She knew everything that went on in that office. I heard she was fired right after the funeral and they wouldn't even let her come back to clear out her desk."

"Did Mr. Lufkin confide in Doris? About things like wills?"

"Not wills, I think, but about his children and Jeannine generally."

"Do you know how to get in touch with her?" "Oh yes, I'm sure I could find out. I spoke to her every few weeks from Florida, but always at the office." Paul underscored her name in his notes.

"Now, why did you leave New Jersey and Lufkin Realty?" Paul was glad he had given the Speech before he asked that question. Nice as Terry seemed, he didn't think he'd get a truthful answer to that question.

"Well, my son Tommy was having problems down where he lived in St. Petersburg, and I thought I should be with him. I didn't want to leave Bob, but Bob said that it would work out fine, he wanted to look into buying buildings in Florida and that he would come down to see me."

Paul didn't buy it. If Lufkin really wanted Terry, he wouldn't have let her move away. Of course it would be easy to prove if he did come to see her.

"Bob bought us two condominiums in the same building in Clearwater Beach, right on the Gulf of Mexico. He didn't think it would look right if he just stayed with me when he came down."

"Whose name were the condos in?"

"Mine is owned by a corporation, I think. The other one is, or was, I should say, in Bob's name." "Do you own the stock in the corporation?"

"I really don't know."

"Do you pay rent or taxes or anything?"

"No, not up to now. But I think Doris wrote the checks, so I'm worried if that will change."

"And did Mr. Lufkin come to see you?"

"Oh yes, but not in the last ten months or so." Hadn't she heard the Speech? Paul began to wonder if Ritzer was right.

Ritzer fidgeted in the dingy waiting room of Mel Weinberg's office, which occupied a small part of a low floor in an older building on Madison Avenue. He wondered how Lufkin had ever found his way there. It wasn't Ritzer's normal practice to conduct a witness interview without an associate or two to take notes, but in this case, he felt it might be easier to forget anything unpleasant without assistance. He knew Weinberg in passing and hadn't elaborated on the purpose of his visit, expecting that Mel would understand.

Weinberg came out himself to bring Ritzer in. "Sorry to keep you waiting Jay, it was just a busier morning than I had planned. You're here about Bob Lufkin, I presume."

"Yes, I've got the children. Not that I know how I'll fit another case into my schedule."

"Bob was a good client over the years; I did a lot of his tax planning. He liked the idea that no one in Jersey knew all his business."

"You drew wills for him as well?"

"Oh yes." "Has anyone been here to talk to you about his testamentary intent?"

"No...No." Weinberg didn't think it was necessary to tell Ritzer that his own client Fred Lufkin had been there days before, or that Weinberg was now on retainer with Lufkin Realty for $200,000.00 a year, ten times what the senior Lufkin had ever paid him in any year.

"How did you meet Lufkin?"

"Oh, I knew his family from the old neighborhood... only the name was Plotkin." This was news to Ritzer, who knew Lufkin had been a member of a restricted club and went to church. Weinberg enjoyed Ritzer's surprise. "Oh yes, Bob was a marrano. Not too many people knew that. He had a good shtick and the looks to get away with it. His parents were on Seventh Avenue. Very successful. They died in a fire when he was in college. I handled the estate. He came into a bundle and decided to be a Goy."

"Fascinating."

"Oh, it happened a lot in the old days. I think you could get away with it easier back then, since once you made the switch, your new friends from Princeton weren't likely to show up at too many bar mitzvahs and hear loose talk about how well you did in Hebrew school." Ritzer didn't think Fred would appreciate Weinberg's publishing his family history. Nothing worse for your reputation at the Club than a skeleton in the closet with a big nose. Ritzer wasn't about to mention that to Fred.

"Anyway, I did wills for Bob and Jeannine over the years. She left him everything she had, so that was simple. Bob changed his will after she died. I assume you've seen both wills."

"Yes, of course. Are there any notes or drafts?"

"Not anymore. Its my practice to destroy all notes and drafts once the instrument is executed."

Ritzer was happy to hear it. "Were there letters to the client during the planning stage for either will?"

"No. Bob didn't like letters about things like that. He would come here and we would talk about it. I knew his situation pretty well anyway, since I did his tax work, so there wasn't much to explain."

"What about letters transmitting the final document?"

"No. He always came here for the signing. Took a copy with him."

"I suppose he was in pretty good shape when he made the last will?"

"Oh yes, sharp as a tack. I remember discussing some other estate questions with him that day. He was thinking about trusts for the children but decided against it. Didn't know who he'd want for a trustee. He thought I was too old and I'd never outlive him. I guess I had the last laugh on that one."

"Was there much discussion before he made the last will?"

"No, he just told me to take Terry Stephens out. Didn't say why. I assumed they'd grown apart, with her moving to Florida."

"You knew about the relationship?"

"It wasn't hard to guess. Good looking woman, bedridden wife, rich man." Weinberg and Fred had agreed that this was the best way to deal with how the new will cutting Terry out came about.

"Did you ever meet Terry Stephens?"

"Once or twice. I remember she was at Jeannine's funeral." "Did you have occasion to speak with her about Bob Lufkin's business or investments on the phone?"

"I can't remember doing that, no."

Ritzer wondered what else to ask. "Mel, you'll call me if Terry's lawyers try to talk with you."

"Oh, yes. Nothing wrong with that new will. I feel sorry for Terry, but she should have got Bob to marry her like she wanted."

"Did she tell you that she wanted to marry him?"

"Not in so many words, no. But I'm sure she did." Weinberg got up. "If there's anything else I can do, let me know." They shook hands. Ritzer had heard everything he came to hear, but something told him it was too good to be true.

CHAPTER III.

Paul was disheartened by his interview with Terry, but Joe Rose heard his dire report without any apparent concern. “I think you're just overcome with the shock of finally meeting an honest client, Paul. They're quite rare, you know, which is fortunate, as honesty can be so inconvenient.”

Paul was used to Joe's refusal to take anything seriously but he really wanted some guidance. “So what kind of case do we have if Terry doesn't know anything?”

“A forty million dollar case with that little bearded monkey Jay Ritzer on the other side. Most lawyers would give their left nut to be where we are now. By the way, I hope you had Terry sign the retainer agreement.” That Paul had done. Thirty percent of the first million, fifteen percent of the next nine million and ten percent of everything beyond that. He wondered if fees like that were legal and whether the firm knew about it.

“Even a bearded monkey can win if we don't have any facts. Terry just isn't any help.” Paul persisted.

“Don't you understand? This case will never be won based on what Terry knows.” Paul was beginning to understand why Joe let him interview Terry alone. “The real question,” Joe continued, “is what the selfless and devoted Lufkin children managed to do behind her back to get dear old Dad to change his will, if he really did. Since they're not about to tell, we have our work cut out for us. You'll have to learn all about the Lufkins. Let a thousand subpoenas issue, let a million questions be asked. But let me see the subpoenas before you serve them." As usual, Joe Rose had put things in a better light but left Paul to do the work.

Still, as Paul walked back to his office he wondered what he could hope to prove, even from the Lufkins. He'd now read enough probate law to know that challenging a will wasn't so easy, especially since many of the standard grounds for a challenge didn't seem to apply. Not undue influence, as Lufkin hardly sounded like a feeble minded victim of coercion. Not a promise by Lufkin not to alter the will that included Terry, as Terry didn't even claim that had happened. Terry, in fact, was no help at all.

Paul decided to ask what his friend and office neighbor Mike Miller thought. Mike was an ex-assistant U.S. Attorney who handled the Joe Rose clients whose antics came to the attention of prosecutors and grand juries. Paul told Mike the story.

"So wait a minute, you're telling me the old broad, Terry went to Florida and the old goat cut her out of the will?" Mike asked. "Why the hell didn't she make sure he died in the saddle before she left?"

"Obviously because she didn't have the benefit of Joe Rose's advice and counsel at the time." Paul's outward respect for Joe ended as soon as he was out of earshot.

"How much money did you say?" Mike asked.

"Sixty million." That figure clearly registered, but Mike continued to yuck it up.

"Well, I'm surprised there weren't broads lined up around the block with make-your-own-will kits, just waiting for Terry to get out of the way."

"I suppose that's one of the things I should ask about. Should `Broads' be a defined term in my subpoenas?"

Mike's limited knowledge of the case didn't deter him from offering an opinion. "I'm sure there's a good enough case out there to scare up a settlement. The kids must have known about the will and done something to get the will changed. Lets get my secretary in here and we'll start drafting subpoenas. Do you know who to go after?"

"Well, there's the office manager, ex office manager, Doris Ryan. She was fired after Lufkin died."

"Well then we certainly don't want to waste our time subpoenaing her."

"Don't you think she'd know a lot?"

Mike shook his head slowly and threw up his hands. "How long have you been working for Joe Rose, Paul? If we don't have to tell the other side we're talking to her, why should we? In fact, if your client had any brains, I'd wire her and let her talk to the old bat instead of us. If she knows anything, the kids made a major mistake letting her go."

"But how do we know what to ask about? I'm not even sure what our cause of action would be. You know the standard for competency to make a will, don't you?"

"Sure. If the testator knows whether or not Captain Kangaroo had a tail, the will's bulletproof."

"And undue influence isn't very promising either."

"I assume there were not scars from a hot poker on the body of the late Mr. Moneybags?"

"None that I know of."

"So then it's just like any other litigation. The better liars will win. Stop worrying about the law and lets think about what questions you should be asking. Now what was the name of the old bat who worked for the Stiff?"

Terry's one useful lead, Doris Ryan, was no longer unemployed. Fred knew better than to leave such a dangerous witness out of his control. Since Doris knew more about Lufkin Realty than anyone, her loyalty to him would be also be invaluable in getting rid of Anne later. At her age there was little chance of her running out and getting another job, so Fred felt the benefits of temporarily interrupting her employment outweighed the risk.

Fred had managed to convince Anne to sign the letter by which they gave Doris notice right after the funeral. "We need new blood Anne. I'm not sure Doris is up to the way we need to do business now. Besides, I'm not sure she wasn't a little too friendly with Terry." Fred knew how Anne felt about Terry. After a little more convincing, Anne had signed the letter.

After rifling her office and letting her sit home alone with her cats for a few weeks, Fred called Doris at home. "Doris? Fred Lufkin here. I want you to know I was dead set against what Anne did. You were so valuable to my father. I thought it was very wrong. I hope you haven't taken another position?"

"No Mr. Lufkin, I haven't. I'm still getting over Mr. Lufkin." Doris had been shocked to be fired, since she had practically run the office for eighteen years. Doris had never felt Anne was particularly hostile to her, but she knew how women could be, and she was prepared to believe Fred.

"Yes, and I shouldn't have let her do such a thing. So now I've let her know that I'm insisting that you come back, no matter what she says. Would you?"

"Well Mr. Lufkin..."

"Call me Fred."

"Of course, Mr. Lufkin. But will it be alright with Anne?"

"Don't even bring it up with her, and I'm sure she'll act as if it never happened. Between you and me I think she's a little embarrassed."

"Oh Mr. Lufkin, it will be so nice to get back to work." "Come in tomorrow if you can."

Fred told Anne that he'd hired Doris back on a temporary basis to help clean things up. Anne, at that time very involved in a refinancing of one of the shopping centers, had been letting Fred handle day to day things at the office, so she didn't question Fred's decision. Fred told Doris that Anne was too busy and Doris should come to him when anything came up that needed the family's attention, which was fine with Doris.

When Paul called Doris Ryan's home, she refused to meet with him and told him she was still working at Lufkin Realty, leaving Paul to believe that Terry hadn't even gotten the story straight. Now she'd have to be subpoenaed, and it didn't sound very promising.

CHAPTER IV.

Paul was still worrying about Terry's case when he got home, but he knew better than to mention the facts of the case to his wife, Sandy, who would be sure to disapprove of someone in Terry's position. Worse yet, she'd want to talk about the case, giving Paul her unsolicited opinions, based on ten years as a parochial school teacher, about how the rich lived and other subjects on which her ignorance was apparently no impediment.

Paul had learned that one did not converse with Sandy, one endured. Any trivial incident was related in real time-it took as long to recount as it had to occur. Even the most minute details of a conversation were regurgitated verbatim for the edification of the victim. Rank speculation was conducted along similar lines that elevated thinking out loud to the status of a public nuisance.

Paul preferred to dream of explaining the case to Lisa LeMieux after a night of passionate disloyalty to Judge Weiss. Sandy was, in any event, not likely to lack for a subject for the evening's conversation.

"I think we're going to have trouble with the carpet people Paul. I called them and the woman who answers the phone, she said she doesn't know when they can install the new carpet and I said well we had an appointment, and I was thinking I know what's happening, Christmas is coming and everybody wants their new carpet and I wanted to say to her how we had relatives coming and we really needed the carpet but I thought everyone's probably telling her the same thing so I decided I wouldn't say that and I was about to say to her that we'd only bought the carpet there because we were promised by the salesman that we'd have the carpet by November first and here it is after election day but then I thought she'd start only in again about Eddy the salesman being fired like the last time I called, when she said she'd check with a different installing company, so then I realized they'd lied to us again because Eddy told us they only used their own installers and I was going to say that, but I didn't want to hear her going on about Eddy again I just want my carpet. I knew my mother was right and we should have gone to Churchills. They've had new carpet from Churchills five times in that house in seventeen years and they've never had a problem."

Paul believed Sandy belonged to an alien species that could inhale through its ears, sent to Earth with the mission of making him miserable. The mention of his mother-in-law, undoubtedly the leader of the pod, caused hatred to begin to replace ennui within him as he drowned in the avalanche of words. Paul had never understood the wisdom of misogyny until he got to know his mother-in-law. Sandy, of course, seemed more like her every day.

The carpet story was reaching its denouement. "So I said to her that I really thought I'd like to speak to the manager because if something wasn't arranged soon I could still go somewhere else. So she put me on hold, for a minute she said only it was a lot longer and when the manager came on I just told him I didn't want to hear about Eddy and how disappointed I was with the service but I knew they would be sure to take care of us and I mentioned that my husband's a lawyer. I said to him, I said couldn't believe they didn't have their own installers and I said to him that I wanted a firm date, because I'd have to stay home from my job at St. Phillips to watch them and I needed to tell Sister Francine ahead of time and he said to me, he said, they could come on Saturday afternoon and I thought that would be better since I'd like you to be here anyway when they come, Paul, you'll be here won't you?"

"When?"

"Saturday, weren't you listening? This is important. Don't you want the house to look nice for the holidays?"

Paul, nauseated by the thought of the Christmas tree astride the hideous new carpet, toyed with giving a truthful answer, but decided for getting dinner at a decent hour instead. He hoped it wouldn't have marshmallows or creamed onions in it for a change.

"Of course I'll be there dear." He was well trained.

Frank Mairone was considering whether to mention the case to his wife. Was it better to mention the case casually without going into the details or not at all? Frank thought it was better to bring up the case in a general way, if only because it would ease his mind. Terry was constantly in Frank's thoughts. Angela had met Lufkin once, but Frank hadn't explained the nature of their relationship or mentioned that he was the executor. She had never met Terry. Frank usually told Angela a little bit about what he did every day and it would be suspicious not to say anything about Lufkin's estate.

"Do you remember Bob Lufkin, Angie?"

"From up in Claremont, the tall man?" "That's right. He died the other day. It turns out I'm his executor. I had to go to court today." Angie didn't ask any questions. She was too busy with their daughter Tina's impending wedding, which would have a cast of hundreds. In Frank's position there were a lot of people that had to be invited. Radin had joked that the Lufkin commissions might just cover the cost.

Frank was more concerned with Radin's serious advice about Terry and cold showers. He already knew he couldn't stay away from her. Did Terry want him? He thought so. The only question was how to get together. Certainly it couldn't happen before the wedding. Fortunately he had business interests in Florida. If he went shortly after the newlyweds came home, Angela would probably stay in Jersey. He could call up, saying he was in Clearwater on business, invite Terry to dinner and let her know how he felt about her. Amore.

Fred had already decided he couldn't count on Ritzer to get rid of Frank Mairone on his own. He wanted to have Mairone followed, to bug his car phone and turn someone in his office. Fred needed money to do that and he didn't want to write a company check. Should Anne be in on it? She was a bit of a goody two shoes, and Fred didn't want her deciding what the investigators did. Better to keep her in the dark.

His father's death had been the greatest moment of Fred's life. Fred had expected the penury and abuse to go on for years, possibly decades more. But rapture is fleeting. Now he was furious that he still had to worry about where to put his hands on a few thousand dollars. He couldn't very well go to Mairone for the money. Anne knew better than to give him a loan, even if they were now millionaires. He'd searched his father's house, where he was now living, for any hidden cash or pawnable items that wouldn't be missed, to no avail. He didn't want to sell any coins, the market wasn't good.

Finally, he decided to create a vendor of convenience for one of the properties and have Doris get Anne to sign the check. He'd done this before, on a small scale. Fred was an expert on the computer and could even set up a past history for the vendor. He'd print the invoice and stationery on his home computer. Leaving the house, he drove to a restaurant and used the public phone to call Jack Butler.

“Sorry to hear about your Dad, Fred.” Jack knew better than to think Fred was in deep mourning. Fred had even beat around the bush with Jack about finding someone capable of giving nature a little push a few times, but jobs like that weren't done cheap or on credit, if they were ever done for guys as squirrelly as Fred Lufkin, so Jack had always pretended not to understand.

“Thank you Jack, it was quite a shock.” When Fred didn't go on at once Jack began to wonder if Anne Lufkin should be starting her own car. A job he definitely wouldn't do.

“What can I do for you Fred?”

“There's a gentleman named Frank Mairone we need to get to know a bit better. He's my father's executor. We need to know everything he says and does for the next few months, especially relating to Terry Stephens.”

“She's in Florida, right?”

“Yes, Clearwater. My guess is he'll be in touch with her. Anne and I want him out.”

"So who is retaining me?"

"Your client is Omega Corporation."

"I don't think I know that company, Fred."

"Will $15,000.00 up front get us started?"

"Does this include interception?" "Car and office."

"Not his home?"

"In the circumstances, I don't think that will be necessary, Jack." While it wouldn't be nearly as much fun as the last assignment from Fred, which Jack would have done for free, Jack saw great future possibilities in the Lufkin account and told Fred he'd go ahead as soon as he got the check. Fred gave him the details.

CHAPTER V.

Tommy Stephens awoke slowly to the pain and nausea of that most grievous of self inflicted wounds - a tequila hangover. It wasn't his first, but he felt a rolling nausea he'd never had before and a dampness. After a minute he realized he was on a boat. Then he remembered that Al DeLucia's brother Joe had a sailboat and they'd talked about going on it last night. Finally the need to empty his churning stomach overcame the fear of the increased pain that he knew would come from sitting up and he made his way on deck. Al's brother Joe and his wife, Pam looked disgustingly well but politely ignored his condition. He knew Al wouldn't be so polite but didn't really care.

"You want a beer, Tommy?" Al called out cheerily. The thought of it prompted a second heave ho, after which Tommy sat zombie like nursing the pain. Joe, probably more out of concern for his topsides than Tommy's well being, offered him a bucket. After a while the sun came out and the breeze over Tampa Bay freshened and Tommy began to feel a bit better. As brain function returned, he tried to remember the night before. Today was Sunday. Tommy concentrated on where he might have left his car, his wallet and his contact lenses. He knew Al wouldn't let on for hours.

The wallet was of particular concern, because hidden in it were five hundred dollar bills he'd liberated from his Aunt Mary the day before. She had come down to visit her sister, Terry. While the sisters were out by the pool, Tommy decided to look through her bag. Flipping through her address book he noticed among listings of various other males, an entry for

Frederick Lufkin, with a beeper number and a home number, as well as an entry for Robert Lufkin.

The listing for Fred seemed vaguely odd to Tommy, as his Aunt denounced Fred as a creep whenever his name came up and he couldn't recall her ever mentioning having anything to do with him aside from bumping into him on occasional visits to the Lufkin office.

Mary worked in a bank a few miles from Lufkin Realty and she used to come to the office for lunch or at the end of the day to see her sister before the move to Florida.

The discovery of 45 crisp hundred dollar bills hidden in a makeup case erased the little black book from his mind. He couldn't imagine his Aunt having walking around money like that. Nor did she seem to be one of those crazy people who carry their life savings with them. Most likely, he thought, she'd made an unauthorized withdrawal from her employer to pay for her vacation. Tommy decided to borrow $500 of the ill gotten gains, figuring that Mary wasn't likely to count the loot every day.

Tommy knew, of course, about his mother and Robert Lufkin. The relationship was one of the reasons he'd run off to St. Petersburg at age 17. He didn't know that his mother had ever been in Lufkin's will or even that she'd hired a lawyer. Her trip to Jersey, he imagined, had something to do with burying Lufkin. Terry had decided that Tommy had little enough motivation in life without factoring in the possibility of her becoming a real estate heiress. She also wasn't too hopeful about her case, for reasons that she didn't admit to Paul Sageman during their interview, but which she shared with her sister.

"I miss Bob so, Mary. The last ten months I kept hoping we'd get back together, but now..."

"I know, Terry. I knew you were apart, but why?"

"That's just it. Bob somehow thought I was unfaithful to him. It just wasn't true and I told him so, but he was like stone, Mary, like stone. He said he'd seen me. But I can't imagine what he meant by that and he never spoke to me again so I never found out."

"He'd seen you? What could he have seen? You loved Bob." "I did. I never looked at another man. And I didn't mind him not marrying me after Jeannine died. I always thought it was because of Tommy. But I'll never know what made him say something like that, Mary, I'll never know..."

At that point Tommy had come to say goodbye to his mother and Aunt with the money hidden in his wallet on his way out for the weekend, interrupting the conversation. Mary was very interested in knowing whether Terry had confided in anyone else, but didn't want to ask the question. "Where are you going, honey?" Terry asked.

"Out with Al. I'll be late. Bye."

"Mary, I haven't told Tommy anything about the case, so please don't mention it when he's around."

"Certainly, dear. I understand." Mary waited for Terry to continue.

"He's a good boy, but I don't want him thinking I'm going to be rich."

"Are you?"

"Well, we just don't know yet. Of course you know about the two wills, Mary. I just don't know whether he made the second one after he told me about, you know, seeing me. But Mr. Rose says..."

From the terrace of a rented condo in Terry's building, Jack Butler watched the sisters through a small pair of binoculars. He'd never seen Terry before and was studying the physical resemblance between the sisters. Terry wore her hair shorter and was, Jack thought, slightly heavier, but still not bad. Otherwise, he thought the sisters could have been twins, though Mary was three years younger.

His new mole in Frank's office had told him that Mairone was flying into Tampa that evening. Fred and Jack had agreed that a stakeout at the condo was worthwhile. He'd already set a recording tap on Terry's phone. Jack imagined that Mary's presence would be something of a complication for Frank. He guessed that Frank hadn't told Terry about the trip and was planning to be spontaneous. Three would definitely be a crowd if Fred was right about the old guinea. Not that a blonde sandwich would be bad, but Jack didn't think Terry was the type.

Frank called in the late afternoon while the sisters were fixing dinner. Terry took the call in the kitchen where Mary was making a salad, but went into the bedroom after hearing that it was Frank on the line. He decided to take advantage of his fiduciary capacity. "I was in Tampa on business and I thought it might be a good idea if we had the chance to chat about Lufkin Realty, Terry. You know the business and I have to decide what to do to protect the estate."

“Shouldn't Mr. Rose be deciding about that, Mr. Mairone?” “Frank.”

“Frank”

“Lawyers aren't businessmen, Terry, I'm sure Bob told you that. They don't understand how things like this affect the people. I don't want to hurt the Lufkins, but I've got to protect everyone involved. When could we get together?”

“Would lunch tomorrow be good? My sister Mary is here for the week.”

“I think we should speak privately, Terry. Could you possibly come to the Marriott for lunch?” Terry didn't think Mary would mind. “I'll be there at 12:30. Where should we meet?”

“The Palm Room. See you then. Goodbye.”

Frank felt like a teenager again when he hung up the phone and began to rehearse what he'd talk to Terry about at lunch. Was it good to talk about Lufkin or not? Could Terry have a new man already? Should he try to smoke that out of her? Frank decided to get her to talk about herself as much as possible.

Jack called Fred to report. “You see, Jack, I knew the old goat couldn't keep away from her. I knew it. Be sure you get plenty of pictures. Do you think you can bug his hotel room or dish them at lunch? If he talks like he's favoring that bimbo too much we might be able to get him out without even using the pictures.”

“Dishing indoors is tough. I'll have to work on the maitre d' at the restaurant so they're steered to a bugged table. You get better quality that way anyway”

“Good, try that. Bug the room too. I'll bet he cons her into going up there.”

"One of your gentlemen callers, Terry?" Mary asked when Terry came back to the kitchen. "Does he have a friend for me?" "No, no, Mary, you know I'm not seeing anyone. It was Mr. Mairone, Bob's trustee. He wants to have lunch to talk about the estate. You don't mind being on your own for an afternoon do you dear?"

"Oh no, honey, of course not. You go right ahead." Terry missed having a man and thought about her lunch date for the rest of the evening.

CHAPTER VI.

"The Riviera, the fucking French Riviera, Radin, that's what we're talking about your stupid dick for brains Guinea client costing me. If I have to spend next August in Point Pleasant I'll never forgive you." Paul could hear Joe Rose bellowing from five offices away and scampered in. "Guess who just called me?" Rose continued to roar into the telephone, "Jay Ritzer, that's who. And he wasn't calling to say hello." Radin knew Rose too well to bother interrupting.

"Do you know where your client and my dumb bitch of a client were last Sunday afternoon? No? Well Jay Ritzer knows all about it. Evidently they had the Spanish fly omelet at lunch at the Clearwater Marriott Palm Court and spent the rest of the afternoon working it off in Frank's hotel room. He's got it on tape, he says. On tape." Joe Rose actually stopped to listen to Radin for three seconds. "Legal? Who cares if its legal? You think Weiss will be able to forget what it is we're trying to exclude when he decides whether to nominate Frank for worst fiduciary of the year? Horny Harry'll probably listen to the tape ten times. Didn't you tell Frank to stay away from her?" Radin confirmed giving the advice. "The only good advice you ever gave and your client doesn't even listen. I ought to send the tapes to his goddamn wife."

Ritzer had been a bit squeamish about using the tapes but Fred insisted. "What kind of fiduciary can that man Mairone be. He can't possibly be watching out for my interests.... or Anne's."

"But the legalities Mr. Lufkin, the legalities. Eavesdropping, taping a man and a woman in a hotel room. I'm not sure they're admissible in evidence... "

"Look, Jay, it won't ever get that far. All we have to do is tell Rose and Radin about the tapes, maybe let them have a listen and give Mairone the chance to fall on his sword quietly. They'd have to be mad to fight that in court. And of course it just proves what kind of slut Terry Stephens is. Then I'll be substitute fiduciary and your firm, I might mention, will be counsel to the estate."

"Well, perhaps if it could be approached delicately, as you suggest, very discreetly. They are remarkable tapes, simply remarkable tapes." Counsel to the estate, Ritzer knew, was an annuity, even with Fred Lufkin paying the bills. He wasn't averse to a little blackmail in a good cause after all.

Radin was very concerned that Frank would throw in the towel when he heard about the tapes. Few men of Frank's generation had antenuptial agreements and he'd be bled dry in a divorce. He decided to tell Frank that any chance Terry had would be gone if Frank resigned and that they'd see about prosecuting Fred Lufkin and Ritzer for eavesdropping, even though Radin knew there wasn't a prayer of any prosecutor touching the case.

Joe Rose, after happily destroying Radin's hearing, turned to Paul. "Well its a little late for damage control, Paul, and I'm not saying I'm blaming you, but you've got to stop assuming our lovely client knows which way is up, though apparently she knows which way is down, from what Ritzer told me. Could be the most expensive blow job in history. You'll just have to go down there to Clearwater and read her the riot act right away. Might want to bring a chastity belt with you. Of course I'm sure you'll miss your lovely wife." Paul knew better than to argue, and he wasn't sure he wanted to, particularly since his in-laws were undoubtedly coming to lunch and dinner to see the new carpet that Sunday.

CHAPTER VII.

After a tearful goodbye from Sandy, who was too upset to drive him the five miles to the airport, Paul immediately removed and stowed his wedding ring and took the morning flight to Tampa. A little sun would soon remove all traces of slavery.

Mary had left the day before and Terry and Tommy met Paul at the airport. Joe Rose had called Terry and while he was relatively diplomatic about it, she knew she'd done something awfully wrong, so she didn't question the need for Paul to visit with her, even though she knew this would make it impossible to keep things from Tommy.

Terry sent Tommy out to the store when they got to the condo. She explained to Paul that she didn't want Tommy knowing any more than he had to about the case, or the money involved, or Paul thought, Frank Mairone. Terry was embarrassed that Paul knew about Frank, but she was more worried than shy and asked for a damage assessment. Joe had told Paul not to get Terry too discouraged, but to make her understand that her conduct was important.

Paul liked Terry and he was fairly comfortable telling her what he thought. "Well, we're hoping it won't be a big problem for Frank, but there's no saying what Fred will try to do. Of course, Frank's a pretty important witness in addition to being the named executor. It wouldn't be good if he got removed. You just have to remember that as long as this case goes on you're probably being watched and listened to."

Tommy offered to show Paul around town after dinner. After a game of eight ball and a pitcher of

Budweiser at a dive in St Petersburg, they went for a drive by the beach while Tommy administered some Colombian truth serum and then checked out a topless joint called Spanky's where Tommy was a regular. Paul, who hadn't seen a decent unclothed female body in years, was having a good time and Tommy waited for him to have a few more beers and a table dance before bringing up why Paul had come down there.

"So my mother's a witness or something in a case of yours?" Paul didn't want to ignore Terry's request, but he was feeling very friendly and a bit talkative, so he decided he could confide in Tommy, who certainly had to have the same interest as Terry in winning the case.

"Your mother, Mr. Stephens, is a little bit more than a witness. Actually, she's kind of an heiress."

"An heiress?"

"If we're lucky, Tommy quite a bit of one." Paul was distracted by a tall blonde who couldn't possibly be of the same species as his wife. "An heiress." Tommy said to himself softly. It had to be Lufkin, Tommy knew, but how much was involved? He didn't know if the lawyer would tell him that. "How about some body shots with Dawn here, Paul?" The blonde came over, attracted by one of Mary's hundred dollar bills that Tommy flashed, and put salt on her left breast for Paul to lick off before a shot of tequila.

"Bottoms up, honey. Can I get you another shot?" Dawn hovered around for the C note.

"Only if I can try the right one." "Anything you want. But Dawn's getting a little thirsty, too Tommy." Tommy ordered a round.

"Forty million dollars?" Tommy asked Paul again. He'd managed to drag Paul away from Dawn before he passed out and extracted some particulars on the drive to Paul's hotel.

"More or less, Tommy, if we win."

"And why shouldn't we win?" "Unfortunately, Mr. Lufkin apparently made another will, without your mother in it. Of course it might be a forgery or something like that."

"What about palimony? She lived for that old bastard." "But she didn't live with that old bastard, which our state seems to require for a claim like that. I'm afraid we need to beat the new will." Paul didn't add that so far they weren't doing a very good job of that.

"What does my mother say about the wills?" Answering that question, Paul knew, might be going too far, particularly as he didn't ever want to know the answer to that question himself.

"Why didn't she ever tell me about this? Its incredible. Forty million dollars. That must be what she was whispering to Aunt Mary about." Tommy remembered the address book, but decided not to mention it to Paul just yet. Before he could ask another question, Paul was snoring. Some lawyer. Forty million dollars. He hoped this Joe Rose guy was some hot shit.

CHAPTER VIII.

Paul reported back to Joe Rose on his trip to Florida, raised the forgery angle and suggested that they consider a document expert. "Experts, Paul, are the most expensive and least satisfying form of prostitute known to man. They know what you want, they shake it pretty good, but in the end they give you nothing but a large bill and a larger pain in the ass."

"But what else have we got?"

"You're right, we can't ignore the possibility that the new will is a forgery. Its been done for a lot less by people a lot straighter than that crook Mel Weinberg. Mel's probably got more hot stoves than a French restaurant. I know Frank Mairone thinks it must be a fake, but then he's a lick or two less than objective, isn't he? See if Mike Miller knows a handwriting expert - one who hasn't done any time - that we can talk to."

Paul went to speak to Mike "Wait a minute, you want an expert to say that the stiff never signed the will cutting out the bimbo? Weren't there any witnesses? Or were they all in on it?"

Paul thought about that. There were two witnesses, Weinberg's secretary and an accountant who worked in the next office. "They could have been. We just don't know."

"You don't know, Mr. Sageman?" Mike pushed his glasses down his nose and attempted to imitate Judge Weiss, "You would malign the integrity of these subscribing witnesses on mere speculation? Not in my Court."

"Well, maybe Weinberg monkeyed around with the document after they signed it."

"So, counsel, now you've abandoned forgery and retreated to monkeyshines. I like a nice consistent line of attack. Did it take you and Mr. Rose long to come up with that? The confidence of the caveatrix, and I use the term tricks in every sense of the word, in her legal advisors is most justified." Mike was not being helpful.

"So what do we do, give up?"

"Paul, how do you propose to get an expert to opine to forgery or monkeyshines, ventriloquism?"

"Couldn't he just look at the new will and the old will and see if there's any inconsistency in the signatures or anything?"

"Not if you want any judge, especially Harry, to listen to him instead of bringing charges."

"What do you mean?"

"I know some good questioned documents guys Paul, but you can't go around suggesting the desired result to them. If the expert knows going in that you represent the bimbo and she's in one will and not the other, you've tainted him. Unlike wives, experts aim to please. They try to tell you what you want to hear so you'll hire them again next time you want to rob graves. Judges know that. What you need to do is get some other exemplars of the stiff's handwriting for the expert to look at and compare to the new will. Do you have any?"

"Well, no."

"Does the Bimbo?"

"I'd have to ask."

"On second thought, better not to ask her. I'll bet there were more French letters than love letters in her life with the stiff. We'll have to figure out some other way."

"Couldn't we just subpoena exemplars from Lufkin's office?"

"Not if you want to win, Paul. With this kind of dough at stake the element of surprise is crucial. And you'll need the best. The best guy I know is Lindsay McCormic, out of D.C. An old timer, retired from the FBI. Incredibly believable on the stand. He saved one of my guys from twenty years on Devil's Island for bank fraud. Proved the ink on the checks came from a different kind of fountain pen. Of course, unlike your client, he doesn't come cheap. But if you need a miracle, he's your man."

CHAPTER IX.

Fred felt good sitting in his father's old leather chair behind the big desk. He hadn't formally taken over his father's office and he hadn't stopped Anne from using it yet, but he was using the room more and more. He thought about where he'd put in a computer terminal after he took over for good. “Doris, can you show me what rate of interest Anne is getting the Company on our float at Union Trust?” A real estate company like Lufkin ran a huge volume of checks through its accounts every month. Fred had a very good idea of the rate of interest, but he wanted to take the position that Anne had been responsible for the waste of money.

“Interest, Mr. Lufkin? Almost all of the accounts are at about 1 and 1/2% on the average balance.”

“Is that all? I think we can do better. Run me a print out of our average balances on all the accounts, would you, Doris?”

“Yes sir.”

Jack Butler, who was now working almost full time for Fred, had been doing a little polite checking on Judge Weiss. Aside from learning more about Miss LeMieux and the Judge than Paul Sageman would ever want to know, Jack found out that Harry's brother Marty was a Senior Vice President at a much smaller bank than Union Trust, Suburban First.

The printout showed that over $150,000,000 a year ran through the Lufkin accounts, with an average balance of fourteen million. “Did my father ever change banks, Doris?”

"Oh, once or twice when they wouldn't give him a loan he wanted, Mr. Lufkin, he would pull the money out."

"So you know the drill?"

"Oh yes, its a little tricky, but the new bank will let you overdraft for a few weeks until the checks on the old accounts are taken care of. Its hell for the girls in the back, but it can be done."

"Well, lets not bother Anne about it until I've looked into the matter Doris." Anne had just refinanced the shopping center with Union Trust and was probably enjoying getting her ass kissed by everyone over there. Another good reason to change banks. "Of course, there would be new resolutions and signature cards if we changed banks, wouldn't there?"

"Yes, Mr. Lufkin."

"See if you can get a direct number for a Martin Weiss at Suburban First Bank, Doris."

Suburban First didn't have many customers as big as Lufkin Realty, and Martin knew who the Lufkins were, so Fred had no trouble arranging an appointment. Fred wasn't about to mention that he knew who Martin's brother was and he hoped Martin was smart enough not to bring it up. Of course if he did, Suburban just wouldn't get the business. Fred got Suburban to arrange a sweep account that would yield a T-Bill rate, a direct hookup to Lufkin's computer system and an unsecured loan of one hundred thousand dollars for Omega Corporation. Martin Weiss was too discrete to ask why. Best of all, the new resolutions and signature cards would have his name on them. Now the only problem was getting Anne to agree to change banks.

"Who the hell is Mary Donnelly, Doris?" Anne was enraged. "How dare she write me a letter like this." Anne read from a letter from Mary Donnelly, Vice President, Administration, at Union Trust to Lufkin Realty. "Union Trust Company has been advised of the passing of its customer Robert Lufkin. It will be necessary for Lufkin Realty and its affiliates to provide proof of authorization of the executor of Mr. Lufkin's estate, Mr. Frank Mairone, in connection with all transactions as soon as possible. Please contact the undersigned to arrange for immediate compliance."

"Don't you remember Mary, Miss Lufkin? She's Terry Stephen's sister." Doris

"Where is Fred, Doris? I want to straighten this out right now."

Fred was found and shown the letter."I thought we meant more than that to Union Trust, Anne. Sending us a form letter like this."

"Fred, it isn't the letter, its who its from."

"Who would that be?"

"Terry Stephen's sister. Frank Mairone must have put her up to this. I'm not sure we should have our money in a bank that would let people like that get involved in our affairs."

"Do you think so? Well, I could look into other arrangements. What sort of interest are we getting on our float there?"

"Oh, two percent, something like that. Doris would know." "What about the shopping center loan you just did? Do we need to keep our accounts with Union Trust under the loan documents?" "I don't think they're allowed to require that any more."

"Well then, I'll see what I can do."

Anne was so anxious to get away from Union Trust that she didn't pay attention to the names on the new signature cards when she signed the resolutions for Suburban First a week later. Fred put the terminal in his father's office the next day. Now he could track all the accounts on a real time basis and make electronic transfers. Mary Donnelly made another deposit in her makeup case.

CHAPTER X.

Paul went back to Joe Rose. “Mike says we need a number of samples of Lufkin's writing to keep the expert on the up and up, but he doesn't think we should ask Anne and Fred for them.”

“Surely you don't suggest that those fine upstanding citizens would be less than forthright in complying with a subpoena, Paul? You no doubt have an answer for this knotty problem? No?”. Rose was actually silent for a moment. Paul wasn't sure if he was thinking or just giving Paul an opportunity to sweat.

“Didn't a little birdie just tell me that the Lufkins had moved all their accounts out of Union Trust, leaving dozens of fine WASP noses at the bank out of joint? Fortunately for her, and you, Theresa Stephens shares me as a lawyer with Lynton Childs. Don't you know Lynton? He just happens to be a Director of Union Trust. I imagine Lynton could arrange for you to sneak a peek at their files. Must be plenty of signatures from old Bob Lufkin in there. After all, if it weren't for me, Lynton Childs would be wearing the stripes on his suits horizontal rather than vertical. Apparently insider trading is an old tradition in the Childs family. Mrs. Dolan.” Joe Rose summoned his secretary with a bellow. Mrs. Dolan, interrupted her morning gossip only long enough to yell back “That's my name.” and returned to her conversation. Rose buzzed her over the intercom several times, with no visible result. “Captivating woman. I don't know what my ulcers would do without her.”

Mrs. Dolan, who could probably give away ten pounds to Rose, looking regal in her beehive finally appeared. "Oh, did you want me, Mr. Rose?"

"Only since first I laid eyes on you, my dear, but since that pleasure has been denied me, would you track down Lynton Childs and tell him he's having lunch with me. Better not be the Club. Make it Solano's at 1:30."

"Aren't there bank secrecy laws or something?" Paul couldn't help asking.

"Why yes, and there are unemployed lawyers as well." Joe paused just long enough to let Paul understand just who might be unemployed. "Besides, Jay Ritzer would lose all respect for me if we acted like we were from some big white shoe firm like Berry & French."

Ensconced at the power table at Solano's, with the mortal remains of two or three calves on his plate, Rose asked about getting a look at the Lufkin archives at Union Trust. Childs wasn't thrilled with the idea. "The Lufkins were very good customers for a long time. It could cause quite a stink if our other customers found out. Anyway, Joseph, I'm really not the man to ask, I'm only a director. I never get near anything like bank records...for any one borrower." His veal was getting cold, so Rose decided not to waste time explaining life to Lynton Childs.

"Big firms like Berry & French, Lynt, they're always having to turn away work, even from former clients, cause of conflicts of interest. And there's some partners of mine, fellows who have nothing better to do, who think its bad for the image of the firm to defend, shall we say market visionaries, like yourself. Now I certainly hope you never need me again, and if you do I'll try to be there for you...of course there are other lawyers out there." Rose paused to put himself outside a cutlet or two.

Thinking Rose wouldn't want to disclose why he needed the records, Childs tried a counterattack. "If I only knew what you needed the records so much for, Joseph, perhaps I could talk to our general counsel about it. Why would you need such records when the Lufkins have left the bank?"

"Surely you don't object to me getting a little inside information for a change, Lynt? Or do you have the market cornered?" Childs could see Rose wasn't giving up or spilling the beans.

"You won't have to take anything out of the bank?"

"No. Of course not. If you don't tell anyone, and I'm sure you can keep a secret, Lynt, no one will ever know. By the way, have you seen the dessert cart today?"

CHAPTER XI.

“I think you'll like these papers, Mr. Lufkin, like them very much. We hit them with both barrels. I'm moving to disqualify Mairone and throw out Her claim.”

“Yes Jay, we can't have Mairone snooping around here.” They were sitting in Robert's old office. Fred hadn't mentioned Ritzer's visit to Anne.

“I assume you'll suggest a substitute executor?” Fred asked.

“Yes, I thought you and your sister as co-executors.” “You know Jay, there's a few things I haven't told you about Anne, poor thing.”

“She's not ill is she?”

“Well, in a sense she is. My late father, Jay wasn't the easiest person to live with and our mother, well...It all had a great effect on Anne. Frankly, Jay, she's been on the couch for a number of years and I'm afraid Mairone could use that against her. It would be very distressing if all that came out. Anne wanted me to tell you that.”

“I understand, of course, Mr. Lufkin, I understand implicitly.” Ritzer considered whether they could get away with it and decided that facing Fred was easier than dealing with Weiss on the subject. “But I'm afraid the Court, the Court, Mr. Lufkin would probably require her to sign a waiver of the right to be an executor of your father's will, as she has an equal right to it with you at law. I could have one prepared and, if those are her true wishes, the Court would go along with it.”

“I think you'll have to do a bit more than prepare the waiver, Jay. Anne understands the problem, but I don't know if she was thinking of signing anything. If you could perhaps give her another reason why our chances would be better by proposing just one executor, without necessarily mentioning the couch. Now suppose we told her that she would be running the business while I just took care of closing the estate as administrator, and that Weiss would be happier dealing with just one administrator than two. Of course if I'm sole executor there wouldn't be any question about your firm continuing to handle the estate..."

"Yes, I'm certain, certain Mr. Lufkin that a single executor would be more appealing to the Court. Should I speak to her today?" Of course Ritzer knew that Anne wouldn't be running the business for five minutes after Fred was appointed sole executor, but it was hardly worth mentioning.

"Why don't we have the waiver ready and I'll think about the best time... When are you filing these papers you were telling me about?"

"They'll certainly be ready by Friday, Friday at the latest."

"Then I think you'll want to go over the papers about getting rid of the old will claim with Anne. I think that would be a good time... Yes, get them ready and have Anne down to your office. Tell her you need her opinion on those papers. Then perhaps you might mention how much it would help getting rid of Mairone to have one executor. Well, thanks so much for coming up." He walked Ritzer out, to be sure Anne didn't run into him without a cover story being ready and returned to what he now considered his office.

Fred thought it might work. The Suburban First switch had gone over much easier than he'd planned.

Still, Fred wasn't about to rely on Ritzer alone. The Terry Stephens claim presented an enormous advantage in that Anne wasn't paying enough attention to Fred's moves. If he couldn't take over now it might be a lot harder later.

Jack Butler didn't really like following Anne around at first. Since he came to the office frequently and she'd recognize him, he could only follow her in disguise. Once he'd bugged her purse though, things got a bit more interesting. He knew what Fred wanted. Something Anne couldn't bear to have made public.

He'd figured her for frigid or maybe a dyke from meeting her in the office. Frigid wouldn't be too helpful, of course. The first few days of following her had been a drag. Hours in the mall, the hairdresser, nothing that appeared to be a rendezvous, straight or otherwise. Then Doris let him see Anne's checks. $250 a week to a Dr. Franca Aletto. Had to be a shrink. He looked up her address, then parked the van across the street. It was a lot easier than following her, and the sound came in pretty good.

"And did you feel abandoned by Jeannine as an adolescent?" Anne really didn't care for Dr. Franca calling her mother by her first name, especially since she was dead, but she'd found all therapists had annoying habits and she hadn't tired of Franca yet.

"I wouldn't say abandoned, because I don't think my mother really had any choice in the matter. Things were beyond her control." By the time Anne was in high school Jeannine didn't get out of bed most days, and her children knew she drank her breakfast.

"But at the time, Anne, how did you feel about it?" Anne expected better questions for $250 dollars a short hour. Embarrassed, rejected, furious, despondent, what did she think?

"Like I really didn't have a whole mother. Angry, sad."

"And you never discussed these feelings with Robert." It wasn't a question. At least she'd figured that much out.

"No." She'd never discussed any feelings with Lufkin. Certainly not about her mother's drinking and for sure not after she discovered that every day in his briefcase her father brought home a bottle for Jeannine. Sometimes wine, sometimes brandy. So much more practical than flowers. Terry got the flowers. Where was Franca going with this, anyway?

"And you knew why she drank." Franca could be aggressive.

Anne didn't respond. "Because Robert no longer loved her?"

If Lufkin had ever loved anyone. "My father could be very cruel."

"He was cruel to you?"

"He was very demanding." Jack, almost falling asleep in the van, wondered if Lufkin had ever slipped it to Anne. Would Fred be jealous?

"Did he beat you?"

"He didn't have to."

Anne remembered trying to play tennis with her father. She was marginally competent and tired easily. Lufkin had learned perfect form and with his height he covered the court effortlessly. One impossibly hot July day when she was fifteen he took her out on the steamy old clay courts at the Club. He ran her around the court. Within a few minutes Anne's feet were burning but Lufkin wouldn't slow down. He cursed under his breath at her insipid attempts at return shots, shook his head in disgust at her weak serves and wouldn't answer her pleas for a break. Finally she was so hot she couldn't run anymore, dropped her racquet and burst into tears. Lufkin walked off the court without a word, got in his Lincoln and drove away without her. Anne, who was shy and really had no friends at the Club, had to ask the mother of a classmate of hers for a ride home. She'd never played tennis with Lufkin again, but he kept paying for tennis lessons.

That same year, she'd finally figured out that something was going on with Terry Stephens, but was too afraid to tell her mother and cause a fight with Lufkin. Of course it wouldn't have been the easiest thing to bring up with your mother, even if you did speak with her regularly, which Anne didn't. She told Fred about it but he didn't seem surprised.

Anne had a few friends at school, plain girls from modest homes awed by Lufkin's wealth. They seemed fascinated by the most mundane details of her life, matching leather luggage, her own charge card at Lord & Taylor, August on Shelter Island. She didn't tell them what a ball it was living with her father and a bedridden mother.

"Was he abusive in other ways? Physically?"

"No, not like that, but we were never good enough for my father."

"But you worked with him after college. Did you have to?"

Actually, it had been Fred's idea. At first, Anne didn't want to be within a thousand miles of Lufkin Realty, her father or Terry, but Fred's argument was compelling. Someone had to watch out for Terry. Anne got along with Robert better than Fred did, which wasn't saying much.

After a while, she'd gotten used to it. Even if Robert didn't respect her abilities, tenants, bankers and other people she dealt with treated her with more respect than she would have gotten working anywhere else. Lufkin rarely berated her except when they were alone. She dreaded lunch with him. Dinner at the house was even worse, with her mother or later on, her ghost upstairs. Lufkin kept a list, in small, precise script, of the things she did wrong and sometimes pulled it out during a meal.

That last night at the house, the list had been rather long. "I had to, yes, Doctor. To protect my mother and my brother. I had to." Jack didn't think Fred needed very much protection. Quite the reverse.

"Protect them? From your father?"

"Yes. We were never sure...He had a relationship...we were never sure he would treat his own family right." Anne had never told a therapist about Terry. With a court fight going on, it might not be such a good idea, but the desire to open up, even to a stranger, was strong.

"What sort of relationship?"

"With a woman who worked in his office. Terry. I don't know if my mother ever understood what was going on, but my brother and I knew."

"Did your father know how you felt about Terry?"

Jack was falling asleep. This Doctor was never going to ask about anything rated higher than PG.

In the end, though, Lufkin had to know how Anne felt. Anne had thought about it through the last six sessions and whenever she wasn't busy working. Franca would never ask the question, but Anne, thinking she'd feel better if someone knew at least part of the story and believing in the confidence of the psychiatrist's office, had to say it. "I never said it Doctor, but I think he had to know. You see, Doctor, I was with my father when he had his heart attack, after dinner at his house."

This didn't sound right to Jack. He'd wondered whether Fred had helped things along when Lufkin died, thought the information might be helpful if Fred needed a little persuading to pay the bills someday, so he'd checked the police report on Lufkin's death. He was almost sure it said Anne had come to the house and discovered the body after Lufkin was cold.

Anne came to dinner at Lufkin's house one Friday every month. The housekeeper left early on Fridays and Anne served the dinner, dessert and coffee that had been left waiting.

Lufkin had been telling Anne how with children like his he couldn't afford to die, because they wouldn't have the sense to hang on to what he'd accumulated. She'd made a mistake a month earlier on a lease with shopping center tenant, costing Lufkin about three thousand a month by screwing up the override formula.

She remembered how after his coffee he took out the book, once again explained the mistake and told her what it meant.

"You just don't make mistakes like that and survive in real estate. That's a twenty year mistake. Two hundred forty months at three thousand dollars a month. Seven hundred twenty thousand dollars. If I have to look at everything, what do I have to pay you for? Even Fred wouldn't have made that mistake. I could just hire someone off the street if I wanted mistakes. Get me another cup of coffee, if you can figure out how to heat it up." Upset, Anne got up and went into the kitchen to heat up the coffee. When she came out Lufkin was gripping the left side of his chest and trying to tell her to call an ambulance.

Anne felt strangely calm. She put down the coffee and watched him from the other side of the table for a minute. "What is it, Father?"

"My chest, call someone..." He couldn't say any more.

"Is it hurting, are you in pain?" Lufkin couldn't speak. He tried to get up from the chair but fell back. Anne didn't move to call. She was thinking about her mother. "Father, does it hurt a lot?" Lufkin, furious at Anne's failure to move opened his mouth but no sound came out. With the idea of crawling to the phone in the hall, he managed to throw himself out of the chair but couldn't move. He mouthed the words "heart" and "hospital". Anne still didn't move. As far as she knew, her father didn't have a heart and she told him so. Lufkin began to realize she wasn't going to help and tried to move again but couldn't. A few minutes later he was unconscious. Anne waited until he turned cold, put away the dishes, then called the police, telling them she'd arrived to find's Lufkin's body.

She told Dr. Franca about most of this now, except for what she told the police, which Franca wouldn't know anyway, it hadn't made the papers.

Jack couldn't believe it. If the police had known she'd been there, maybe even served him some cafe Sayonara, they'd at least have done an autopsy. This went beyond leverage. He'd have to think about whether Fred ever learned about this. After all, Lizzie Borden might pay a higher price for Jack to bury the hatchet than Fred would pay for the information.

CHAPTER XII.

"Wait a minute, what the fuck is the Omega Corporation?" They were sitting in Mike's office. Paul had been telling Mike Miller about Lindsay McCormack's disappointing oral report. Lynton Childs, who had no intention of giving up the stock market and wanted Rose in his corner, had arranged for Paul and the expert, McCormack to secretly inspect documents bearing Lufkin's signature that were still in the possession of Union Trust.

McCormack, who looked like he could have been Paul's long lost Irish grandfather, had arrived from Washington that morning on the train in a trench coat and Harry Truman hat, carrying a large metal suitcase. Paul drove him straight to a coffee shop a block from Union Trust headquarters. From there, they were actually smuggled in through the loading dock by a Vice President who had solemnly pledged on his pension never to reveal the name of the director who asked for the little favor, and placed in a small room inside the main vault that just happened to contain the Lufkin records.

Paul rifled through three bankers boxes of corporate records and set eight documents and the two wills on a table in random order while McCormack set up his equipment, consisting of a traveling microscope and what looked like a small chemistry set. McCormack spent almost two hours scoping the documents, taking minute ink samples, photographing the signatures with an ancient camera that actually revealed a bellows when unfolded and whispering to himself.

Finally he spoke to Paul. “Do you want the dope now?” Paul thought about that. He'd actually set up a fair inspection, which he felt ought to be witnessed by some third person, but couldn't very well arrange that in the circumstances.

“I guess so, just by the numbers.”

“Documents one through six and eight are consistent and presumably genuine. Document number seven was not signed by the same person as documents one through six and eight, though there was clearly an attempt made to cause it to appear to have been signed by the same person. Beneath the ink on number seven are pencil tracing marks, disclosed by analysis of the sample I took. The appearance of the letters further confirms my conclusion. Its a fairly amateurish job.” Too bad, Paul thought, they had been amateurish on the wrong document.

McCormack had unwittingly concluded that the old and new will were signed by the same person--undoubtedly Lufkin--who signed the wills and a number of other loan agreements and other notarized documents. Document number seven, however, was a stock power assigning 51% of the shares of Nikful Corporation to Omega Corporation. Paul wondered if the conclusion could have been affected by a less scrupulous presentation.

Describing it all to Mike, Paul didn't see how that helped Terry. “I don't know what the Omega Corporation is, but what good does it do us?”

“I assume you know what Nikful owns and who owns Omega?” “Well, no...”

“Then you don't know how it could help you. Maybe somebody just signed Lufkin's name to save him a ride down to the Bank. Or maybe Lufkin never knew about the stock transfer. Who did you say the named executor was, Mr. Hotpants?"

"Frank Mairone, for the moment. Ritzer's applying for his removal and asking that Fred be substituted in."

"But for now he's the presumptive executor, right? So get him to do a little digging. Its his fiduciary duty after all."

Paul went and explained the Omega angle to Joe Rose, without necessarily mentioning Mike's contribution. Rose actually listened.

"So what you're trying, in your own inarticulate way, to say is if we found out that Fred or Anne are behind Omega, Harry might not be so quick to replace Marcello Mastrionni. And it just might leave a very bad, inky taste in Harry's mouth when the children's credibility is put into play on the will contest. That's a good idea, Paul, a very good idea. I'm glad I thought of it. Let me explain what we want to Radin in person. Meanwhile run a search on Omega and Nikful right away."

"A corporate search?"

"And what else, Mr. Sageman? Prove to me your name isn't third degree false advertising, won't you?" Paul thought. Nikful, Lufkin, Lufkin Realty.

"Or should I trade you in on a Polish exchange student?"

"A title search to see what real estate they own?"

"The rain in Spain falls mainly on the Plain." Rose was singing now. "The rain in Spain falls mainly on the Plain. By George, Mrs. Dolan, I think he's got it. The Rain in Spain... Get me Radin."

Radin was flushed out and connected while Paul remained in Rose's office. "David, I've made a little discovery." From now on it really would be Rose's idea. "No, it isn't my feet, David. We may have something to divert Weiss's attention from Romeo and Juliet, if that's possible. I think its your turn to buy lunch." Paul, whose attention had been diverted from Rose's appropriation of his stolen idea by passing the test on searching, walked out happy. When Mrs. Dolan had returned to her desk he asked how to order the searches. Mrs. Dolan, who liked Paul, didn't mention his ignorance to Rose.

Nikful, it turned out, owned ground leases on seven shopping centers, and in turn leased the ground to the operating entities. The short form recorded leases didn't mention the rent, but Radin might be able to find that out. Nikful also owned outright something like one hundred-eighty acres of land in Western Jersey that was apparently being held for development.

Omega didn't show up as owning any real estate, but its incorporator and sole director was none other than Mel Weinberg and it had been incorporated about eighteen months before Lufkin's death. Paul couldn't find out who owned Omega from a corporate search. Nor, he found, did Omega have a listed phone number in the state. If Mairone couldn't come up with the answer, they'd have to pry it out of Weinberg.

CHAPTER XIII.

Tight Ends was the slickest of the go-go bars, with the best looking girls and the most action in the parking lot, so Jack knew Judge Galante would show up there eventually, and it wasn't a bad place to be staked out. For a dollar you got a good look and a quick feel. Some of the girls were intrigued by his looks and his private investigator badge, so he wasn't lonely. Ella, the bartender, knew him and introduced all the new girls after a short resume on how far they would go for how much. On Omega's expense money, that was pretty far. But not tonight, until the Judge showed.

Judge Galante was a municipal judge whose wife either thought court sessions lasted until 3:00 A.M. on Thursdays or didn't care. Defense attorneys knew Thursday nights were the rocket docket in Galante's courtroom and some used the threat of long winded expert witnesses to get adjournments of DWI cases. Mrs. Galante also didn't know the Judge owned three go-go joints through clients, including Tight Ends, his biggest money maker.

The Judge sometimes used Jack to solve problems, like girls who thought their dealers should get some of the 50% cut of all tips that belonged to the bar, instead of the Judge. Jack sometimes took payment in kind. He'd thought about running a shakedown operation targeting suits that spent too much time in the parking lot, but he wasn't sure the Judge would like the idea. It might be bad for business or the Judge might want his 50%. Tonight he was here about a different kind of shakedown and he wasn't about to give away 50% of that.

Jack knew he didn't want to play his hand without knowing what the hole cards were. He might not be the only one doing any taping and he didn't want to approach Anne without knowing how to avoid an extortion rap. He also wanted to know just what her criminal exposure was for letting Lufkin eat the dining room carpet as his last supper, knowledge that might affect the price. Judge Galante might not be a legal scholar but Jack was pretty sure his scruples wouldn't get in the way.

There were a lot of Russian broads working Tight Ends that night. Jack thought they were a bit of a pain in the ass. Sure they knew where the parking lot was but communicating with the more recent arrivals was a hit or miss proposition. Most of them learned English by watching American reruns with subtitles while they were back in Kiev or St Petersburg. He was working on a new young blonde one, Svetlana, while he waited for the Judge. “A private investigator? Is that some kind of Doctor?” Jack wanted her to investigate his privates for a fifty but he didn't know if he could get through to her. Maybe the Judge should pay for some English lessons.

The Judge came through the door with two Spanish models hanging all over him. Jack signaled that he had to talk to the Judge, who got rid of the girls for a few minutes. “Juanita, Pilar, go get ready to audition for me. How's my favorite Dick, Jack?”

“Judge, I need a good lawyer.” “If you think you find good lawyers in go-go bars, I'd say you need more than a lawyer. Ella, darling, a double Remy for me and a Shirley Temple for Jack Boy here. Put it on his tab, honey.”

The Judge lit a small dark cigar and leaned close to Jack. “So what did you do, Jack, leave a glove at the scene of the crime?”

“I've got a client whose a little worried about something, Judge. His mother died of a heart attack. He was visiting with her at the time and one of the paramedics made a stink why he didn't call an ambulance sooner. She was stiff by the time they got there. Some cop overheard and may be snooping around.”

“Any dough involved?” What was he a mind reader too? Jack knew that big Eyetalian nose was sniffing around for a cut. “Dough? Naah, why? I mean he owns a liquor store down in some shine neighborhood...he pays me, slow like... for checking on his wife”

“No, the old lady.”

“Maybe a couple of rentals, two families, her husband left her and a few bucks. But what's that got to do with it? He just wants to know if the cops can do anything to you for watching someone croak and not doing nothin’ about it soon enough.”

“Jackie, I shouldn't be giving out free advice like this, that's my problem, that's why I'm so poor. Besides its against union rules.” Jack knew the Judge was looking to see if he'd offer to pay anything, but if he did, the Judge might smell blood in the water. It only took a drop. But he needed the information.

“Could Pete represent this guy if it went anywhere?” Pete Giresi was the Judge's law partner.

“If its not in my town, sure, why not.”

“Okay, this guy's very worried, he's got a bitch of a sister who might push things. What if we retain Pete for this? This guy really wanted me to get him the advice."

"Yeah, let him call Pete in the morning. But if you got a retainer for me now it would be easier." Like Pete would ever see it. Juanita and Pilar came out dressed in platinum G- strings and draped themselves over the Judge. Jack wondered if the Judge would share. He liked the look of Pilar and he was sure she knew what to do with those big lips of hers. "Duty calls, Jack, I've got to make sure these ladies have no hidden contraband." The Judge started to move away towards the back office.

Jack didn't want to wait for Pete, so he said the magic word. "I think I've got the retainer here Judge, but this guy would like to get an idea of what he's up against." He pulled out twenty hundred dollar bills.

"This will get us started on the criminal matter, Jack, but the civil matter, that's separate." "Civil matter?"

"Sure, you said the bitch of a sister's after the swag, didn't you?"

"So? What's that got to do with it?"

"Don't you know, Jack that a person who's criminally responsible for a death, in any degree, can't inherit? If he gets hit for depraved indifference, not impossible without a good lawyer like Pete, the sister walks away with everything. She'll be blowing the prosecutor like a trombone to go after your client." The Judge took a drag on his cigar and a pinch of Pilar's thigh while Jack recovered from the shock. He had a twenty million dollar tape recording sitting in the back of his van.

CHAPTER XIV.

Ritzer knew he had to tread a fine line with Anne. How to convince her that the position of executor was not too important to renounce without raising the question of why, if the post was veritably ministerial, Judge Weiss would care whether there was one executor or twenty. Distraction, he knew, was the better part of chicanery--focus the mark on the pot of gold rather than the details of the mining operation.

"Even with the evidence we have, Miss Lufkin, it is less than certain, less than certain that Judge Weiss will remove Mr. Mairone or end the will contest now. Given his relationship with your father's...that is with Ms. Stephens, it is vital that he be removed, especially if the Court allows the contest to continue. We need to create the path of least resistance for the Court, give that woman nothing she can point to regarding the alternative to Mairone that would give the Court pause." He felt that this was as far as he could go in alluding to the couch, but that a sensitive person would perceive the unmentioned potential objection to Anne as an executor. Looking at Anne across the conference table he wasn't sure how Anne felt about the subject or whether she was picking up on his subtly expressed concern.

She had liked the papers Ritzer's people had drafted seeking to remove Mairone and dismiss Terry's claim, making a few suggestions that Ritzer made a show of appreciating, but when he'd changed the subject to the real reason for the meeting, she had become rather quiet.

"A single executor is always preferred in these circumstances, Miss Lufkin, always preferred. And of course the executor wouldn't be running Lufkin Realty, just making sure your father's estate was properly closed." This bordered on fraud, Ritzer knew, but in a good cause, a good cause after all.

"Of course I could always ask to be named as an executor later if I felt the need to, after Mairone and his girlfriend are gone couldn't I?" This was a troublesome question. The renunciation, which he hadn't showed Anne yet, or even mentioned, was quite clearly to the contrary.

"I cannot, of course, guarantee that the Court would do that, but I can't see any reason why not if there's a need...but you would need to sign a document for the Court's benefit renouncing the position for now." Ritzer didn't mention that if Fred objected, she wouldn't have a prayer of coming in later.

"But aren't there commissions, Mr. Ritzer? I don't know that I want to give those up."

"I'm certain, Ms. Lufkin, certain that your brother would renounce the commissions if you so desired." Ritzer had no idea that Fred would do any such thing, but it would be years before an accounting and he counted on Anne to be scatterbrained enough not to memorialize that little promise. Ritzer pulled out the form of renunciation but didn't hand it over. "We'd like to file this with our papers Ms. Lufkin. Then Judge Weiss will know you and your brother were united as to the Estate and he'd be more inclined, much more inclined to remove Mr. Mairone."

He handed Anne the renunciation. She studied it in silence for a few minutes before ruining Ritzer's afternoon. "I'll have to think about this Mr. Ritzer, talk to Fred." Ritzer knew this was a big setback. If Anne really thought about it she'd never renounce. Maybe she'd even talk to some one and find out that the line about gentlemen preferring single executors was pure eyewash. Still, Ritzer didn't want to look any more anxious than he was already.

"Perhaps if we could just confirm about the commissions, Ms Lufkin?"

"No, Mr. Ritzer, I'll need to sleep on it I think...we Lufkins don't like to make rash decisions. But I'll take the waiver with me so that if I decide to go ahead we won't lose any time." There was still hope, but Ritzer had a sinking feeling. Once a wedding is put off, or the mark gets out of your office without a sale, the odds of the deal closing fall.

"Of course, of course, Ms. Lufkin." Ritzer manufactured a smile. "But do remember, we really should file these papers soon."

CHAPTER XV.

Donald Morton was just finishing the latest issue of The Salmon Fisherman and thinking about how good his first Beefeater Gibson at the club would taste when his secretary Jeanne Lee buzzed. "There's an Anne Lufkin on the wire. She sounds a touch upset. Will you speak to her?"

"Well, what does she want?"

"She needs to speak to a lawyer right away, says her brother's trying to kick her out of their father's company." Morton didn't know anyone named Lufkin, and the firm of Ferguson & Mather usually didn't take on clients they didn't know, but he couldn't very well ask Jeanne Lee to find out how much dough was involved, and he hadn't had a new client worth spitting over since losing the Hartmann & Hartmann will contest the summer before, so he picked up the phone.

"Don Morton, here Mrs. ..." Damn, he never could remember names the first time.

"Lufkin, its Miss Anne Lufkin. Lufkin Realty is our company." If she expected Morton to have heard of it, she was disappointed, but she continued. "My father Robert Lufkin died last November 11th. Now my brother Frederick Lufkin is trying to get me to renounce as executor, and he's gotten people to threaten me."

"With what?"

"Well the person he had call was a bit vague, but I'm sure Fred was behind it. He said he was some kind of Judge and that I should meet him to discuss some very serious problem I have. I'm very afraid."

"Don't you have a lawyer already?"

"Well my brother and I have been using the same lawyer, Jay Ritzer, for the will contest, but Mr. Ritzer was the one who asked me to sign the renunciation yesterday. Then last night, I got a call at home, on my private, unlisted number, from this person who called himself Judge, Judge Galante, I think and said we needed to meet right away." Jay Ritzer? Morton had run across Ritzer before, always wondered where he hid the horns and the pointy tail. Hadn't he been disbarred yet?

"And you never heard of this Judge fellow before? Maybe you should call the police." Morton didn't know if he wanted to get involved in some penny ante case with this dizzy broad so he decided to get to the critical facts. "Where did you say your company was?"

"Lufkin Realty is in Claremont, Mr. Morton." He'd heard of Claremont. Pretty nice town. There might be something to talk about here after all.

"And what does Lufkin Realty, I gather it belonged to your father, do?"

"That's right Mr. Morton. Lufkin Realty and its affiliates own and manage two-thousand five hundred and seventy five residential units, eleven shopping centers and other properties in North and Central New Jersey." Morton wrote that down. The gibson would have to wait. Even if F & M ended up with only a quarter of the estate, it might be a worthwhile case.

"Did you say there was a will contest?"

"Yes, a ...friend of my father's Theresa Stephens was in an earlier will. My father cut her out but she can't accept it and now, believe it or not she's actually sleeping with the executor my father appointed. Mr. Ritzer has it on tape."

"She'd do better to sleep with the probate Judge, wouldn't she?"

"Really, Mr. Morton."

"I'm sorry, I know these are serious concerns you have. I think we'll need to meet. We don't have a New Jersey office you know, and it doesn't sound like we'd better meet at your office, Ms. Lufkin. Could you cross the river, perhaps tomorrow morning?"

"Certainly Mr. Morton. Are there any papers I'd need to bring?" Other than a check?

"You're way ahead of me Ms. Lufkin, way ahead. The wills, of course and copies of anything filed in Court. Anything describing the organization and ownership of your businesses."

"What shall I say if that awful man calls again?"

"Ritzer? No, you mean the Judge. Turn on your answering machine Ms. Lufkin, and don't erase the tape. We're at Park and 53rd. Ten o'clock alright?"

"Fine. Thanks so much Mr. Morton. Bye now."

Morton buzzed Jeanne Lee "Get what's his name, Pedersen, in here, he needs to give me a crash course on Jersey probate law right away, assuming there is any law out there. And we need to find out if there's really anyone named Judge Galante." Jay Ritzer, for God's sake, in Jersey. He'd probably need a rabies shot before this was over.

CHAPTER XVI.

They were fishing off a pier in the Gulf, downing Buds to beat the heat and Al DeLucia had waited through almost the entire story with uncharacteristic patience, but could restrain himself no longer. "You have to be the single stupidest sack of shit that ever leaked, Tommy, I just can't even believe you're sitting the fuck down here in St. Petersburg jerking off while a bunch of half assed Jew lawyers throw away your winning lottery ticket."

"What am I supposed to do, Al, I ain't no lawyer. They wouldn't listen to me. They probably wouldn't even talk to me."

"Lem'me tell you something Tommy, all those fucking lawyers are doing is trying to figure out how fast they can sell you out. Your mom, she's nothing to them. The other side has all the dough, all the power. What do you think is gonna happen? The only way to even the score is to give this Rose guy something to worry about. Ask questions, get in their face. Be there. You and your mom."

"She doesn't even want me to know what's going on."

"Cause she was doin' the old guy?" Al was a good enough friend to get away with that one and it was a pretty good guess.

"So I should make her go up to Jersey, get more involved?"

"Yeah. Like right away. Just remember me when you're a rich fuck. I'm giving you the best free advice you ever heard." Tommy figured Al was right.

"But how do I convince her?"

"Hey do I have to think of everything? Listen, Joey's had a few go rounds with lawyers trying to shaft him. That's the way the contracting business is. Maybe he could talk to her. She's met him a few times." Joe DeLucia was at least half way respectable. Even if Al wasn't his mom's favorite person, it might work.

"Okay, but I still don't know how he's going to bring it up if I'm not even supposed to know what's going on."

"Hey we'll blame it on that kid lawyer who was down here. Paul what's his name. Say he blabbed. Isn't that how you found out? And that'll give her a clue how you can't trust them too much." Tommy had to admit, Al was pretty smart for a University of Miami dropout. But Al was still trying to figure out how to cut himself in for a slice on this deal. Maybe Joey could think of something.

CHAPTER XVII.

Judge Galante had already figured out how to cut himself more than a slice. He'd seen through Jack's story in five seconds. The Judge knew Jack had been living off the Lufkins for months and he'd heard enough about the case to figure it had to involve one of them. After Pilar had softened Jack up a little in the back room, the Judge dropped the Lufkin name on Jack and he broke like an eggshell. A short but colorful lecture on how easy it was to go down for extortion when your victim was a big name and Jack had agreed that the Judge should handle things.

The tape was copied and secured in a safe deposit box in someone else's name outside the jurisdiction, he told Jack to get a copy of the police report and then the Judge made the call to Anne. Jack told him enough about Fred Lufkin for the Judge to know he wouldn't go near the guy. Fred would have nothing to lose turning Jack and the Judge in and getting a third of the estate for nothing. Anne had everything to lose.

He figured the best option was to tell her enough of the story that she'd know she was cooked and let her make an offer. Not a word about the tape. She might figure the shrink was mouthing off, or that her brother had dug up the information some other way but she'd mostly be scared, too scared to figure out that you never stopped paying. Maybe he'd name his next club Annie's Fannies.

Anne hadn't returned his first call, so he left a second message. Instead of Anne, Don Morton returned the call and agreed to meet in the bar at Il Turvino, a restaurant on the Judge's turf, without even asking what the story was. Could Anne have guessed? Or were things just a bit slow at Ferguson & Mather?

The Judge had seen the smooth routine before, but this Morton guy was the tits. How do you start a shakedown when a guy's talking about dry flies? Morton had apparently checked out the Judge and found out he was in municipal court because when he was done with the fishing stories, in a transparent attempt to establish camaraderie, Morton told him about how he was a justice of the peace out in Southampton when they'd busted a hooking operation run out of a waterfront mansion where the johns could arrive by yacht and get their booms vanged.

After the waiter delivered a second round, the Judge decided to cut out the bullshit. The Judge had done a run through of the story with Pete, who suggested a formal tone and a careful avoidance of any demand.

"It's come to my attention, Mr. Morton..."

"Please Judge, call me Don."

"It's come to my attention that your client may have a serious exposure in connection with the death of her father."

Morton couldn't quite hide his surprise. "I'm sure you know she told the police that she found her father dead on the floor. The story she told the police about Robert Lufkin's death doesn't jive with what's she's since told others. This information is reliable and verifiable." Morton didn't respond. "She told the police that she didn't arrive at Robert Lufkin's home until he was dead. That apparently isn't the case. She served him his last meal that night at his home. Only the two of them were there. I don't need to tell you what the implications of that discrepancy are, or what might happen if that information got into the wrong hands, particularly with a will contest going on." The Judge felt he better make sure Morton didn't fuck things up by not knowing that Fred was the wrong hands he had in mind. "At this point none of the other parties has this information. None."

"Then you're not representing any of the contestants?"

"No. But I'm sure an expert such as yourself understands that any responsibility for the decedent's demise could affect her rights as an heir."

Morton, like Anne, had figured this was just a maneuver by Fred and Ritzer to dump her as a fiduciary. It could still be, but Morton was beginning to think he had a few more questions to ask Anne Lufkin before he went any further. Like whether Lufkin had been cremated. On the other hand, he sure wanted to find out what the Judge was after if he wasn't working for Fred.

"Who do you represent, then Judge, if you don't mind my asking?"

"Are you sure you want the answer to that question, Don? Its really not necessary and it might be, shall we say, inconvenient."

"This has nothing to do with whether my client resigns as a fiduciary?"

"That's none of my business, but I'd have to say I don't think it would be a good idea to resign based on what I've heard about her brother."

This guy couldn't be working for Fred. Which meant Anne Lufkin really did have some big problems.

And Ferguson and Mather would need a big retainer if it was possible she could be disinherited.

"I appreciate the advice Judge. Naturally I'll need to discuss this matter with my client. Can I get back to you tomorrow?"

"Certainly, Don. Let me give you my private line at City Hall. I'm on the bench tomorrow." The Judge was happy that Morton was the one asking to follow up. It meant he was scared and it eliminated the need for the Judge to suggest the price of silence. He began to think about how to cut Jack out entirely.

Morton retreated from the restaurant and told his driver, Jimmy, to find a phone booth. This wasn't one of those calls you made on a cellular phone. While they drove, he decided what he had to do. He needed to ask Pedersen what degree of homicide they'd have to prove to divest Anne. Was a conviction required or could responsibility for the death be proven civilly? Then he had to talk to his client in person, though he didn't relish the thought of dining with her after she knew he was in on the secret. A home cooked meal was out of the question. It never occurred to Morton that she was incapable of murder. In his experience, broads could convince themselves that anything they did was justified.

Pedersen was a good man, said he'd get right on it. Anne agreed to meet him by Bloomingdales in the parking lot of a mall at five o'clock. Morton felt like he needed another drink. Hell, he'd been in Jersey for an hour and found out from a judge who was trying to blackmail his new client that she was probably a murderess. It made Manhattan look like Disney World.

Jimmy held the door of the Lincoln open for Anne. Morton had been thinking about how to approach this interview while Jimmy found Bloomingdales and he'd decided he had to know the real story sooner rather than later so he could decide whether a strategic retreat from the case wasn't his best option.

"I don't know you very long, Ms. Lufkin, but I hope you can trust me to help you make some very important decisions."

"This sounds serious Mr. Morton. Wasn't that Judge person just another attempt by my brother to get me to step aside?"

"I can't be certain, Anne, but I don't think so. I'm afraid I'm going to have to ask you about the night your father passed away."

Anne clenched her fists and stared straight ahead. "I found him, Mr. Morton, on the floor of the dining room in our family home in Claremont. He'd apparently had a massive heart attack, which surprised all of us since he took very good care of himself."

"This Judge fellow says that's what you told the police but he knows better. He says you were there before your father had the attack. That you even served him dinner." Anne continued to stare straight ahead. "Now I don't want you to get upset and I don't want you to tell me whether he's right or wrong. But I think you have to know what the implications of that story are. And you have to consider who would be telling a story like that."

Anne knew the only person who could have told that story but she was a little hazy on the implications.

"Just what do you mean Mr. Morton? This is all very shocking."

"Well, someone could seek to institute a criminal proceeding based on suspicion that you were somehow involved in your father's demise. And if you were, you couldn't inherit your share of the estate."

Now Anne understood. That whore Terry must be the one telling stories to the Judge. If Fred believed the story he would never have told Anne or anyone else. He'd have gone to the police in a New York minute to double his share. But Terry, Terry needed something to make the Lufkins settle. But how could Terry have heard this story? She'd only told Franca last week and Terry was down in Florida, didn't even know Franca. And Franca wasn't supposed to tell anyone anything Anne said during a session, Anne had checked that out years ago. She had to keep Morton believing it was all nonsense.

"I just can't imagine who would make up such a yarn, Mr. Morton. Of course my father's ex girlfriend might have a reason to. But what do we do about this Judge?" Morton didn't have the answer to that question yet and he needed to talk to Pedersen before he asked Anne any more questions about it or decided what to do.

"A very good question, I don't mind saying, Ms. Lufkin. Can you sit tight for a day or so?"

"I don't see where I have a choice." Morton considered telling her the old line that there were ten guys in Sing Sing as a result of shooting off their mouths for every convict who was there for shooting off a gun, but he thought she might take it the wrong way. "Naturally, Ms. Lufkin, it's important to be careful who you speak to about these...events until we get a better handle on things."

By now Anne had figured that out for herself. She was wondering how bad it might look to discontinue her sessions with Franca. It would be worse if Franca wanted to go back and talk about that night though. Anne decided just to claim she had to reschedule due to business.

CHAPTER XVIII.

Mary Donnelly wasn't too happy to hear that Terry and her no good kid were coming up to stay with her, but she couldn't very well say no. She had two extra rooms in her townhouse. When she told Fred Lufkin about it, though, he was elated. "I wouldn't discourage her, not at all. I'm sure we can make suitable arrangements as to any expenses you might have." And Mary could get a look at anything Joe Rose sent Terry that got left around the house. Fred thought Jack must have one of those spy cameras to lend to Mary so she could photograph papers on the sly. Not that he'd tell Jack just what he wanted the camera for, the way Jack had been acting lately.

Tommy still couldn't believe how well Al's plan for getting Terry to come up to New Jersey had worked, but he wasn't really sure how to go about leaning on the lawyers. Of course he had a little leverage on Paul Sageman after their night on the town, so he decided to start with him.

Paul was happy to be able to say that they'd finally have made some progress when Tommy called. He tried to explain about the documents at the bank and what the forged stock transfer form for Nikful meant and how they were close to getting Weinberg to admit that the Omega Corporation belonged to Fred, which would mean Fred couldn't kick Mairone out as executor while that accusation was hanging out there, but to Tommy it sounded like more jerking off, or worse.

"I can see what that does for Mr. Mairone, but what does it do for my mom? Isn't that who you're working for? What you're telling me is you've now proven that the old guy did sign the second will, right? I think we need to talk to Mr. Rose about this, right away. I'd like to bring my mom in tomorrow."

Paul felt bad that he couldn't convey the importance of the forgery to Tommy, and worse that Tommy and his mother would insist on talking directly with Joe Rose about it, when Paul knew a big part of his job was to run interference for Joe. He was surprised when Joe agreed to the meeting and directed Mrs. Dolan to book the board room, Berry & French's largest conference room, and order lunch from Oscar's.

Terry asked Mary to come meet with Joe Rose but she begged off. "Oh, I'm much too busy at the bank today dear, the year end reports and everything." Of course Fred would have wanted her to go, probably would have paid good money for the story, but she just didn't feel comfortable having to sit there with Terry's lawyers. Anyway, Terry would probably tell her all about it and she could hit up Fred that way.

Joe greeted Tommy and Terry like old friends, even listened to Tommy's concerns. "You're quite right, Tommy, but don't worry, I've been keeping a close eye on this case. And Sageman here isn't as dumb as he looks, though I admit that would be a challenge. Quite candidly, I never expected that the second will would be a forgery, even if it was drafted by Mel Weinberg. In all my years of practice I've found remarkably few will contests involved forged instruments, despite what you may read." If Tommy could read, Joe thought. Paul knew this was Joe's first will contest but didn't think he'd mention it.

"We simply looked into the forgery issue to cover all the bases. That's why stumbling across the forged stock transfer form was actually such a bonus for our team. Once we find out why someone went to the trouble, and I'd bet my seven layer cake that it'll be Fred, we'll have shown the court just how devious the young Lufkins are. And that's what the case is really all about. How did they fool Bob Lufkin into changing the will?" Not that they were really any closer to the answer to that question than they had been before. "I've convinced the Court to let us look into things and I promise you we'll put the Lufkins under a microscope. Anything you can remember, Terry, that could help us with that question, anything at all that you haven't told Sageman already could be of inestimable value."

But Terry couldn't remember anything else that she was interested in telling Joe Rose. Lufkin's final words to her didn't appear helpful. She only came to the meeting to placate Tommy, figuring it was the least she could do since she had really come back to Jersey to be near Frank Mairone.

"So what are you doing with this great discovery?" Tommy asked. Joe had an answer for that. "I think its about time we have a little chat with the esteemed Mel Weinberg, Esquire. Under oath."

CHAPTER XIX.

Though unaware that Rose had discovered the Nikful transfer, Fred was enraged when he learned about the subpoena for Weinberg. Even though he didn't expect Mel to tell the truth, considering what he was being paid not to, stranger things had happened. Fred believed, correctly, that Terry's lawyers didn't have a clue as to the reasons why Lufkin had written Terry out of the will and Fred wanted to keep it that way. He called Ritzer.

“What kind of lawyer are you, Jay, letting Rose get the jump on us like that? If anyone should have to testify its Theresa Stephens.”

“Mr. Lufkin, surely you don't believe, don't seriously believe that Rose gets to depose anyone just because he serves a subpoena? My people are already working on a motion to quash the subpoena and stay all discovery until after our motion to get rid of her complaint on legal grounds is heard, and I believe the Judge will be receptive, particularly with what he now knows about Terry and Frank Mairone.”

It didn't escape Fred that Ritzer was now relying on the very evidence he'd been too chickenshit to use until Fred practically bribed him. He also wasn't too pleased that Ritzer had failed to get Anne to renounce as an executor, but Ritzer hadn't made any promises in that regard and Fred knew how difficult Anne could be.

“Shouldn't you be trying to take her testimony?”

“I'm afraid that would blunt our argument for why Mel shouldn't testify, Mr. Lufkin, much as I would enjoy deposing Terry.”

"You really think we can keep Rose from deposing Weinberg?"

"I do, Mr. Lufkin." Fred decided he'd better have another discussion with Mel, just in case. He arranged for a meeting in a new restaurant Mel picked near Weinberg's office that looked like a Palm wannabe.

"To what do I owe the pleasure, Fred? I'm not sure your Dad ever bought me a meal. I hear the lobster cocktail here is A-1." Fred had to admire Weinberg for the cute way he reminded Fred who held the cards.

"I'm sure you haven't spoken to Rose about anything, Mel."

"Not Rose, no, though I received his calling card, of course. Not to worry. Though I do think the Estate better triple its reserve for legal fees."

Was Weinberg trying to jack him up? Fred decided to let the suggestion dangle. Mel explained: "I heard Don Morton's getting into the case."

"Don Morton?"

"He's a big name in New York. Head of Trust and Estate litigation at Ferguson & Mather, where they're so white shoe they wouldn't step on a Jew, we used to say."

"Is he replacing Rose? That won't triple my fees."

"'Fraid not. Apparently your sister consulted him last week on the QT." Fred couldn't believe it. Anne hiring her own lawyer? It could spoil everything. Was it too late to stop it?

"What do you know about this Morton?"

"Well his stock hasn't been too high lately, I must say. Lost that Hartman & Hartman case, three hundred big ones. He's got a big reputation as a schicker, too. Beefeater Gibsons before the sun's over the yardarm." Mel laughed. That sounded promising to Fred, if he could get someone else to fill Anne in on these details.

"But you've got to understand, Fred. Ferguson & Mather, it's an institution. They handle the biggest cases, hire the smartest kids out of Harvard and Yale. Even out in Jersey I imagine they'd command some respect."

The thought of Anne adequately represented was appalling. Why hadn't Jack Butler told him about this?

"How much does Morton know about Anne, anyway? I imagine a fancy firm like that screens its clients pretty carefully, Mel. Do you think Morton could be scared off?"

"If Morton learns how big this estate is, I seriously doubt it. Of course Ritzer's got a problem now. If Anne's interests become adverse to yours, he might have to withdraw." That concerned Fred, not because he had Jay Ritzer confused with Perry Mason, but he doubted a more legitimate lawyer would let him call the shots like Ritzer had. On the other hand, he might need a bigger gun if Anne was prepared to fight him over running the estate once they got rid of Mairone.

"Still, Morton might not know that Anne's spent over two hundred thousand dollars on shrinks. Do you know him well enough to give him an idea of what he's dealing with?" Mel was busy consulting the wine list.

"Chassagne Montrachet 'eighty nine? Tart but tasty, I'll bet. Used to say that about Terry Stephens, come to think of it." Mel laughed. "No Fred, the last thing you want is for me to seem to be taking any position in this case. Anyway, Morton'll see soon enough that he shouldn't rock the boat, so long as he gets paid."

CHAPTER XX.

"Where to play this weekend, Chris? Decisions, decisions", one waspy young associate confided to his chum as they rode up in the elevator, ignoring Paul's existence. Decisions. Like whether to take it up the hooter or down the throat from the country club partner this faggot fawned over, Paul thought. What a place. Who talked like that? Paul hated all of them. Golfers, sailors, figure skaters, deacons of the Episcopal church, the place was crawling with Dartmouth and Princeton Grads who wouldn't know a bagel from a blintz and exhibited no visible concern over how they would become partners and hire more of their own, perpetuating Berry & French, while Paul worried about whether he'd have a job next week and broke out in a cold sweat thinking about Joe Rose's cholesterol level.

A message to call a Don Morton, with a New York area code was on his chair when he reached his cubbyhole office. He'd never heard of Don Morton, but he returned the call, which was answered Ferguson & Mather. Everyone knew who they were. Paul was fairly certain it wasn't a recruiting call, since he graduated from Rutgers Law and hadn't argued before the United States Supreme Court before he turned 29.

"Paul, Don Morton. I understood your partner Mr. Rose was on vacation, so I took the liberty of asking to speak to you about the Lufkin estate."

"What can I do for you...Don?" Paul didn't mention that he wasn't a partner, because he figured Morton really didn't care.

"I'm new in the case, you understand, and I want to see if we can't have a Pow-wow before anyone gets scalped."

Pow-wow? Had the Indians foreclosed on their $24 dollar mortgage on Manhattan?

"I think I should tell you sir, that I'm of Native American heritage." Morton laughed. "Anyway, you haven't told me who you represent."

"Oh, sorry Paul, I figured if Mel Weinberg knew, the world couldn't be far behind. I've got Anne Lufkin." As Mike Miller would have said Forget the Pow, this was Wow. Somebody representing one of the Lufkins wanted to talk settlement with Terry Stephens. And something must have blown up between Fred and Anne. Paul started to worry whether he should be the one having this conversation but was dying to know whether this was serious.

"What sort of Pow-wow did you have in mind, Don?"

"Well, I'll bring the peace pipe, but I don't know if we'll be smoking on the first date, Paul."

"Would Jay Ritzer be bringing the tobaccy, Don?"

"Far as I know he's still got war paint on, Paul. This would be just girl talk. Anne and Terry. But no clients of course."

"I'll need to check dates with Joe Rose, of course, but I can't see why not. Your Wigwam or ours?"

"Oh, this is a New Jersey case. I'd be happy to come see your Mr. Rose. Why don't you let my secretary, Jeanne Lee, know when he's available next week? A pleasure doing business with you Mr. Sageman." Morton hung up. Next he had to call Anne and convince her of the reasons why buying Terry off was in her best interests.

Paul ran down the hall to tell Mike

"Wait a minute, Ferguson & Mather? The Ferguson & Mather? You Park Avenue pooch you. This case is really going places. Who from Ferguson & Mather called you? The shoeshine boy?"

"Don Morton." Paul didn't expect Mike to know who that was, but Mike remembered. Lawyers always remember big cases other lawyers lost.

"Don Morton. Don Morton... No wonder they want to settle. He got his head handed to him in the Hartmann & Hartmann case. He needs something he can call a win. Wait a minute, why should Anne settle this case? Doesn't our own expert says the stiff signed the will cutting out our round heeled client? And they don't even know that we know about Nikful."

"But how do we know they're talking any real dough?"

"Cause its Ferguson & Mather. Jay Ritzer would be good enough to offer you fifty grand nuisance money. Something's going on. Of course you've got a big problem now, Paul. A real lawyer might even want to work on a case with Ferguson & Mather in it. Better not let them hear about it in the bone yard up on fifteen." Paul hadn't thought of that. He did think he needed to tell Rose.

Mrs. Dolan decreed that news like this was grounds to interrupt the Rose vacation "As long as its not meal time."

Rose got on the phone. "So Sageman, what happened, lose your skate key?" Paul told Rose about Morton's call. Joe almost took it seriously.

"Ferguson & Mather. The great white shoed sharks are beginning to circle, Sageman. I'm counting on you to save my retirement. I guess the loving Lufkin children must have had a little falling out. Didn't you think to try to find out why Anne got her own lawyer?" Luckily Joe didn't dwell on that but moved on to more important subjects. "How serious did he sound? Seven figures?"

"I think it must be pretty serious, to bring in Ferguson & Mather. This doesn't include Fred, of course."

"A separate peace. Well it almost worked for Kaiser Wilhelm. Guess we'll just see what he's got to say. I forgive you for interrupting my second honeymoon here Sageman, but Mrs. Rose never will."

"Should I tell Terry?"

"Terry...Oh, I guess you have to. That punk son of hers would go ape if we met with the enemy without letting them know. But tell her not to expect too much."

CHAPTER XXI.

"Now why would Anne run off and hire her own lawyer, Jack? I just don't understand it. You and Ritzer have really let me down. Do you have any idea?" Jack had a pretty good idea but he wasn't about to tell Fred Lufkin.

"Maybe she got spooked over Ritzer asking her not to be an executor?" Jack hoped Fred would focus on Ritzer, who he'd complained about before in Jack's presence.

"No. That isn't like our Anne. If she didn't like what Ritzer was doing I'm sure she'd tell me. You should know her pretty well by now, Jack. Is that like our Anne? Perhaps you've overheard something about her chats with this Don Morton fellow?"

Jack had been hoping Fred wouldn't ask that question, but he'd been expecting it since Fred had asked him to take a ride with him over to one of the shopping centers.

"I think the battery in that purse bug must have burned out and Anne hasn't been in the office much lately, so I haven't had a chance to check it."

Total bullshit. "Well Jack, maybe you better find out what Don Morton's up to then." Fred was getting a very bad feeling about Jack. Lucky he had a few other sources.

When he got back to the office, Fred had a message from "Katherine", Mary's code name when she wanted Fred to beep her.

"You know Anne has her own lawyer, Fred?" Mary whispered.

"Of course, Mary. Old news. Did you have me page you just for that?" Fred wasn't going to pay for stale information.

"Well, I know something else, something important. I just found out from Terry." Terry? What would she know about Anne?

"Oh. Will you be letting me in on it?"

"A shy girl like me needs a little encouragement, Mr. Lufkin."

Tramp. Worse than her sister. "Do we need to meet?"

"Don't sound so happy about it Fred. The Racquet Club bar. 5:30." Fred wondered if he'd get it cheaper if he let Mary think he was interested.

She made him wait until almost six and buy her two drinks before getting down to business. Was it hard for her to betray her own sister? More likely she thought stalling a bit would raise the price. "So, Mary, I simply can't imagine what Terry would be able to tell you regarding Anne."

"Well, for five thousand dollars you won't need to imagine." Mary normally wasn't so direct with him.

"Our arrangement was that I would pay for information regarding your sister, not mine."

"But this is about my sister, too."

"Three thousand if I haven't already heard it."

"Am I supposed to depend on your honesty, Fred? Okay, I'm sure you don't know how much Anne's lawyer offered Joe Rose to settle the case this afternoon. But if you guess right on the first try, it's free." Anne offering to pay Terry a dime was news to Fred.

"You win. How much?

"Didn't we agree on Five thousand dollars?" Mary lit a cigarette.

"Thirty-five hundred for the whole story, Mary. What was the offer?"

"Okay." Fred took the cash out of his jacket and passed it to Mary, who took her time stowing it.

"One million-five hundred thousand dollars, payable over five years if the will contest is withdrawn and a two hundred fifty thousand dollar consulting fee to Mairone if he waives the right to be executor."

"Impossible. The estate won't pay blackmail like that. Terry doesn't have a case. And Mairone is going down with her." Mary laughed too loudly at the unintended double entendre.

"An old guy like that Mairone. I doubt it Fred. Anyway, don't worry. The offer was out of Anne's share. And Rose turned it down."

"He'd have to be whacko to turn down money like that. The old clown is just trying to get Anne to tweak the offer a little bit to justify his fees." Fred was now certain he had to find out why Anne was doing this. Even the prospect of getting out of the case for free and getting rid of Mairone wasn't as important as knowing. Especially since Terry didn't have a case she could ever prove and Mairone was on the skids. He'd stop the settlement himself if he had to. It might be the only way to get rid of Anne.

CHAPTER XXII.

Tommy lifted a ten dollar phone card at the convenience store he was working at for beer money and called Al. "A million-five, Al. I can't believe this. And Rose tells Mom to turn it down. What the fuck is going on?"

Tommy didn't have it quite right. Rose was too smart to ever actually tell a client not to take a settlement, even if he didn't want her to. He'd even told Paul to do a letter to Terry setting out the risks of not settling and confirming that it was the client's decision not to take the offer. But now Rose smelled blood in the water, even without knowing who was bleeding or why and he thought five million was possible. Joe complimented Terry by telling her that she could expect to be around many more years than she'd been with Lufkin. He told her you only had to read the papers to know that Social Security wasn't what it used to be. Most important, he told her that Bob Lufkin had obviously meant for her to have more. None of which would appear in the letter, of course.

Al had his own take. "Come on Tommy, you never take the first offer." Of course it could all be a setup so Tommy's mother would look like a pig to the Judge. Maybe they never meant to pay, just gambled that she'd turn it down, or figured they could weasel out of it some way even if she'd called their bluff. "Was the offer in writing? How do we know they even made it?" Tommy hadn't thought of that.

"Oh, Mom said some new lawyer came over from New York and met with Rose."

"Did Rose tell them your Mom turned it down?"

"No, she wanted to think about it."

Terry called Frank, who'd already heard from Radin, but didn't tell her that.

"What should I do, Frank?" He'd known that was coming. The right thing was to tell her to take it. A measure of financial security for Terry and the kid, a big downside in going ahead with the case. Considering that Radin was sure he could arrange it so the tapes would be destroyed and Frank could walk away with $250,000.00, a homerun for Frank Mairone. And Radin said the will contest wasn't going anywhere, even with the Nikful forgery, which might have nothing to do with the will anyway.

On the other hand, it wasn't nearly enough money so he could leave his wife and move to Florida to be with Terry permanently. And it meant that piece of shit Fred Lufkin was getting off cheap. "This isn't an easy decision, Terry and I'm not exactly in an objective position. Could we meet to talk about it? Not here, in the city." He knew she wanted to.

"I'd really like that Frank." Terry and ten million of Fred Lufkin's money, Frank thought, now that would be paradise.

Anne hadn't been easy to convince. She still suspected that Terry was somehow involved with Judge Galante, just the kind of lowlife she probably knew. Morton too hated to end a fight like this so quickly, but he really had Anne's best interests in mind. Of course if Anne stayed in as executor, there would inevitably be a battle with Fred, and Morton didn't think Anne was likely to change counsel, so it wasn't like he would lose all the fees from the will contest.

Morton had Pedersen write up the whole parade of horribles for his meeting with Anne, including some Morton hadn't even thought of, like being held without bail.

She looked like hell. Hadn't cried but it was touch and go. Morton had his partner Skip Thiessen and Pedersen in for the meeting, figuring he needed witnesses for a decision like this.

Morton and Pedersen had come up with the settlement amount in advance. Enough so Terry would be very, very nervous about turning it down and Mairone would be happy to walk away if he had any sense. No haggling. Anne could stay in as executor and the fees and commissions would practically pay for the settlement. They didn't see how Terry could turn it down. It didn't even occur to them that Fred would object.

Probably the best thing for Ferguson & Mather, too, Pedersen thought, what with the mess the charges against Anne would be and Don Morton meeting with Judge Galante, hearing that story and not immediately blowing the whistle.

Judge Galante was a little harder to handle. Morton figured that his price would go down if the estate was settled first. Worst case, they'd make the judge a silent partner in one of the properties after Anne and Fred split up. If he got too greedy, Pedersen had come up with the idea of a judicial misconduct inquiry. It was a great idea because judicial misconduct proceeding in Jersey were conducted in secret and lasted for years. After meeting Judge Galante, Morton told Pedersen, he figured there was probably a terrific backlog of judicial misconduct inquiries over in Jersey and if they made them public, there probably wouldn't be ten judges left sitting in the whole state.

Once an inquiry was underway, Galante wouldn't dare pass the information on to Fred or the prosecutor's office until he was cleared. Even Morton knew that delay was always the ally of a criminal defendant. In this case, he thought, the evidence was quite literally disintegrating.

Anne almost cried, but she knew what would happen if Fred ever learned about what Judge Galante knew and she couldn't imagine Terry turning down money like that.

CHAPTER XXIII.

For the price of a lunch, a Kingdom was lost, Fred thought, after a short but successful meeting with Jack. Casting about for a solution to the puzzle of why Anne, of all people, would offer Terry over a million dollars of her own money without even asking Fred to pony up, he'd decided to see what Jack had been up to. Doris brought him Jack's reports and expense vouchers. There it was - ten dollars for a certified copy of a Claremont police report that Jack, the cheap bastard, had put in for just three weeks ago. It could only mean one thing - something he'd learned from following Anne had led him to look into their father's death. Of course, Jack had told him the whole surveillance of Anne had been a dry hole, but Fred couldn't believe it now. Within a week after Jack gets a copy of the police report Anne tries to end the whole estate fight. And she'd hardly showed her face in the office the last few weeks. Doris had even asked if she was on vacation. No, coincidences were for suckers. But how to get Jack to cough it up. Was he peddling the information to Rose? Or blackmailing Anne?

Fred decided to pay the police detective who investigated his father's death - if you could call it an investigation - a visit, get a copy of the report and try to figure out what Jack was up to. Doris set up the appointment. Fred was confident she wouldn't say anything to Anne.

Lieutenant Napoli was smart enough to know who the Lufkins were - he remembered the mansion where the old man was found - two million dollars, at least - and he was eager to please. Napoli commandeered the vacationing chief's office and had the file brought in. He wanted to know why people were suddenly so interested in the investigation. There had to be some dough in it, people like that. But the file confirmed his recall. It was just another cardiac arrest - even the rich aren't always lucky enough to have someone around to call an ambulance. The daughter hadn't even gotten there 'til he was cold.

Fred didn't necessarily want to suggest it was anything more just yet. On the ride from the office he considered the consequences of opening up the question of his father's death. Could he prove his whereabouts that night? Would the police suspect that brother and sister, whose interest in the estate had tripled just months earlier with the will eliminating Terry, were both involved? Would Anne if cornered try to implicate Fred? She couldn't be trusted not to try but Fred doubted she could devise a story that would hold up without any evidence. If anyone was in the line of fire, it was Anne. Fred thought he would move forward one step at a time. At the least this might be the leverage to get her out of the company for good. It didn't occur to Fred to be grateful to his sister if she had done in their father

Napoli met him at the sergeant's desk and escorted Fred to the Chief's office. “I understand you'd like to see the file on your father's, uh, passing on, Sir. Sometimes relatives find these things upsetting. I should warn you.” He passed the file to Fred across the Chief's desk and began to work on a report. Napoli had decided not to ask why Fred was suddenly so interested. Maybe he was just a ghoul. Fred gave him creepy vibes, dressed in a dark grey almost black suit and a black pattern tie, like a funeral director, reading the thin file, silently, actually making notes in a little black leather bound pad.

There wasn't much to the file, Fred saw. They hadn't even done an autopsy. Then suddenly he had to work to conceal his excitement. Anne said she didn't arrive until almost 9:00 at night at 314 Mountain Avenue. That was a Friday. Fred knew that if his father had Anne over on a Friday, it was always for dinner, which was never after seven o'clock. Lufkin was careful with his digestion and regular in his habits. Anne would usually have cleared out by nine-thirty at the latest. But Jack wouldn't know that, would he? Jack must have more incriminating information. There was something to it, he was sure now. Could the police help him squeeze Jack? Did he want the police there if Jack cracked, or did he want to take a shot on his own? If the police were there, Fred couldn't help Jack with his story and he'd lose control. On the other hand, Fred was sure he'd only have one shot with Jack and the element of surprise might be important. If this Napoli would agree to a meeting at Lufkin Realty with just Jack and Fred, it might all come out.

“Lieutenant, I'm afraid there may be more to my father's death than meets the eye.” Napoli wasn't surprised to hear this. He'd only be surprised if the suspect wasn't a competing heir. Napoli decided not to make it too easy and didn't respond right away, so Fred continued.” “I believe an individual I employ from time to time may have important information he hasn't disclosed to the police.”

"Well it says in the report your father died of cardiac arrest, Mr. Lufkin. Do you have any reason to doubt that?"

Fred saw he could lose Napoli if he implied that the police weren't doing their job. "I really couldn't say but I'm certain this individual knows facts at variance with the statements in the file, things the police had no way of knowing."

"And when did you learn these facts, sir?" Napoli wasn't going to waste his time unless this guy was good for it. Of course he wasn't going to find that out sitting in the Chief's office.

"Only yesterday, Lieutenant. I wonder if someone could meet with the witness at my, our, office, perhaps tomorrow?" I feel it would be more productive than asking him to come here. I'm sure you understand, Lieutenant."

"I would still be the investigating officer." If there were anything to investigate. "How is one o'clock Lieutenant?" Napoli agreed, and Fred left, stopping to visit his safe deposit box at Suburban First on the way back to the office.

Napoli wasn't kept waiting when he arrived at Lufkin Realty in an unmarked. He didn't tell the receptionist who he was, just that he had an appointment with Fred and he was escorted into Robert Lufkin's office by Doris, who closed the door when she left the office. Jack had been asked to be there at 1:30 for a new investigation -- Fred told Jack he suspected Terry had been embezzling while she worked at Lufkin and wanted him to look into whether any unusual deposits or purchases could be traced. It sounded to Jack like the kind of tree Fred would bark up, and

Jack's desire for more work won out one of his fear that Fred would figure out Jack was working his own angle on Anne.

Napoli could not understand why Fred didn't seem in a hurry to get to the point. "Do you have any children Lieutenant?"

"A boy, he's eleven, Mr. Lifkin."

"Any hobbies? I was always a collector, even as a boy." "Well, they all sit in front of the computer these days. No one seems to collect baseball cards like when I was a kid."

"I enjoy the computer myself. But I collect old things, coins and stamps. Is your son interested in ancient Rome? I have a lovely gold Justinian here - from 415 A.D." Fred pulled a gold coin from the gray velvet case on his desk and handed it to Napoli. Napoli had never held anything like it in his hand before. It was larger than an old silver dollar and heavy. "415 A.D. - really?"

"Its absolutely genuine, I've had it checked out." Think your son would like to see it?"

"Well..."

"Consider it on loan Lieutenant, from my collection to yours." Napoli put the coin in his suit pocket. Fred sat down.

"This individual's name is Jack Butler. He holds a private investigator's license." Napoli was wondering what the Justinian was worth. "He's undertaken a few investigations for our company. I think he ran across something that led him to believe my sister Anne Lufkin was responsible for my father's death."

"Was he checking her out for you?" Gold coin or not, Napoli needed to know what he was getting involved with. "My sister has some emotional problems Lieutenant, I believed it was prudent to monitor her behavior if she was going to help me run the family business." Sure, Napoli thought perhaps hire private detectives all the time to check on their sister's emotional problems. "I wonder if you could ask him why he went and got a copy of the report? Whether he's spoken to my sister about it?" Napoli knew what to ask this Butler - why hadn't he told the police he knew Anne Lufkin had lied to them? How much was she paying? Obstruction, accessory after the fact – blackmail. But, the important question was, would the DA look at any of that? Would the DA look at Anne for murder? How many coins could Napoli 'borrow' to get him to go to the prosecutor? If Jack said too much probably none - he'd be forced to go. But how could that be? Cardiac arrest, no bruises. Napoli had to assume his earlier investigation would be used against him. Could the failure to order a post mortem bite him in the ass if they looked at it? That would stop this parade cold - but Napoli knew one guy in the DA's office who'd never point the finger - Jeff Connery, an ex-cop who'd been on more than a few 'hunting' trips with Napoli in the old days. Connery would never screw over an old pal who knew how many beaver pelts they'd tanned. But was Connery still homicide? Claremont rarely gave the homicide bureau any business and he hadn't talk to Connery in months.

"I'll need to decide what questions are asked, Mr. Lufkin." Lufkin shouldn't even be present, of course, but Napoli understood what Lufkin was paying for, and he was sure he could gloss over that slight irregularity, especially since the report wasn't necessarily going to mention that Lufkin had fingered his sister before Napoli even spoke to Jack Butler.

"Shall I ask Mr. Butler in Lieutenant?"

"I believe that would be fine Mr. Lufkin so long as we're in agreement that I will be asking the questions." Lufkin buzzed for Doris to bring Butler in. Butler made Napoli and froze.

"Sit down Jack. This is Lieutenant Napoli. He has a few questions."

"Why don't you tell us what led you to obtain a copy of the report on Robert Lufkin's death? Mr. Lufkin tells me he never asked you to look into his father's death."

Jack couldn't deny getting a copy of the report. The judge was going to kill him for putting in the expense voucher. But who, was going to say what Fred had asked him to do beside Fred? He decided to try it on for size. "Don't you remember, Fred? About a month ago."

"Are you telling me Mr. Lufkin came down to the headquarters to see a report you gave him a month ago?"

"I didn't say I gave him the report."

"What are you saying, Jack?"

"That Fred asked me to, uh, check upon his sister and that was part of the investigation."

"But you didn't tell Fred, uh, Mr. Lufkin, what you found or give him the report. Do you really think I came out here just because you ordered a report, Jack? I've got better things to do. We know you've been shaking down Anne Lufkin." That, Jack knew, could be pure bullshit, but a denial now could be very embarrassing later if Napoli had heard what the Judge was up to. He said nothing.

"Blackmail, obstruction of justice, accessory after the fact. More important people than you have gone down for that Jack. Mr. Lufkin never asked you to do anything like that did he, Jack?" Probably only because he hadn't thought of it.

"Of course not." That answer alone should be good for another Justinian. Napoli thought. He wrote it down.

"You know we're not really looking to hang you up Jack, but if we don't know everything you know pretty damn quickly, this may have to go official. Which means, at the very least after this you'll be a security guard for the rest of your career if you're lucky."

"If I had anything to tell you I'd need Mr. Lufkin's promise that my name will be kept out of the case and your promise that I won't need to testify." Jack though that would slow them up.

"Jack promises are made so lawyers can break them, you know that. You want to give me a reason not to bust you, then we'll talk to the DA."

"Let's just say I've got the reason, Lieutenant. You haven't got anything on Anne without me, and you've got nothing on me, but you push too hard and your chance could disappear." Jack knew Napoli was slime and this was probably the last shot he'd ever have at a more comfortable retirement. Could there be a deal made for the tape with Fred? It didn't look like Anne was going to make a deal anytime soon. Without the tape Fred had no way to prove Anne was lying. "On the other hand gentlemen, if I were asked to look into the matter there might be a very substantial upside for all of us. Fred nodded at Napoli. Jack would be more expensive than Napoli, but it would be worth it to get rid of his sister. The question was, did Fred have enough for Napoli to run with? He didn't want to pay both of them for nothing. Jack wanted to make sure Fred knew what this was worth. "I assume you know that Anne can't inherit if she was mixed up in your father's death."

"And was she?" Napoli asked. Fred was struck dumb. He hadn't known the law was so definite. Someone must have told Jack about it. If Jack was right, Fred would have the entire estate. But could Jack prove it? Jack answered Napoli's question. "I heard Anne say she watched him die."

CHAPTER XXIV.

Terry knew Frank didn't want her to take the settlement even though he might be out $250,000 if she turned it down and Fred succeeded in kicking Frank out. They'd been awake half the night talking about it. Wasn't it strange to be in another man's arms talking about Robert's money? But Terry was sure Frank wanted her more than the money.

A friend of Frank's had loaned him a suite on Central Park South. They'd made love right on the carpet then sat holding each other and looking out over the park while they talked. Frank couldn't understand why only Anne seemed to be making the offer, but he didn't think it meant there was any chance of an offer from Fred.

Mary, doing Fred's bidding, had told Terry the offer was completely inadequate -- it wasn't enough to live on, it wasn't even 5% of what Bob had intended for her to receive, she deserved more.

Frank figured that conservatively invested the settlement would yield about $7,000 a month of which Tommy would eat $2,500 for the foreseeable future, especially if he got his own place - an unstated condition for a relationship between Terry and Frank. Anne hadn't thrown in the condo Terry lived in - owned by the estate, so she'd have to pay for that, buy medical insurance and provide for everything else - it would, he said, be a little tight. Unless she went back to work - but hardly poverty.

Terry knew Frank would lose a lot of his property to his wife if he got a divorce and she understood what he was saying - the settlement might not be enough to permit them to live the good life and she wouldn't ask him to give that up. Of course, she could get nothing. Paul had told her that was possible - unless they found out why Bob changed his will or came up with something else that the Lufkins couldn't let see the light of day.

She'd told Mary what the lawyer said. Mary played dumb: "But what could that be Terry - what kind of secret could mean more to Fred Lufkin than money? Nothing the bank ever knew - Lufkin Realty was clean as a whistle. Still, I can't understand how they tricked Bob. But it will all come out in the end dear."

After the night with Frank, Terry called Paul and told him she couldn't accept Anne's offer. Paul went to tell Joe Rose, who was happy with the decision. He had a crapshooter's confidence that this case would be a big score, though Paul couldn't see why.

"Gut instinct, my boy. Gut instinct. Never fails me, except occasionally in selecting my assistants. I hope you're putting together a good outline for Mel's deposition. He knows something's rotten - he's probably shaking down the kids himself. Must figure out some way to make him fess up....Tell me Sageman - didn't it occur to you to see if we can find out what kind of fees uncle Mel is pulling down from the Lufkins these days?"

But first, they'd have to beat Ritzer's application to put Mel's examination off while the motion to dismiss Terry's case was being heard - and Paul wasn't too confident about that.

CHAPTER XXV.

Tuesday morning, Jeff Connery would have moaned aloud if they couldn't have heard him through the rickety partition to his office. Even as first assistant for homicide you didn't get much privacy. He just had to give up those nights out for Monday night football - winning the pool didn't help - they wouldn't let him out of O'Meara's until he bought the house two more rounds after the game and he couldn't let all those losers drink alone. He tried to read the file Napoli had sent over - such as it was -- zero forensics, an inadmissible hearsay 'confession' no way to know if the old guy had even been murdered. What was Napoli up to? Well he'd only asked Connery for a fair shake - and Jeff guessed he owed him that much. Nappy was one of the all time great alibi witnesses - kept Connery out of divorce court on numerous occasions. Coffee with three sugars and a handful of aspirin was beginning to take the edge off but it couldn't help this case. Circumstantial wasn't the word for it - Connery didn't think he could get his own mother to vote an indictment - motive - sure - forty million motives - and the old guy had apparently been a 24 carat asshole - but cardiac arrest wasn't like a bloody dagger with prints on it.

Napoli was bringing his star witness in that morning. An ear witness, Jeff though, not an eyewitness. Even if you believed Butler's statement, if Anne Lufkin watched her old man turn blue there was no way to prove that calling an ambulance would have saved him - not without an autopsy - the attack might have been too sudden. You couldn't tell much of anything from the 'crime' scene shoot - Lufkin prone on an oriental carpet in a suit, one hand on his chest.

Napoli knocked and walked in “Hey, Connie, heard you took the points last night.”

“Nappy, you shouldn't just barge in like that. How'd you know I wasn't giving my secretary some personal dictation.”

“Cause Mama Cass ain't had a breakfast that tiny in years, Connie. This is Jack Butler, Jeff.”

“Pleased to meet you, Mr. Butler.” He hoped Nappy had enough sense not to drag Fred Lufkin in to the office too.

“You read the file Jeff, but I wanted you to hear what Mr. Butler had to say.” Nappy had something cooking here, but Connery didn't want to take the lid off the pot. Connery knew that if Robert Lufkin lived in a third floor walkup Nappy wouldn't be here.

The prosecutor wouldn't even look at a case this flimsy, neither would most cops.

Napoli knew he had to motivate Connery without letting him in on the deal -- not that Connie was any angel, but you take even a good cop, turn him into a lawyer and you just couldn't trust him.

“Mr. Lufkin was a very prominent citizen of Claremont, Jeff”...Napoli believed every prosecutor wanted only one thing more than guilty verdicts - his mush on the front page of the Ledger - and if this case went anywhere it would definitely get mondo coverage. Connery hadn't ever mentioned the desire to run for office, but most first assistants dreamed of it. Even if you ended up in private practice a few headlines couldn't hurt.

“Did you bring any evidence with you, Lieutenant that wasn't mentioned in your report? Like a confession?”

“Well, that's just what we're here to discuss.” Napoli and Jack had talked it over. Without the tape the case was dogshit. With the tape, they might be able to spook Anne Lufkin into an admission, if she was dumb enough to talk to them without a lawyer. “We need to talk about the big I, Connie.” Immunity.

“You know I never talk about that on the first date, Lieutenant. Why Mr. Butler hasn't even bought me a drink yet.” That's what Napoli needed him for - Butler knew cops, even homicide Lieutenants, couldn't make that deal. But immunity from what? Not anything to do with a homicide -- that only Big John Martin, the DA could hand out - Butler piped in “suppose Mr. Connery you could be sure Anne said to her doctor, what I heard - hear it for yourself. Could we have an understanding on that?” Butler had a tape, Connery understood and was looking for cover on whatever he did to get it.

Illegal surveillance, Connery thought, maybe breaking and entering - a shrink's office- that he might have to ask Big John about. It could look bad. Of course Connery wasn't sure such a recording could ever be used in court - which also made granting immunity a little delicate if the shit hit the fan. “I'd need to hear it and I'd need your sworn statements to how it came about. And you only get a pass for the circumstances of the recording. If you held the old guy down while his daughter fed him a pillow, that wouldn't be included, understood?”

"Of course, Mr. Connery you got nothing to worry about." Sure. Nothing for the career like being a witness in a malicious prosecution action - if it ever went to the grand jury at all.

"So how did you hear it?"

"Let's just say Ms. Lufkin had an extra lipstick in her Gucci purse."

"So you didn't need to go into the doctor's office?"

"Well a few visits wouldn't have hurt after working for Fred Lufkin, but no, I didn't need to wire the couch."

"I don't suppose you ever learned anything helpful when Ms. Lufkin wasn't with the shrink?"

"Sorry, no."

"Well Nappy, I'll need to run this by Big John but I think we can accommodate you."

Napoli hustled Butler out of Connery's cubicle. "Let me know what the verdict is, Connie, so I can send an engraved invitation to Ms. Lufkin."

CHAPTER XXVI.

Fred still couldn't quite believe it. A year ago he was expecting another twenty years of servitude under his father and a sixth of the estate. Now the old bastard was gone and he had a good shot at cutting out both Terry and Anne - leaving him with sixty million or more.

Better yet, Ritzer had told him, he had two bites at the apple with Anne. Even without a conviction she could be disinherited in a civil proceeding -- although it didn't happen very often and a conviction was clearly preferable. There was also a nice point of law over whether just letting someone die was enough. Fred hadn't heard the tape but apparently Anne hadn't admitted to doing anything to cause cardiac arrest, just sitting back and watching the show.

Even that showed more sange froid than Fred would have expected from Anne, but then she'd been closer to what was left of their mother than Fred and hadn't had the reprieve from their father that Fred had enjoyed at Combaf. Fred had trouble believing Anne had done nothing to hasten the process. If she hadn't in fact poisoned or throttled him, she'd taken the risk that the old bastard would survive - then he surely would have thrown her out of the Company and disinherited her.

Napoli was working hard for the chance at a few more Justinians and Jack had come around quite nicely but Fred hated to leave it up to them. He couldn't bribe the District Attorney of course and he definitely had to stay in the shadows on the investigation but what if they were missing a trick? Shouldn't they be searching Anne's car, her apartment? What about her desk at the office?

Fred had tossed her office before he'd heard about the police report, looking for something to convince her to retire, without success, but then he hadn't been looking for evidence of patricide. He'd been over every inch of his father's house but he doubted Anne was stupid enough to leave any leftover Belladonna behind on the kitchen counter anyway. Coming up with evidence of how, Fred concluded, was improbable, especially without a post mortem, but what about evidence of why? As a child of Robert Lufkin, Fred knew why, but for those who hadn't had the pleasure, evidence of motive could be very helpful.

The tape might help of course, but would Anne have opened up to anyone else? If she had any friends, Fred didn't know them. Her secretary Kimberly wouldn't give Fred the time of day. He couldn't wait to can the bitch. Was Anne the sort to keep a diary? He'd never seen one but by now she'd have ditched it. Fred believed in writing down as little as possible and keeping less. Mel Weinberg, the Jew bastard, was no fool, throwing out all his notes and drafts.

Fred suspected this wasn't Mel's first case of third-party estate planning. Mel had told Ritzer that Robert didn't like written advice but that wasn't why the file was clean as a whistle. His father did write things down, often leaving terse instructions for his children and other employees in his fine hand, always in black ink. Not to mention the black book. Fred had the book, in his father's roll top desk in the study at the house on Mountain Avenue. The study was Fred's favorite room now. But he hadn't thought to check the black book. They'd found it on the dining room table but the Claremont detectives hadn't even bothered to read it. Fred logged out and told Doris he'd be back in an hour. Driving to Mountain Avenue he thought about whether he should hand it to the detective or the prosecutor or merely encourage them to reinvestigate the crime scene and happen upon it themselves. In any event, he'd be wearing gloves when he read it just in case - Anne had conveniently placed it in the desk the next day when they straightened up. She'd been a cool customer that day Fred thought, though she rarely vented in front of Fred, except about Terry.

Fred slipped on the felt tipped cloth gloves he used to handle his collection, sat in his father's carved mahogany desk chair and began to read. A shiver went through him as he read the last month's entries. "Tell A How Poorly She's Handling Crown Centre lease up... Couldn't find a credit tenant if one fell on her... No more basket weaving schools...Ask A why is she putting up with slow payers at Sussex Plaza. Where are default letters?" If we go out of pocket to pay mortgage next month its out of her pay check." "A.- never sign a repaving contract without me seeing it first - too high - giving away money. Fred would do better. Throwing away rent." The final entry, the day of his death. "Must take A through mistake she made in override lease at Broomefield Center. My own child bankrupting me. If Anne can't handle responsibility. I'll hire someone who appreciates the job." Dad really came through for me in the end, Fred thought. He'd driven Anne to whatever she'd done then left a road map. There was no time to waste - he picked up the phone. “Lieutenant Napoli please.” They put him through. “Lieutenant, could you stop by Mountain Avenue this afternoon? I've stumbled across something you ought to review. And bring one of those evidence bags.” Fred had no doubt he could convince Napoli to tell the prosecutor that Napoli had found the black book.

CHAPTER XXVII.

Napoli brought Connie a copy of the black book entries. "I decided to take a look through the Lufkin place. Now that we have a question about the circumstances, Connie."

"And you found a strychnine bottle with Anne's fingerprints, Nappy?"

"Well I wouldn't want to make it too easy for you Connie, but the deceased's calendar has some interesting notes - it looks like he was really beating up on his daughter the last few weeks." Nappy was really flogging the file, Connery thought.

"Give." Napoli handed him the copies. Connery read them. "Very convenient Nappy. If the decedent actually wrote them."

"I'm sure we could prove that Connie. You'll notice the date of the last entry."

"Just before the Last Supper I believe." There was just one problem. Would any Judge let this stuff in? Any law student worth his salt remembered the case, a golden oldie, New York something or other versus Hillmon, a case that went not once but three times to the Supreme Court of the United States back in those palmy days before civil rights, when they had time on their hands.

Mr. Hillmon insured his life for a fortune. Mrs. Hillmon tendered his alleged corpse and demanded the loot - except it turned out that the body might belong to someone else. The insurance company came up with the real body's letter in which he said he was going to meet up with Hillmon - The question was whether the letter was inadmissible hearsay or admissible to show that the corpse knew Hillmon and actually met him. Lufkin's diaries indicated the intent to beat Anne up but she could deny that her father ever actually did. And she had to deny they ever talked the last night or her goose was cooked. "Don't know, if I can use it Nappy, but there is nothing to stop you from asking. Does the tape corroborate any of this?"

"From what Butler tells me not specifically but its certainly consistent." Better, than a kick in the head Connery thought. And it was dynamite for the press coverage even if the jury wasn't allowed to see it. "DAD'S DEATH DIARY DISSES DAUGHTER." He'd take this case if Big John approved. And if Nappy got him the tape.

CHAPTER XXVIII.

Judge Galante hadn't given Jack a receipt for the tape and to his way of thinking the storage fees were very high and getting higher if brother and sister were in the bidding. Jack knew it could be very unhealthy to ignore a call from the Judge, and he needed the tape, so when summoned to Tight Ends he went - but had Napoli stationed across the bar just in case.

The Judge pulled him into the back office. "Nice of you to show up, partner. I've been a little worried about you, not dropping by to see Pilar."

"Just been a little busy Judge. But since I'm here, Judge I think we can make something happen if I could have my uh, property back."

"What property would that be Jack? I didn't think you owned anything but an old van and some gum shoes." Could Anne be paying Galante? If she was, why would Galante be calling him? The proximity of Tight Ends to the Great Swamp began to concern Jack. By the time Napoli decided to act like he got lost on the way to the men's room and knock on the office door, Jack could be fish food.

"Judge I really think we can do very well with this my way..." Since Anne wasn't acting like she was interested in paying, the Judge listened. He assumed Fred was willing to pony up, but he wasn't going to turn anything over until he got paid for his trouble.

"I like the 'we' part, Jack, but how well is very? After all, there's more than one way to do this and I've got to believe you're only talking about a one shot deal. Whereas the people I'm speaking to represent a long term relationship for our partnership." The Judge was already considering hiring a real estate lawyer to handle the Lufkin Realty account, probably the cleanest way to extract payment if Anne was the successful bidder and stayed in the business.

"Let me have one more chat with my friend Don Morton before I take Fred's offer - If we can't arrange things, you'll get the tape when your employer makes a suitable contribution to our favorite charity. Meantime, Mr. Morton and I will go fishing."

Morton didn't think he could turn down a friendly invitation to fish with the Judge, who had a surprisingly nice 45 foot sport fisherman that he docked in Belmar. Hell he'd bill a client for a fishing trip any day - and he was just as happy as the Judge that you couldn't tape over the noise of twin diesels at 18 knots.

The problem was, how could a lawyer put himself in the middle off a deal like this -- paying off a Judge to avoid a murder prosecution? Even Jay Ritzer probably hadn't done that more than three or four times. Morton didn't think that his partners at Ferguson and Mather would appreciate his picture on the cover of the American Lawyer in handcuffs.

The Judge was one step ahead of him though. They'd hooked up on some keeper striped bass and were alone on the fly bridge on the way home. "Don, I'm sure you've had the experience, even at a firm like yours of knowing when it's in the client's best interest for your firm to step aside and let local talent deal with local problems."

"I have Judge, I have, though I personally hate to walk away from a fight." And, they both thought, a seven figure fee. The Judge had heard that Morton was no longer hitting the strike zone but figured he wouldn't be anxious to hand the ball over. “I'm happy to let you continue to handle the competing heirs, Don, but Ms. Lufkin's little problem that we spoke of has a complication we didn't get to discuss at lunch.” Even out here the Judge felt compelled to whisper in Morton's ear. “There's a very incriminating tape, Don, and I may be in a better position than you are to be certain it doesn't fall into the wrong hands.” Jesus, a tape, Morton though. If I get out of this one with my license I'll never set foot in Jersey again. “If your client were to retain my partner Pete Giresi, who has great experience with matters of this nature, I'm certain we could keep her off the hook.” This guy has the fucking tape. “Your firm wouldn't need to be involved, and I can't see how you could do better for your girl otherwise.” The Judge concluded.

“Well, thanks for an interesting day of fishing Judge.”

On the ride home, Morton couldn't help brooding over the fix he was in. Could he hand his client over to a vampire like the Judge? Morton was sure he'd put the big squeeze on Anne for years to come because there was no way to be sure the tape hadn't been copied. Morton hadn't any doubt there was a tape, and little doubt it was incriminating. Could he just walk away from the whole case? Worst of all, how would he respond when Anne asked him what to do? Morton didn't think he could ask Pedersen or even one of his partners for advice on this one - which just proved how deep in it he was already. Of course, the Judge had tried to make it easy - hadn't said he had the tape, and Morton wouldn't need to be in the middle of the ransom negotiations, but no matter how you sliced it he was still at risk.

"Pull over at the next watering hole, Jimmy." Morton had decided to sleep on the problem, since it wasn't going away. Maybe he'd even do a little research on his own, tomorrow, if he could remember what floor the library was on. Just what were the elements of obstruction of justice, anyway?

CHAPTER XXIX.

Judge Weiss didn't even give Ritzer a hearing on the motion to prevent Weinberg's deposition, mailing it back with "Denied" scribbled across the Order. So now Terry's lawyers could take Mel's deposition. "Sageman you're almost thirteen now and its time you became a man." Rose had summoned Paul to his office and actually asked him to set down. If the door had been closed, Paul would have been sure he was getting canned.

"Guess who's taking Mel Weinberg's deposition next week?" Paul couldn't believe it. Rose must have decided the case really was a loser if he was letting someone else take the deposition, especially since it was the only one they could take before Ritzer's dismissal motion was heard. "Now I don't want you to worry, there's only your career and a five million dollar fee at stake, so I'll let you in a little secret. I only care about one question and one answer, cause Mel's gonna lie about everything else anyway. I don't have time for the Socratic method this morning, so I'll connect the dots for you. Had Mel done any work for the young Lufkins before the date of the last will?" Paul wrote down the question and waited for Rose to explain two thing. Why would Weinberg tell the truth about that and why was the answer so important. "By the blankness of your stare Sageman, I see that time will need to be wasted explaining the obvious. Appearances to the contrary notwithstanding, ours is a noble profession. Our Supreme Court in its wisdom has recognized the limits of that nobility, however, by deciding that, if X employs a lawyer and X's doddering old father Y employs that same lawyer to draft a will leaving Y's million to X, that will is tainted and is subjected to a higher level of scrutiny. If Mel ever billed either of the children for anything, I don't think he'll risk his ticket to deny it, since paper has an awful habit of avoiding obliteration. Bills, checks, files - these are our friends Sageman. I'm counting on you, the client is counting on you. Berry and French is counting on you. Most importantly, Mrs. Rose is counting on you, Sageman. Mrs. Rose, I might add is far less forgiving than any of the aforementioned."

Paul knew where to start - for whom had Weinberg incorporated Omega? Mike Miller could help him with the rest of it.

Mel Weinberg wasn't surprised that Ritzer couldn't stop Rose from examining him, and told Fred not to worry. "It was only me and your father in the room, Fred, when he told me why he was changing his will and one of us isn't talking." Fred believed Mel would follow the party line, but he expected Mel to hit him up for more dough, claiming that perjury wasn't included in the retainer. Mel thought a payoff after the fact would be less dangerous than a bribe.

This was Paul's biggest assignment yet at Berry & French. Even though Rose had said he was concerned only with the answer to one question Paul knew he expected more. Mike told Paul it wasn't just what you asked but how, especially in a fraud case. Mel would flout the oath and deny the deniable, but based on the facts he'd have to admit Paul should seek to create the appearance of suspicion.

"What are the ten most important things you need to know before deposing this guy?" Mike asked.

Paul was stumped. "The digits of the stiff's kids' telephone numbers. Wait a minute, you did ask for this slime ball's phone bills didn't you?" Luckily he had.

"But if they called him or he called at the office those numbers wouldn't show up."

"And if they communicated by smoke signals it wouldn't either. But we have to hope he returned calls at least once in a while, hopefully in the period before the last will."

"But he could still lie about what was discussed."

"Sure, but we're expecting that."

Mike told Paul to set the deposition for Mel's office - it was harder to 'forget' to bring documents to your own office. So Monday morning there they were in Weinberg's cramped alley view conference room. Ritzer, manning an oversized Mont Blanc fountain pen and one of Weinberg's yellow pads, Don Morton and his sharp-nosed associate Pedersen, Fred Lufkin and the court reporter filled all the chairs. Radin, to maintain the illusion of neutrality among heirs and wills, was absent. Paul fumbled his outline and redrope of exhibits out of his trial bag, worrying over whether he'd forgotten anything, while Morton chatted up Ritzer and Weinberg.

"Say Mel do you charge time and a half for testifying?" "Oh, no Don, I doubt I'll break a sweat this morning. Telling the truth is easy." Fred was used to Mel's antics and continued to study the glossy coin show brochure in his lap. Paul had the court reporter swear the witness, then he questioned Weinberg about the subpoena for his records. Mel pulled a shoebox full of phone bills out from under the table and pushed them across the table to Paul. Lucky, he thought, that

Fred's biggest coin collection was the sock full of quarters he used to make sensitive calls from phone booths. Mel always had his secretary "Mrs. Green" call Fred at the office and leave a message with a non-existent return number. Paul asked for copies. "Twenty five cents a page Mr. Sageman. Got to make a living somehow." Paul went over the rest of the subpoena with Mel and learned of his sound policy against retaining those pesky draft wills and the lack of notes or advisory correspondence. Mike and Paul had decided not to mention Omega in the subpoena.

Mike had told Paul not to back Weinberg into a corner by asking whether he did work for Anne or Fred before the last will. Once he denied that he'd have to fight harder over the issue of who he'd set up Omega for -- and who owned it now. Paul plodded through the outline. Mel stuck to the script on the new will. "Yes, Mr. Sageman, he just told me to change it. Nope, didn't say why...Didn't I ask why? No, son, that's none of my business...No, I didn't ask about his relationship with your client, that wasn't my business either." True, in a way. Mel hadn't had to ask, Lufkin had volunteered an earful. Whatever Fred did to convince the old man that Terry was stepping out on him had sure done the trick, the old philanderer was hot as a pistol, couldn't wait to cut her loose. Lufkin had waited while Weinberg's secretary ran off the new will, cause Mel told him if he got run over crossing the street after announcing the intent to disinherit Terry but before he signed, Terry would still be in the driver's seat. Mel didn't remember that detail for the record.

Paul took Weinberg through the history of representing Bob Lufkin and his companies, but the name Omega didn't come up. Weinberg remembered Nikful, Crown Center Limited, Broomefield Plaza Associates and half a dozen others, but not Omega. Paul asked if those were all the companies Robert Lufkin owned. "All I can remember off the top of my head, Mr. Sageman, but Bob had companies like your dog has fleas, just like all the real estate operators I represent."

"Did Mr. Lufkin own all the companies you've listed for us at the time of his death?"

Fred touched Ritzer's arm below the table. Ritzer said "I'm afraid Mr. Sageman that nature calls and we'll have to take a little break. Do I need a key Mel?"

Mike had warned Paul about this. "Just try to hold out for a couple of more questions Jay."

"Can you answer the question Mr. Weinberg?"

"So far as I know, Bob liked to hold onto things. Never was interested in family partnerships, living trusts or any of those tax planning vehicles."

"You suggested them?"

"Sure, its my obligation to present the client those alternatives." Which of course turned Doreen and her word processor into a profit center every time the tax laws changed. Mike had given him the next questions.

"And those alternatives would also include life time transfers of interests?"

"Yes." "But Mr. Lufkin didn't make any transfers of interests to his children?"

"Not that I know of. 'Course he could have been two timing me with some local guy over in Jersey. And he did have investors. I believe your Mr. Mairone was one!" Without knowing just why, Morton began thinking that Weinberg was forgetting what a dangerous sport fencing could be, and that Sageman was not just bumping about aimlessly and Ritzer apparently knew it.

Fred hit Ritzer again. "Mr. Sageman, I hate to interrupt, but." "Just a couple more questions, Jay. Just so we're clear Mr. Weinberg you're not aware of any transfer by Mr. Lufkin of shares in an existing entity other than as consideration for an investment."

"No, sir, I'm not aware. But I could have forgotten, or someone else might have done it." Mel, unaware of the Nikful stock power, was trying to figure out where the kid lawyer was going with this. Was Terry going to claim Bob was on the pay as you go plan and had gifted stock to her? Ritzer, also in the dark, was thinking the same thing and felt Mel's last answer disposed of the issue for the moment. Fred was worried by the mention of Nikful but didn't see how Terry's lawyers would know about the forged stock transfer. Would it be better to tell Ritzer, or Mel, about it now? Paul, approaching the subject of Omega hesitated over the next question.

Fred tapped Ritzer again. This time Ritzer got up. "Mr. Sageman, this seems like a natural breaking point." Ritzer steamed out of the room before Paul could stop him. "Guess I'll check my messages." Mel excused himself, followed by Fred. Paul now had to think of how to handle the conference now in progress when questioning resumed. Still, Paul thought, Fred had signaled for the time out and believed he must be getting close to the cheese.

Out in the hall, Fred sent Ritzer to the can and whispered to Mel about Omega. Then Mel remembered. Back before they'd really teamed up, Fred had first approached Mel, probably as a pretext for later hijinks and asked him to set up a way to insulate Fred from future trading losses, of which incorporating Omega was a part. Lucky he hadn't sent Fred a bill individually, because that would not be deniable. Could he assert privilege, if any, if this came up? Mel decided to try and told Fred not to worry. They returned one by one to the conference room. Paul having failed to prevent the conference, did the next best thing and put the fact of the break and disappearance of the three stooges from the conference room on the record. Ritzer replied at length, alluding to the innocent cause of the interruption and the scurrilous nature of the accusations implied by Paul's comment, threatening to terminate the deposition if such aspersions were again cast on the right honorable Mel Weinberg.

"I'm sure your client appreciates your zeal Mr. Ritzer, but I haven't quite forgotten where we were when you interrupted the proceedings." Paul hadn't listened to Joe Rose for three years for nothing.

"Would you tell me Mr. Weinberg for whom you incorporated Omega Corporation, a New Jersey corporation." Paul pulled the certificate of incorporation from its folder, squelching Ritzer's foundation objection.

"No sir, I believe that would be privileged." Mike had anticipated this and told Paul what to do next. "I take it then sir that you incorporated Omega for a client of your legal practice."

"Yes sir that's correct."

"Did you issue shares in Omega?"

"Not to my recall." Nor, Mel was happy to learn out in the hall, had anyone else. To Mel the decision was simple - just say Omega belonged to Robert Lufkin. Fred and Anne were almost certain to inherit the whole pile anyway. But Mel knew from thirty years of practice that greed is infinite. He didn't know - because he'd instructed Fred not to tell him - just what Lufkin loot now bore the Omega brand.

"Do you know who owns Omega Corporation's stock?"

"No, sir."

"Do you have the corporate seal, bylaws, stock register or blank certificates for shares of Omega Corporation?"

"No, sir."

"Did you ever?"

"I don't recall."

That information, Paul had learned could be obtained, so Mel's lack of recall was inevitable.

"Did you incorporate Nikful?"

"Yes sir."

"For Mr. Lufkin?"

"Or one of his entities."

"Is Omega an asset of the estate of Robert Lufkin?"

"At this time, it is not my understanding that a Form 706 has been prepared, and I don't believe Mr. Mairone has rendered an account - at least to anyone other than your client, so I couldn't answer that question."

“Do Fred or Anne Lufkin have any interest in the stock of Omega.”

“I don't know.”

“Have you ever discussed Omega Corporation with Fred or Anne Lufkin?” Weinberg was beginning to break a sweat. Lying about a chat with Bob Lufkin was one thing, but Weinberg didn't want to put his ticket in Fred's hand, and he couldn't be sure that wasn't some document that would make it clear that there must have been such a discussion. Ritzer, who was beginning to see where things were going decided to let Mel make the call.

“Any such discussion would have been privileged.”

“So Anne and Fred were your clients?” Paul thought he had Weinberg on the ropes, but Weinberg had a few moves left in him.

“I didn't say that, Mr. Sageman. Anne and Fred are officers of Lufkin companies that I have represented.”

“So you have had occasion to discuss matters of Lufkin Realty business with Fred and Anne Lufkin?”

“Yes, of course.”

“While Robert Lufkin was alive?”

“I suppose so.”

“Before the date of Mr. Lufkin's purported will of October 11, 1996?”

“I don't recall.”

“What matters did you discuss with them?”

“The affairs of which ever entity happened to be in issue.”

“So if the estate waived the privilege you could testify to those discussions?”

"If the estate can do so."

"Then we'll be coming back to that subject."

Paul pulled out a copy of the stock power. "Do you know why Robert Lufkin would have transferred the stock of Nikful to Omega?" Fred maintained a poker face, though he was stunned and he didn't know how Terry got wind of it. Was that tramp Mary, who had access to records at Union Trust, working both sides of the aisle?

"I didn't know he had, so I guess I wouldn't know why."

"Did Robert Lufkin ever discuss transferring shares of Nikful to Omega with you?"

"Not that I recall."

"Did Robert Lufkin ever discuss Omega with you."

"Not that I recall."

"What was the business of Nikful?"

"I believe it was a vehicle for holding some land out in Jersey."

"Was that land mortgaged?"

"I don't recall."

"So is it fair to say you know Robert Lufkin owned Nikful, the vehicle for holding the land, you don't know if he owned Omega, there is a stock power purporting to transfer ownership of Nikful to Omega, you incorporated Omega and you won't say who you did it for?

"Objection to form." Ritzer weighed in.

"Could you answer the question?"

"What I said was, if someone directed me to incorporate Omega, that would be privileged."

"But it wasn't Robert Lufkin or one of his companies?"

"No."

Was this enough, Paul wondered? There still wasn't any proof that Anne or Fred had anything to do with Omega, though it was a good bet Fred would be warming up the shredder as soon as he got home.

Paul believed that he was entitled to an order requiring Weinberg to cough up the identity of the client, but he'd been around long enough not to have confidence that it would happen. Would it be enough if Weinberg simply failed to deny that it was Fred or Anne? "Mr. Weinberg, can you tell me that it wasn't Fred Lufkin who directed you to incorporate Omega?" Ritzer objected, but Paul knew he'd asked the right question.

"No sir, I can't say yes or no." Paul decided not to ask about Anne.

CHAPTER XXX.

Three days had passed and Judge Galante hadn't heard from his old fishing buddy Don Morton. The Judge had gotten wind of the game Jack was playing with Napoli and the Mick Assistant DA and had come up with a way to use it to turn up the heat.

"Jack, boy, I'm beginning to think you may be on the winning team after all." Jack was glad to hear it. Napoli had been badgering him for the tape all week. The Judge had summoned him to chambers at Town Hall, poured Jack a drink and filled him in on the fishing trip. "This guy Morton, he's either too greedy to step aside or too scared to explain life to his girl. I'll give him one more chance to shit or get off the pot, then we sit down with Mr. Lufkin and see if he'll trade Boardwalk and Park Place for Anne's get out of jail free card." "Seems to me Morton's had enough rolls of the dice, Judge."

"Jack, you and I, we've been around the block. This is all new to Morton and his girl. Maybe they think we're bluffing. But a call from your friend at the Hall of Justice might just change their whole attitude."

Now Jack knew why the Judge had called him. But Connery was too careful to bring Anne in without the tape. "I don't know that I can get that call made without a piece of additional evidence, Judge." But once the tape was in Connery's hands, the game was over, since he wasn't a member of the Lufkin early retirement plan that Jack and Napoli were working feverishly to fund.

"Supposing, Jack, that the next District Attorney could be sure of the existence of the tape and exactly what was on it, without our actually turning it over to him."

"You wouldn't give him a copy?" Jack would be buying a new van and Napoli would get a hernia from carrying around all the gold coins if that happened.

"No, Jack, just a chance to listen to it. That should be enough to get him moving."

"Listen in?"

Napoli didn't have an easy time persuading Connery to make a field trip to a filthy phone booth by the Medical Center the next afternoon, but peace appeared to have broken out among his usual customers the crack dealers and Connery had time on his hands. He was won over by the promise of a personal intro to one of the Judge's 'friends' from Tight Ends. The phone was ringing when they pulled up. As soon as he picked up, he realized that he was now probably a witness, but his curiosity got the better of him as he heard a distinctive and somewhat refined female voice say "I told him he didn't have a heart, Doctor. A few minutes later he was unconscious. I don't really think he suffered enough." The phone disconnected within a minute to avoid a trace.

Connery stumbled back to the car dumbfounded. "That's incredible Nappy. If it's for real, I don't think I have a choice."

"Trust me, Connie, it's for real. The brother didn't know nothing about it 'til Butler gave it up."

"Could Butler have spliced it?"

"He don't strike me as that sophisticated." "Course you know Nappy, that its absolutely inadmissible."

"So she's got to be spooked into admitting it before she calls a lawyer. That we always knew. Do you think she should get away with it?"

"But even if I believe it I still don't have the tape." "If I just repeat the words 'I told him he didn't have a heart' to her, there'll be quite a puddle on her chair, tape or no tape. Can we bring her in?" Connery didn't answer. "Come on Connie, just for a chat. There'll be no arrest unless she coughs it up. No one needs to know you were in the loop if it's a dead end." Meaning Connie would 'forget' the promise of immunity for Butler and hang him out to dry if need be.

"Okay, go ahead. But I gotta tell you, that's a very tricky interview. Could she be dumb enough to say word one without a lawyer?"

Napoli had given that a lot of thought. He'd prefer not to bring Anne to the Claremont Police Headquarters, since he'd somehow forgotten to tell the Chief about reopening the investigation, but he knew Connery didn't want her down at the Hall of Justice either. She wouldn't be nearly intimidated enough in her own house and Fred wouldn't want it to appear that the shakedown had been at Lufkin Realty. Anne didn't live in Claremont but in a townhouse in West Ridge. Napoli had some friends on the job there. Could she be pulled in late at night, when it was hard to get through to a lawyer, on a vehicular charge and then sideswiped? He talked it over with Jack. If Jack could tail her and give the West Ridge boys a shout if she was coming home late one night, Napoli would join the interview in progress and maybe get Anne to cough it up. If some defense lawyer later said these were KGB tactics, Connie would deal with it somehow.

CHAPTER XXXI.

"A touch slapdash, Sageman, a bit hurried, but overall, I have to admit, mission accomplished." Rose held the transcript of Mel's examination in his hands. Compliments, being free as the air, were not unknown in the Rose lexicon, though Paul rarely heard one that wasn't backhanded. "Now young Mr. Darrow, what's the next step?"

"Don't we have to wait for Ritzer's motion to be heard?"

"He who hesitates, Sageman is unemployed."

"But we can't take any more discovery until then can we?"

"Cross move, Sageman, cross move in the interests of justice. A change in circumstances. Strong evidence that Bob Lufkin's purported last will was prepared by Fred's running dog Mel Weinberg, a New York lawyer. A New York lawyer, Sageman, Harry doesn't like them very much. Be sure to say that three or four time a page in the brief. Serve subpoenas on anyone who might have a scrap of paper having anything to do with Nikful or Omega. Maybe even Union Trust. Stir up a shit storm, my son and watch them run for cover. Get me Radin, Mrs. Dolan, so I can tell him how I saved his bacon once again."

The moment Ritzer found out Mel had been working for Fred before the last will was signed, he was sure the motion to dismiss had no more chance than one ticket in the lotto drawing but there was an art, an art to letting the client know how bad the news was. Ritzer didn't want Fred thinking he should be looking for his own Ferguson & Mather, so he knew he couldn't tell Fred the whole truth. At the same time, it could be fatal to let Judge Weiss be the first to tell Fred he might be going to a full scale trial and the estate would be tied up for years. Fred wasn't going to make it easy. They were sharing a cab so Fred could be dropped at Penn station on the way back to Ritzer's office.

"So Jay, I don't suppose they can make anything out of what Mel said, can they?"

"Ultimately, Mr. Lufkin, ultimately no."

"What do you mean ultimately?"

"Rose will make an argument, just an argument, that perhaps there's a suggestion that Mel might not have been acting entirely for your father when he drafted the will. I am certain, certain Mr. Lufkin that ultimately that argument will go nowhere."

"I'm not clear on what you mean by ultimately, Jay. I want that case dismissed now." So that with Terry out of the ring Fred would be the executor and could turn his tender attentions to his sister. "Are you telling me that what Mel said could affect that?"

"It's a slender reed, a slender reed, you understand, Mr. Lufkin but a judge just might give Rose a limited opportunity, limited of course, to make sure that the possible dual representation had no effect on your father's will."

"Based on what, Jay? Suppose Mel did a bit of unrelated work for me. What does that have to do with my father's will?"

"There's a case, nothing at all like our case, of course, nothing at all like it, in which a court decided that the dual representation slightly affected the presumptions to be applied. But the facts, the facts were entirely distinguishable and we will be sure to address that."

"Are you telling me we are going to lose the motion, Jay?"

Clients did ask the darnedest questions. "Not at all, Mr. Lufkin, not at all. But I did want you to understand the argument that I anticipate Rose will make."

"You better win that motion Jay." Fred gave his parting command as he left the cab.

CHAPTER XXXII.

Morton's hesitancy in passing the baton to Judge Galante was at least in part a result of his realization that the estate fight was going to go a few extra rounds as a result of Mel's testimony. Pedersen had showed him the Jersey case about dual representation and Morton couldn't see how Ritzer was going to get around it. Morton didn't have too much else going on and a two year fight with plenty of depositions, motions and hearings didn't sound bad. He knew that once Judge Galante got his proboscis under the tent he'd try to cut Ferguson & Mather out of the whole case. Of course if your client was in jail she might have a hard time writing checks monthly. And if Morton didn't get out of this thing soon, he might need his own lawyer to avoid ending his career in a cell in Trenton.

There was only one right answer in the client's best interest. Tell Anne she had to make a deal with the devil. But it wasn't an easy message to give the client. The immediate question was, just how soon could the shit hit the fan? He needed to figure out just what to say and not to say and Pedersen couldn't help him. Would he need to tell Anne there was a tape? What if she asked him about paying to obtain the tape? Or destroying it once she got it? Could he risk having a conversation like that without a witness? But who could be a witness?

Morton decided to think about it over the weekend and call Anne on Monday.

That Friday Anne had been invited to a dinner theatre show by Bill Mintz, a visionary among realtors, who believed that Lufkin Realty would break up and the properties be sold off as a result of the inevitable battle between Fred and Anne. There would be big dollars in commissions if he could only get the listings for some of the properties. Why should the lawyers drink all the blood spilled in a family tragedy? Mintz was divorced and not hideous, so Anne accepted.

After a few glasses of chardonnay the show had been enjoyable, Mintz, if not gallant certainly gentlemanly and Anne was in a good mood driving home in her new Mercedes.

Jack, following in his van, clocked her at 50 in 35 and called Napoli. "Lieutenant, I think we have some serious lawbreaking going on here on West Ridge Avenue."

"We'll take it from here, sir thanks for your public spirit." Two West Ridge patrol cars scrambled and before she knew it Anne had failed her first field sobriety test and was in the back seat of a police car feeling nauseous and alone. Who could she call? It didn't seem like the kind of thing to call Morton about. He was too far away and Anne wasn't sure she wanted him knowing she was being charged with drunk driving anyway. Anne imagined what her father would have said. She decided to wait and see just how serious it was before trying to reach a lawyer. They couldn't lock her up could they? It wasn't as if there had been an accident.

At the West Ridge station Anne submitted to the blood alcohol test, since she didn't think it was possible that three lousy glasses of wine could put her over the limit but they wouldn't tell her the result. Instead she sat alone in a cold interrogation room for 45 minutes before Napoli entered the room with Clarence Mayes, a black detective from Connery's office and the arresting West Ridge officer, James Tucci. Napoli had told Mayes that Connery wanted him there, though it wasn't exactly true. Anne stood up, as if she was ready to leave.

"Officer Tucci, I'm sure you have my test results by now. Unless I failed, I'd like to go home now."

"Ms. Lufkin, we're still awaiting the results but in the mean time these gentlemen would like a word with you."

Napoli advanced into the room hand outstretched. Anne reluctantly took his paw. She had the feeling she had seen him before, but couldn't place him. "Lieutenant Napoli, Ms. Lufkin, and this is my colleague Sergeant Mayes."

Napoli had taken Anne's statement after she called in to report her father's death, but it had only taken a few minutes and her memory bank for lower rung public servants was limited. "When can I go home, Lieutenant?"

"Soon, I'm sure. In fact I'm here to help, because Lufkin Realty is quite an important institution in Claremont and I'm hoping we can avoid any embarrassment for your family."

"How kind of you. Perhaps we could just get the test results so I can get home, I've been here over an hour."

"I understand. Could you tell me, Ms Lufkin, in confidence, how much had you had to drink?"

"Shouldn't you be reading me my rights, Lieutenant, if you're going to be asking questions like that?"

"Well, I don't know if that's necessary, but if you insist, Ms. Lufkin." Napoli gave the Miranda warning and Anne signed a form confirming she understood it. It was unsettling that two detectives were there to interrogate her over a drunk driving charge, but she didn't want to appear nervous or evasive.

"Since you asked, I had two glasses of wine with a five course dinner at the Old Mill Playhouse. I hardly think that I could be intoxicated, and I would imagine you have more serious matters to investigate, Lieutenant."

"Well I'm just trying to make sure that if we can keep this quiet I won't regret it later. Do you drink regularly, Ms. Lufkin?"

"I would say occasionally, Lieutenant, not regularly."

"Good, good. So no record or anything?"

"No, Lieutenant."

"Are you on any prescriptions, tranquilizers, things like that?"

"No."

"Good. I had a concern if you had a substance problem, because..."

"Because why, Lieutenant?"

"Well, Ms Lufkin, can I call you Anne?"

"If you like."

"Well Anne, I had heard that in your family."

"I can't see what that has to do with me, Lieutenant." Where did this slob hear about her mother?

"I'm on your side Anne, just trying to make sure there isn't a larger problem here before I speak to Officer Tucci, you understand."

"I appreciate that, Lieutenant, though I'm at a loss as to why you've taken such an interest in a stranger."

"Oh, don't you remember me, Anne? I took a statement from you the night your father passed away." Anne was suddenly much more nauseous. Could that Judge person have gone to the police? Could she stop answering questions now? Should she ask for a lawyer? Anne decided it was best not to show fear. She had thought through what she would say if the subject ever came up.

"I'm sorry, I'm afraid I don't recall." But now of course she did.

"Yes, I believe you told me that you got there after 9:00 and your father was already dead from a heart attack, isn't that right, Anne?"

"Yes, Lieutenant."

"But if that's so, Anne, when did you tell your father that he didn't have a heart?" Since hearing what Judge Galante had to say, Anne had on occasion envisioned the interrogation she might face and chosen a course of action, so after the initial shock of realizing that Napoli was actually investigating her father's death she was able to maintain.

"But I never actually said that to him, Lieutenant." That was how Anne had decided to deal with the issue. Whatever they had overheard, she would just say was invention after the fact, what she would have said if she'd had the chance. Napoli was disappointed with the effect of his question, but the next one was really more important.

"You know, I don't think I asked you where you happened to be that night before you got to 314 Mountain Avenue."

"No, I don't think you did Lieutenant."

Mayes jumped in on cue. "Perhaps, Ms Lufkin you could tell us just where you were that night. I'm sure we could find out when you left your office." That answer Anne hadn't thought through completely. May or whatever his name was, was probably right, no one was ever in the office after 6 on a Friday and the cleaning crew came in then. There was a pause, then she said "I imagine I went home after work, like any other night Sergeant May."

"Mayes, Clarence Mayes. You mean you don't remember what you did the night your father died? I'd think someone would recall a night like that."

"I believe I went home."

"Then drove all the way back to Claremont, for what? Couldn't you have just spoken to your father on the phone?"

"If my father wanted me there in person, I would have gone, Lieutenant."

"Why would your father want you there?"

"To discuss some business issue he considered urgent at the time."

"And what issue was that?" Anne thought about whether she should attempt to recall something or say she never found out. The latter seemed safer.

"I never had the chance to find out."

"How did you know your father wanted you there at 9:00?"

"He told me, Sergeant, earlier that day." Anne had decided out not to say there was a phone call, which she figured could be checked.

Napoli took over again. "Did you have disagreements with your father about how you handled Lufkin Realty business?"

"I'm sure from time to time there were minor questions, but he had complete faith in me. I was authorized to negotiate and sign leases, mortgages and what have you."

"But did your father ever tell you you'd made mistakes with leases or what have you, major mistakes that cost Lufkin Realty money?"

"I don't recall him ever saying anything like that."

"Did he ever say he'd considered reducing your authority?"

Could this all be part of Fred's campaign to take over the office, Anne wondered.

"No. Not once." Napoli was happy with these statements, but he didn't feel that overall they'd moved the ball. The key was going to be showing she was there before 9:00- at least they'd nailed her down on that statement.

"Is there anyone who could tell us that you went home after work that night? Did you maybe pick up something for dinner, have a guest, make a call that you can remember?"

"Not that I can remember, but then I had quite a shock that night Lieutenant." Anne felt she'd held them off pretty well. She was quite certain it looked better not to refuse to talk and she didn't want to call a lawyer. Her instinct was that it was very unlikely that there was a reliable witness who could place her at 314 Mountain Avenue earlier that night. People in Claremont didn't hang out on the sidewalk or their front stoops. They hadn't asked about the housekeeper, who would know that she had set out dinner for two before leaving, but Anne thought it would be easy to confuse the addle brained Gladys on why she put out dinner for two that night. Gladys could easily have confused her father's statement that Anne was coming over later that night with the direction to set out dinner for Anne.

"Had that ever happened before?"

"Had what happened?"

"That your father asked you to come over so late on a Friday?"

"It's hardly past my bedtime Lieutenant"

"But 9:00 on a Friday is a bit irregular in the real estate business, wouldn't you say?"

"A family business like Lufkin Realty, Lieutenant is not a 9 to 5 job."

"But you still haven't answered my question, Anne, had you ever gone to see your father on business as late as 9:00 at night on a Friday before?"

"I don't recall specifically but it wouldn't surprise me."

"Why wouldn't your father have just had you over to discuss whatever it was at dinner? Didn't you commonly do that? Wasn't it sort of a regular thing?" Anne was beginning to think Napoli knew too much.

"Sometimes we did, sometimes we didn't."

Napoli signaled Mayes and they left Anne alone. She wished she could have a cigarette, but that would make her look nervous. Could they keep her there indefinitely?

"That's one stone cold bitch Lieutenant. She don't crack easy."

"But Clarence, it takes a stone cold bitch to watch her father croak without lifting a finger."

"You're right, Lieutenant. She could be good for it at that." Napoli wanted that message delivered to Connie so he'd have the backup to find a way to prove when Anne got to her daddy's house that night. If he could find that, Napoli thought, he'd need two safe deposit boxes for all the gold coins.

Tucci came up to Napoli "She blew a .06 Lieutenant, I'm afraid I'm going to have to cut her loose."

"That's okay, Jimmy, we're done for now. Say goodbye to the lady for us. And thanks."

"What are friends for, Lieutenant?"

CHAPTER XXXIII.

Anne was in shock driving home. She'd been cool, she thought, under fire but now she was beginning to have a reaction to the seriousness of what had just happened. Someone, Terry or that Judge Galante, had actually told the police about what she'd said to psychiatrist, they'd checked it against her statement to that grease ball Lieutenant and they were taking it seriously. They could charge her with her father's death. She understood now what Napoli was driving at. What if someone said she had been seen at 314 Mountain Avenue before 9:00? And where did Napoli get his other information. She didn't think she'd ever described the Friday night routine to Dr. Franca. Terry could have known about that, it was going on even before her father had kicked the tramp out. Anne assumed a number of people knew about Jeannine's problem. But what would all this do for Terry? She'd already turned down Anne's offer and she had to know that a higher offer was out of the question now.

Could anyone but Fred be behind this? Anne decided she'd made a mistake talking to Napoli and that she'd better let Morton know what was going on. As soon as she got home she called Ferguson & Mather and they tracked Morton down at his beach house. Anne told him the story.

Morton couldn't believe she'd been questioned. They really played hardball over there in Jersey.

That Anne had been pig headed enough to think she could make it all go away with a couple of snappy answers didn't surprise Morton. Either Galante had decided to turn up the heat or tired of waiting for capitulation and sold the tape to Fred Lufkin. They had to assume the worst What was the next step?

Morton felt the situation was now beyond him and decided he had to let Pedersen know enough about what was going on so they could figure out what to do. He hated to get the kid out of bed at 2:00 in the morning but he'd need answers right away.

Morton knew enough about criminal law to understand that it was now critical to intervene before the DA went to the grand jury. Morton didn't know how fast that could happen in Jersey. He told Anne to try to remember every question. "Write down the questions, Anne, not the answers." She agreed to come to Ferguson & Mather the next day at 11:00.

Morton called Pedersen, who managed to sound wide awake and to suppress his disgust at how badly Morton had fucked the whole thing up. Now there was no way to make a deal with Judge Galante. At least two cops apparently knew the whole story. Maybe they even had the damn tape already. And there were exceptions to the Doctor-Patient privilege that Morton was counting on to keep the tape out of evidence. Nor did Pedersen mention that there was no way he could find out at 2:30 in the morning how fast the DA could act in Jersey or how to stop it. Good Ferguson & Mather associates didn't complain.

CHAPTER XXXIV.

Napoli had convinced Mayes to spin the interview in a positive way to Connery, practically a tacit confession that she had said to her father the words Connery had heard from the tape. The Lieutenant wanted Connery to call the Chief and say he wanted the investigation reopened so they could canvas for a witness to Anne's arrival time. He called Connery as soon as Mayes had softened him up.

"Connie, if I say I decided to reopen it there'll be a thousand questions. You can just snap your fingers and the Chief will roll up his sleeves. It's a good case, I'm telling you. This broad, at a minimum, watched the guy die slowly and painfully. She's got no proof she wasn't there. Her story's bullshit. She's gonna have to admit she said the words. Whose gonna believe she made the story up to impress her shrink?" "Look Nappy, if I do that I better not be reading anything about this in the paper. Anyone hears we're doin' this and we have a big problem, understand?"

"Connie, of course, we'll be cool about it. Don't I know how to keep a secret?" Connery called the Chief and said that there should be a limited inquiry, just to clean up some loose ends, avoid a charge that the Claremont department was too kid gloves because it was the Lufkins. But it had to be kept under wraps. The Chief understood. Connery then brought in his assistant, David McCann, and told him to very quietly do some research and start drafting an indictment. If Nappy got the goods, Connery didn't want Anne to wise up and start throwing some legal muscle at Big John before Connery could get to a grand jury.

"So, Paulie, I guess things are looking up for the jilted tramp you're proud to represent."

He hated being called Paulie. "What the fuck are you talking about?" As if there was any doubt that Mike would tell him, in his own annoying way, whatever it is he knew Paul didn't know.

"Wait a minute. Didn't the well informed Mr. Rose hear yet? Or perhaps he hasn't bothered to fill the underling in."

"Hear what?" Was Mike gonna make him beg?

"I guess it pays to have worked at the Office." Ex Assistant U.S. Attorneys always called their former fraternity 'the Office.' Like everyone else worked in a fucking factory.

"And why would that be?"

"Cause my old friend Rob Cohen, from Robinson & Gray happened to be slumming it in state court yesterday and thought we might want to know."

Whatever it was, was it important enough to go through this?

"Might want to know what, Mike? How big an asshole I have an office next to?"

"No, Paulie, who they're fixing to indict for murder."

"It might be me if you don't get to the point sometime soon."

"You're gonna like this, Paulie." Paul just waited.

"What if the stiff didn't depart this life under his own steam? Say he had a little push into the great beyond? Would it be of interest to you?"

"Not if I have to wait this long to get a straight answer."

"I'm sure you'd be interested to know that its one of the children of the stiff."

"Fred?"

"No."

"Anne? They're indicting Anne Lufkin? But the father died of a heart attack."

"Don't women cause ninety percent of all heart attacks?"

"But they don't usually get a murder rap out of it, just the insurance."

"Not this time, Paul. Apparently she was sipping sherry watching Dad turn blue on the carpet rather than calling an ambulance. That, my friend, is depraved indifference. And since the conscientious constabulary of Claremont failed to ask for even a rudimentary autopsy, for all we know she may have done more than watch."

"How did your friend find all this out before there was even an indictment?"

"The secrets of the Office cannot be revealed to mere civil plodders like yourself."

"But doesn't it just slow my case down?" Paul couldn't see the point.

"What planet are you from? Daddy changes his will to cut the slut. A few weeks later little orphan Annie makes sure he'll never change it again. Suggestive of anything about the new will?"

"Maybe, but we don't even know if the kids were aware of the new will."

"Don't take my word for it, Mohamed. Go to the Mountain, the Mountain of a man and see what he thinks. I'm sure he'll see it my way." Paul often worried that he was slow on the uptake. Was it really so obvious that even if Anne did let Lufkin die, it made it more likely that she had anything to do with his changing the will in the first place?

Rose, of course, saw it exactly that way. “I knew this case had legs, Sageman. Never doubt the gut instinct of a man with a gut like this.” Rose slapped his belly like a tom-tom. He wanted to call Big John Martin right away to make sure he didn’t get cold feet. “Courage, Sageman, unlike greed, is a trait foreign to all politicians. We don’t want to give him time to think about all the money the Lufkins could spend on a governors’ race and making the greatest mistake in the history of law enforcement by letting Annie off the hook.”

Paul managed to restrain him. Whoever it was at the state prosecutor’s office shouldn’t have told Mike’s friend about the case at that stage. Paul convinced Rose that it could be counterproductive. “I suppose this means we can’t tell the client anything either, Sageman. I’d like to cheer her up. They tell me Frank’s in Italy for two weeks.”

Connery’s assistant, McCann, a raw recruit anxious to ingratiate himself with a partner at a major firm like Robinson & Gray, had spilled the beans. Connery didn’t know yet. He wasn’t about to indict until they could find some evidence that undermined Anne’s story about when she got to 314 Mountain Avenue that night. Nor was he thinking of going public. There was always some risk that the detectives canvassing the neighborhood would set off someone’s alarm bell but that wasn’t the same as holding a news conference. There’d be time enough for that later.

CHAPTER XXXV.

Napoli wondered if he could have bluffed Anne with a story that there was a witness while he and Mayes were shaking her down. If he'd thought about it at the time he might have tried, but he doubted she'd have caved without a name. So Napoli and two uniforms were questioning the neighbors. Napoli didn't hold much hope for an eye witness. They spent the afternoon going from house to house but half of them were empty and the other half no help. It looked bad. People who lived in mansions on five acre spreads just didn't spend their time looking out the window.

Of course they could get lucky at Lufkin Realty. Napoli was sure Fred could come up with an ambitious employee who would 'remember' that Anne said she was going to have dinner with her dear old dad at 314 Mountain, but that would only be a last resort. The cross examination was just too easy and the whole case would hang on it. Fred and Jack were pestering Napoli for an update but he'd been vague about the interview and hadn't brought up the timing issue. Jack, after all was a competitor and there were only so many Justinians to go around.

Napoli told the uniforms to call it off for the day and went back to the station. He passed Al Decker, Claremont's canine unit, and his dog Prince on the way into the station. "Hey Sniffy, how you doin'? Where're you and the mutt goin? To split a Pizza at Trezzoni's?"

"Nah, Lieutenant, just Prince's usual after dinner exercise."

"Don't forget the scooper, Sniffy, or I'll have to write you up for depraved indifference to my new shoes."

Napoli didn't even say hello when Connery picked up the phone the next night."What's fucking Columbo got that I don't, Connie, except an eyeball you clean with Windex?" Connery knew there must have been a break.

"I don't know Nappy, a dirty raincoat and a million bucks?"

Napoli wouldn't be asking Fred Lufkin for the raincoat.

"Connie, I'm sitting here with Mr. Brian Pendleton of 245 Mountain Avenue, who was nice enough to join me at the station after walking his Gordon Setter Felicity this evening. I think you'd better listen in on speaker while we go over what Mr. Pendleton told me."

"Now Mr. Pendleton, you walk Felicity every night when you get home?"

"That's right, lieutenant. Usually around 7:15. I work on the Street and I normally take the 6:35 out of Hoboken."

"I take it you mean Wall Street, Mr. Pendleton?' Connery asked.

"Oh, I'm sorry, yes of course. Merrill Lynch. I trade telecoms and cable." Beautiful, Connery thought, the jury would be sure he was too rich and waspy for Fred to bribe.

"Did you normally pass 314 Mountain on your walk?"

"Unless it rains, Felicity likes a nice walk. Mom doesn't really let her out to stretch her legs during the day."

"That's Mrs. Pendleton, sir?"

"Yes, my wife Abigail."

"And how far is 314 Mountain from your home."

"About half a mile, I'd say."

"Now when I met you and Felicity, what did I ask you?"

"Whether I ever noticed cars going in and out of the homes along Mountain Avenue."

"And what did you tell me?"

"That I did if they were people I knew or if Felicity and I had to stop for the cars."

"Did you know the Lufkins?"

"Actually I did. Bob Lufkin and I played tennis once in a while at the Club."

"Did you know his children?"

"I've been introduced, but that's about it."

"And you knew Bob had passed away."

"Yes, the night it happened. Abby and I were coming home from picking up some videos in town and the ambulance passed us. I saw it turn in at 314. So when I gave Felicity her last walk, I went by and one of the officers told me what had happened." Connery hoped the videos weren't too racy. A good defense lawyer would check.

"And had you walked Felicity when you came home that night?"

"Yes."

"And what time was that?"

"The usual time, 7:10, 7:15."

"Did you notice any cars pulling in or out of any of your neighbor's driveways?"

"Yes. I saw a woman in a BMW pull into Bob Lufkin's driveway."

"Did you recognize her?"

"I think it was Anne. But I've only met her a few times."

"You're sure it was a BMW?"

"Yes."

"And you're sure it was 314 Mountain?"

"Yes, because when I saw the ambulance pull in there I remembered it." Incredible, Connery thought, yet believable.

"Thank you Mr. Pendleton, for agreeing to come down."

"Say what's this about anyway? I thought Bob had a heart attack."

"At this point it's confidential Mr. Pendleton. But we'll let you know as soon as we can." Napoli wanted to hug the guy but restrained himself.

Napoli walked Pendleton out and called Connery back. "The luck of the Guineas, Nappy, how did you dig that guy up?"

"Brilliant police work, Connie. Nah, I'll level with you. I was walking into the station this afternoon and I saw Sniffy and his dog. And I figured the only way someone was out on the street at night in Claremont is if they were trying to squeeze a load out of their pooch. So I walked up and down Mountain Avenue 'til I met Felicity and her boyfriend. Good lookin' dog by the way."

"You've got to get out more Nappy."

"Anyway, I've got our conversation with Mr. Pendleton on video for later use. I'll send you a copy. Do you think we can get him in to the grand jury soon?"

"Oh, I think that can be arranged."

Of course they still needed the tape. Connie wouldn't let him arrest Anne without it. Napoli would have to get Jack, the lazy bastard, moving on that project. Now, especially since he dug up Pendleton, Napoli thought the Judge's cut should come out of Jack's share. Napoli figured getting Anne out of the will should be worth at least 500 grand to Fred Lufkin, maybe more. He decided to give Fred an update. They met in the parking lot at Broomefield Plaza.

"Mr. Lufkin, I think we can definitely establish that your sister didn't tell the truth about when she arrived at your father's house the night he died. That's a very valuable fact."

"Really, Lieutenant, didn't we know that already from her own statements?"

"Let's just say she had a little wiggle room before and we've shut that down. It took a good deal of police work, but we've got a very good witness statement that I'm sure will stand up. If we can get the tape, I can practically guarantee that the district attorney will seek an indictment." If some greasy cop could fix this, Fred thought, why couldn't Ritzer get rid of Terry's case? Maybe Ritzer was just stringing it along for the fees.

"Indictment? But there'd still need to be a trial. Could she be convinced to plea bargain?"

"With what's at stake here, Mr. Lufkin, I wouldn't expect that."

"Of course if we had a forensic report, Lieutenant, the district attorney's bargaining position might be stronger." And that, Napoli understood wasn't the only bargaining Fred was thinking about. Maybe the indictment needed to be held up pending a substantial down payment.

"I could talk to the DA about exhumation, Mr. Lufkin. The lab boys can do amazing things these days. But I think we'd need the tape first."

"Of course. You know Lieutenant, I really appreciate the work you're doing. Perhaps you could have a word with Jack's friend about the tape?" Napoli thought Fred was offering him Jack's share but he wasn't sure he wanted to take the risk of a meeting with the Judge. Napoli believed the Judge had to be under investigation by an entire alphabet of federal and state agencies and he didn't want to be caught on any surveillance talking about buying evidence.

"I think we'll let Jack handle that end, Mr. Lufkin. But I wanted you to know that we're doing everything we can."

"Well then, please let Jack know just how critical it is that we get the tape for the DA, Lieutenant."

"Will do, Mr. Lufkin."

CHAPTER XXXVI.

It didn't occur to Fred that he might be getting the cart before the horse by having Anne indicted before Terry had been disposed of, but he wanted to turn up the heat on the Terry front as well. Fred didn't trust Ritzer's expressed opinion on the odds of the motion succeeding. He knew Mel's deposition and the Nikful deal were a problem and was considering the Mel's advice that Omega be thrown into the estate, assuming it wasn't too late.

Nikful had been Fred's first attempt to increase his share. The property, which his father had purchased years before was, became more valuable when it turned out to be just two miles from the route of the newly announced interstate loop. Being undeveloped and held free and clear, Fred had figured there might not be any reason for anyone to look into its ownership until after the blessed event of his father's passing, so he'd traced his father's signature and inked it, then planted the stock power in the bank records. Fred hated to dump it back in the estate, but he'd asked Mel how it could be done.

"Simplicity itself, Frederick. When they do up the estate tax return, just put Omega on the list as if it always belonged there."

"But what about your testimony? Doesn't it suggest that you incorporated Omega for me or Anne, not father?"

"Not to worry, you can simply recall that you were carrying out your Dad's orders and Omega always belonged to him. You just borrowed it from time to time."

"But why would he transfer Nikful to another shell?"

"Let me play the shell game, son. I'm sure I'll be able to remember why that would have been done when the time comes."

"Shouldn't we be telling Ritzer all this?"

"My sense is no. At this stage if we put those facts in we'd be running scared, dignifying this molehill the kid lawyer dug up. If we ignore it we've got a shot at never having to explain it. If Terry's still on her feet after round one, then we'll put the horseshoes in our gloves."

CHAPTER XXXVII.

Frank Mairone came back from dragging his wife around Italy for two weeks with blue balls for Terry and a knot in his stomach over the content of Ritzer's motion to remove him as executor, which was on for the next week, together with the motion to throw out Terry's case.

Radin had run over to court and obtained a sealing order from Weiss the day he saw the transcript of Frank's work out session with Terry. That kept the transcript from becoming a public document.

Radin couldn't promise that the subject wouldn't come up at argument, but he had a plan. Weiss had scheduled a special afternoon hearing for the motion to get rid of Frank and the motion to throw out Terry's case. Normally Ritzer would have been up at bat first, creating the risk that he would spill the beans in open court. Radin filed a motion to seal the courtroom, to give Weiss a chance to protect Frank and to give Radin a shot at arguing that the transcript was irrelevant and that even if it was relevant, the privacy interests of the parties merited protection.

Paul in the meantime was attempting to get Joe Rose to pay attention to getting ready for the motion. "I don't know what you're worried about Sageman. There's just not a chance of Weiss tossing this case until he goes out on a couple of dates with Terry."

"Isn't she a little old for him?"

"Oh a little powder, a little paint and forty million could make her look like what she ain't. Of course if you hadn't talked me out of calling Big John I could probably be walking in there waving around a murder indictment against Anne. Now that would have been a show stopper. As it is, all we've got going for us is the shifty eyed Mel Weinberg and the fact that Ritzer will be arguing for Fred and Anne. If we lose, I'll be forced to blame someone in this room. But don't worry, I'll be ready."

The day of the motion Rose instructed Paul to have Terry in the courtroom and he called up let Radin know Frank should not be there. "Cause if they lose control and Harry has to call in the fire department to hose them down, it won't be good for our cause, David."

Radin agreed. Besides, Radin said, Frank shouldn't look too anxious to hang onto the gig.

When everyone was at counsel table Weiss pointed at Ritzer and gestured that he should come forward and in the same gesture silently instructed the court reporter not to record the sidebar conversation.

"Mr. Ritzer, are you listening? I don't care what you pull over in Fun City. You will not turn my courtroom into an instrument of blackmail. I don't want to hear any mention of the activities involving the caveatrix and the executor. Do you understand?"

"But it seems to me your honor that the best interests of the estate are implicated by such a relationship and the court should consider it in connection with the appropriateness of Mr. Mairone's service."

"Mr. Ritzer, this isn't the place for a lesson in trust and estate law, but suffice it to say that there is no requirement that an executor be disinterested, only that he discharge his duty to all beneficiaries. Now at such time, if any, as Mr. Mairone is a witness with respect to the wills, I will of course have to consider the evidence with respect to his credibility, but it is irrelevant to his service as executor. Just so we're clear I will hold you in contempt for immediate commitment, Mr. Ritzer if you disobey. Now do you agree to abide by my instruction?"

"I have no choice, your honor but I do think that the impropriety of the relations does bear on his ability to serve as well."

"But I'm the man wearing the black dress, Mr. Ritzer. Now return to counsel table."

"We're on the record. Mr. Radin, your motion to seal the courtroom is moot. Mr. Ritzer do you have anything else on your motion to remove the executor?"

"Apparently not your honor." Ritzer wasn't going to risk a visit to Essex County Jail for Fred Lufkin or anyone else. Weiss, the sneaky bastard, had scheduled the hearing for the late afternoon for just that reason. If Ritzer been thrown in jail at four o'clock they'd have a very hard time finding an appellate judge to spring him that day. Fred, sitting directly behind Ritzer figured they had simply miscalculated. Weiss had too much empathy for someone in Frank's position, so to speak, as a result of his own cavorting. Still, it didn't seem like Ritzer had put up too much of a fight. Radin was happy but not surprised.

"The motion to remove is denied. I will hear you on the motion to dismiss the claim of Mr. Rose's client, Ms. Stephens."

Ritzer made a very good argument about the insufficiency of the claim but didn't mention Mel. Weiss let him jabber on for a while so it would look like he was actually considering the piece of shit's argument. He also figured it would look better if Rose, rather than the court, brought up the implications of the conflict of interest engaged in by the shyster Mel Weinberg. "In conclusion your honor, this is nothing more, nothing more than a strike suit. There is no evidence, no evidence at all that my client was unduly influenced, of unsound mind or otherwise lacked testamentary capacity at the time he made his last will. That will address the natural object, the natural objects of his bounty, his children, Anne and Frederick Lufkin." Morton figured that tune would change soon enough as to Anne, who was not present.

Ritzer was winding up. "As a matter of policy Your Honor, of policy and judicial economy, it would seem that the law should require more than a naked allegation such as this to sustain a claim against a duly witnessed entirely regular and unquestionably genuine last will and testament of a man of sound mind. Such a bare allegation does not deserve, does not deserve any more of the time of the court, the estate or the true beneficiaries and I respectfully urge that it be dismissed." Ritzer sat down. Morton had gotten admitted on behalf of Anne and stood up to join in the motion.

Weiss greeted him. "Yet another esteemed member of the bar of New York, Mr. Morton of Ferguson & Mather. Our fair state must be coming up in the world."

"Thank you your honor. I join in Mr. Ritzer's motion and agree with his argument. There is no basis for this claim. I'm a visitor to your state but I understand the law is the same here as in New York or anywhere else. A man has a right to change his mind as to his testamentary plans. It's a basic American freedom, except as to wives of course, who get an elective share whether you like it or not.

There is no dispute that Mr. Lufkin was of sound mind. He was successfully operating a large real estate business at the time of his demise. He was not just sound but strong. And strong willed. He, not his children, was running the show. Judge, you've met men like Mr. Lufkin. Is there any likelihood that his kids forced him to change his will? None. It didn't happen. Ms. Stephens has presented no evidence that it happened. It was over between them, he changed his will. Happens every day of the week. There's just no case here." Morton sat down.

Weiss was actually impressed with the notion that as a matter of experience with guys like Bob Lufkin, no one was telling him what to do with his dough.

Joe Rose hauled himself to his feet. Weiss recognized him. "Mr. Rose, I assume you'd like to respond?"

"A man and a woman have a relationship for fourteen years Judge. Fourteen years. This was no mere dalliance. Perhaps it cooled off. But it was by all accounts a serious, devoted relationship. They worked together in the real estate business as well during those years. I'm not saying the law recognized it as creating an involuntary obligation, or that it should. But just because it cooled doesn't mean that Mr. Lufkin didn't appreciate the relationship he had with Ms. Stephens over those many years, feel some continuing love or gratitude. There is no evidence that Ms. Stephens was replaced in Mr. Lufkin's affections by anyone else. So I find the assumption that Mr. Lufkin tossed her aside like a used kleenex both callous and improbable judge. Now I'll be honest, Judge."

"Turning over a new leaf Mr. Rose?" Everyone laughed.

"If that were my whole case, I think I'd be forced to agree with Mr. Morton and Mr. Ritzer. But for two reasons I can't. First, I haven't had the privilege of questioning either of the people who will so greatly benefit from Mr. Lufkin's last will if it is probated. Second, its clear to me that Mr. Weinberg, the drawer of that will was representing one or both of those very same people at the time. He danced around it, Judge, he bobbed and weaved, but he could not deny, he did not deny that he was representing them. That, as the court knows, changes everything. In the Haynes case - same situation - our Supreme Court said such dual representation shifts the presumption of the validity of the will. Now I know what Mr. Ritzer and Mr. Morton will say. They do a yeoman job of trying to distinguish Haynes. They say Mr. Lufkin was not a candidate for undue influence by Mr. Weinberg or anyone else, that Mr. Weinberg was a mere scrivener, that the witnesses to the will saw a man of sound mind determined to make a change.

But Judge, Mr. Weinberg wasn't some guy in a storefront office that Mr. Lufkin had never met before. Mr. Weinberg had represented and advised Mr. Lufkin for a number of years. He was in a position to influence Mr. Lufkin's decision. In answering Mr. Lufkin's questions about the change, couldn't Mr. Weinberg have been affected by his representation of the children and his desire to continue to represent Lufkin Realty into the next generation? We're not done questioning

Mr. Weinberg Judge, whatever he may think. These questions need to be answered. I believe the Haynes case alone compels denial of this motion and entitles the party challenging this will to a complete investigation of the circumstances under which it came about. Thank you your honor." Paul had to admit, Rose had made a good point about Weinberg's interest in the matter. Paul had expected more wind, but Rose knew that Weiss thought the Gettysburg address was a page too long and rarely thought that argument added anything to what he already knew.

Weiss sat quietly for what seemed like a long time, then picked up the volume of the New Jersey Reporter containing the Haynes case.

"Before me is a motion to dismiss a complaint seeking to bar probate of the purported last will and testament of Robert Lufkin, late of Claremont. While I agree with the proponents of that will that the caveatrix has failed to articulate a coherent theory as to how or when their father was wrongfully induced to change his will, I am also mindful that there appear to be open questions as to the existence of conflicts in the dual representation of testator and beneficiaries by the attorney who drew the will, Mr. Melvin Weinberg of the New York Bar. The proponents argue that there is absolutely no evidence that Mr. Lufkin was feeble minded and indeed to the contrary he was vigorous and strong willed up to the moment of his unexpected and sudden demise. They further argue that the will benefits the natural objects of his bounty and that Mr. Lufkin's admitted relationship with the challenger had terminated, making the change in beneficiaries the most natural thing in the world. That may be. I feel compelled, however by the Haynes case to deny the motion. It would appear that the presumption in favor of validity, in the case of this particular will may not be justified and I must permit the challenger to explore these matters further. I will warn you Mr. Rose, that if you fail to find a stronger basis for this challenge, I will entertain another motion and I will award fees to the beneficiaries and I imagine they would be substantial, though I am certain Berry and French could afford them. If the good offices of this court can be of service in resolving the matter by referral to mediation or otherwise, I would be only too pleased to help. Thank you. Mr. Rose will submit an order."

Weiss rose. Fred was enraged but said nothing and walked out without waiting for Ritzer. Rose shook Radin's hand, patted Sageman on the back and leaned over to Morton. "That's law West of the Pecos Mr. Morton. I hope you'll be able to spring Anne for her deposition." Paul couldn't believe Rose would let the cat out of the bag like that. He hoped Terry and Tommy sitting behind the rail hadn't heard. Morton wouldn't take the bait.

"I'm sure Ms. Lufkin will be able to take time out of her busy schedule running her father's company to answer any questions you may have." But it was bad news, Morton knew, if Rose had sniffed out the possibility of a prosecution of Anne and he had no intention of ever producing her for a deposition if she might need to take the Fifth.

CHAPTER XXXVIII.

Terry was thrilled that the case lived and that Frank was still the executor. She couldn't resist smiling as Fred went by. Tommy understood that the judge was saying they still might not have a case but he was starting to trust Rose a little more. What, he wondered, did they need to prove and how could they ever prove it? Paul had the same question, but was, like any lawyer, thrilled to win the battle.

Once they cleared the court house Morton told Pedersen there was no time to waste. Someone had to step in front of this runaway train before Anne was indicted. Morton was not without the arrogance for which Ferguson & Mather was known, but he was too smart to think that walking into the prosecutor's office cold was the way to go. "We need a local boy, Pedersen, but I can't bear the thought of sharing a cell with Judge Galante and his partner. There must me someone in this hellhole of a state that we can trust who knows the DA. I want to do it now."

Pedersen was two steps ahead of Morton. "I took the liberty of putting together a short list after our chat the other night. They tell me that the best man for the job is Sherman Brown."

"Sherman Brown? What firm is he with?"

"Brown & Brown. Apparently he's the dean of the criminal bar and the most successful black lawyer in the state. More important, they tell me he got the DA his first job."

"It won't look too contrived? Going to this guy's mentor? Another black guy?"

"Not from what I'm told. First, if it would rub Martin the wrong way, I think Brown would tell us, because he wouldn't want to fuck up his relationship with the DA. Second, I read a few articles about him on Nexis, and he defends plenty of white people, corporations, even lawyers."

"Jersey lawyers? Jesus, if he can keep them out of jail he must be good. Can we see him today?"

"I'll call. I assume we can say Anne will pay his usual retainer?"

"How much?"

"From what I'm told, 150."

"Shit. Well lets see if we can get a meeting first." Pedersen flipped open his phone and mumbled for a few minutes. "Five o'clock. His office is a few blocks from here."

"You've really got this covered. I suppose you can tell me where I can get a decent drink in the meantime?"

"The best we can do is the bar at the Downtown Hilton. I'd like to be sure I understand how you want to handle the tape issue before we meet with Mr. Brown." Pedersen was smooth.

Sherman Brown knew who Morton was and figured that Ferguson & Mather didn't want to consult him over a DWI, so he made time for the visit and had them come right into his office rather than a conference room. Morton laid out the situation, but for the specifics of Morton's knowledge of the tape and his dealings with Judge Galante, and mentioned that Rose had apparently heard something. "You were right to come in. We have no time to lose. Rose will be pushing for an indictment and a press conference. He's buddy's with the City Editor at the Ledger. Once this goes public we'll have a lot harder time smothering it. I suggest, I strongly suggest, you get your client to authorize me to prevent that right away." Morton wanted to ask how Brown could do that, but Pedersen gave him a sharp look.

"If I can speak to my client." Brown had his secretary take Morton to an empty office. This was not an easy call to make. He reached Anne at home. "Anne, I'm afraid that Terry's suit isn't over yet, and that's the good news." He told her that they needed to get Brown on board right away if she didn't want to be an instant celebrity.

"I can't believe this is happening Mr. Morton. Is Fred really behind this?"

"That, I don't know. But for God's sake, don't talk to anyone unless Mr. Brown says its okay."

Anne wanted to know, but didn't ask Morton, if Fred could still stop the train. Maybe a deal could still be made. She'd gladly get out of the company to avoid being charged with her father's death. "I suppose I need to speak to Mr. Brown myself, Mr. Morton."

After meeting with Anne and hearing and disbelieving the story that old man Lufkin was already blue when she got there, Sherman Brown strolled up the hill to Big John Martin's office. He didn't need an appointment. When Brown walked in Big John shooed the foxy young assistant prosecutor out of his office and closed the door.

Brown smiled, "Life be pretty good for the Big Man." Martin laughed.

"Just remember what happened to Judge Lackman, getting' caught with his gavel where it had no business being."

"Don't you worry, Dad, its casual."

"Let me tell you Big John, there's other ways than pussy to get messed up in this job. I hear you've got a homicide assistant who's hiring out to rich white folks to settle their family feuds."

"You hear more than I know." Martin knew Brown had to be talking about Connery and Anne Lufkin, but didn't want to give that up until he knew what Brown was up to.

"Well then you better be knowing more."

"You here just as a public spirited citizen, Mr. Brown?"

"In a manner of speaking. I've got a client but I've also got a friend I don't want gettin' no egg on his face."

"There's been no charges filed. It's just an investigation."

"You best be sure that investigation is damned private."

"I have no intention of publicizing any charges unless we have grounds to indict."

"Grounds to indict, my ass. You better have grounds to convict, or I'll buy a jet plane with my contingent fee on the malicious prosecution suit. You've got a death certificate that says natural causes, no physical evidence and no witnesses. Any fool can get an indictment but now you know she's got a real lawyer, you can't think you can convict, assuming you get to trial at all. In the course of my defense I'm sure I'll be able to prove who was pushing the charge, and why and if I have to turn your homicide bureau and the Claremont police department upside down and start shaking to do it, I will. It's never good to lose a murder case on the front page. It's worse if it looks like your boy Connery was fronting for some slumlord honky like this Fred Lufkin. And if you were any greasier than this Detective Napoli you could slide up the banister on the courthouse stairs. It's just not a pretty picture."

"Thanks for the warning, Sherman. If I don't think it's a strong case, I won't let Connery take it inside. But don't be so sure that there ain't no witnesses. Your girl be talking out both sides of her mouth and you may hear some shit you don't want to hear. But I will make sure Connery knows its hush hush." Martin walked Brown out. He'd have to make sure Connery wasn't full of shit, but he was far from ready to dump the case. The depraved indifference angle cried out for national press and Martin saw more good than bad in pushing such a case, even if he couldn't convict. With any luck Martin would be a U.S. Congressman before Anne Lufkin's civil suit got out of the starting gate. Plenty of elderly voters out there who might appreciate him standing up for an old man. And Fred Lufkin had plenty of money to spend on a campaign, that Martin knew.

CHAPTER XXXIX.

"Now that I dodged that bullet, Sageman, I'm sure you know what we need to do." Rose had actually invited Paul to lunch without a client, a rare event.

"Order dessert?"

"Oh, ho, never bite the hand that feeds you Sageman. And let me make the jokes. Your mission is to get the loathsome Lufkins in the chair for their depositions as soon as possible. Though perhaps Anne is more worried about another kind of chair right about now. A shocking thought, eh? You know she hired Sherman Brown? Not a bad move, considering the complexion of the average Essex County criminal jury. He's a damn good lawyer, Sherman."

Brown had called Rose and performed an exceptional rim job over the phone, telling Joe how he wouldn't think of going up against him in the civil suit and what great things he heard from the US Attorney about the miracles Joe performed to keep his clients at liberty. Of course he'd also managed to make it clear that dropping a dime with the papers wouldn't help anyone. If it went public Anne couldn't possibly settle, but otherwise settlement was exactly the course of action he would recommend to his new client. Actually Brown was considering just how to shoulder Ferguson and Mather aside, and take over the will contest but he knew it was one step at a time.

When he got back to the office, Paul started the process of setting up the depositions. Rose wanted Fred first of course. Anne would take the Fifth, and useful as that would be, Rose didn't plan on giving Fred early warning as to the subjects on which he would be deposed.

Ritzer knew Fred would rather walk over hot coals than be deposed. Not that his client was afraid to lie of course, but there was always the chance of getting tripped up or contradicting whatever paper trail there was linking him to Weinberg and worse. Ritzer demanded that Terry be produced first. With any luck the process could be slowed to a crawl. Paul also asked for another day with Mel. This time Rose would be there. Ritzer objected to that as well. No one would be deposed and everything would eventually wind up in front of Weiss. While Ritzer didn't have too much faith that Weiss would force Terry to walk the plank first, he had little choice but to try.

Fred agreed with the strategy. Delay would give him more time to figure out how to get Weiss off the case. Jack, now on the team again, was put to work. Fred also promised Jack a large bonus if he could put the tape in the hands of the prosecutor without further delay. He made the same offer to Napoli, but Jack had the inside track because Napoli was afraid to meet with the Judge.

CHAPTER XL.

Judge Galante sensed that Anne had dropped out of the bidding and felt the price of the tape was peaking. Pete had pulled all available information on Lufkin Realty and figured that after taxes the estate was good for $40,000,000 or so. The Judge thought 1% was a modest price to pay, but he had to build in a little haggle room. They met at the club, with Napoli hanging around outside.

"$750,000 Jack boy. You can make your own deal with young Mr. Lufkin of course, but I suggest you get paid before I turn over the goods."

What fuckin' balls on this guinea crook, Jack thought, its my deal and he tries to take it away. "Judge, you're way up in the sky. Lufkin won't pay that kind of money. Anyway how could he pay you that kind of dough without someone finding out?"

"Lovely fishing in the Cayman Islands Jack. A wire here, a wire there and no one the wiser."

"But the money has to come from somewhere Judge. He can't just write a check on the company, you know."

"I hear tell your boy is quite a collector. I'm sure he could liquidate part of the collection in say Hong Kong, the chinks are mad for gold these days. I might even take delivery in gold myself, but there'd have to be a premium for the trouble of selling it, of course."

"Judge, I just think you overestimate the amount of dough he can get his hands on."

"Well I won't know that til I hear an offer. This ain't no dutch auction. Let him tell me what he'll pay and how."

"Judge, if it made sense to me, maybe this could get done." The Judge knew Jack would need to be cut in, but he wouldn't discuss the cut until he knew how big the cake was.

"Just see what your boy can do, Jack, then we'll hash it out. Now let your cop chauffeur take you back to the boss man. But I suggest you move quickly. Anyone serves a warrant on me either I got to turn the thing over or it disappears forever and that don't do any of us any good. There's already been too many meetings and too many people know about it. Now get out of here."

Jack told Napoli that the Judge wanted a million bucks, no sharing. "That greedy fuckin' whore." Napoli didn't think there was any way the Judge should do better than him, or even than Jack and he didn't trust Galante.

"That shifty motherfucker, what if he gets our dough and sells the tape to Anne anyway? Or erases it? We really gotta think of how this exchange goes down."

"Nah, if he fucks us we blow his cover on the dough." "Easier said than done. That just raises other questions. And you told me yourself he's not the kind of guy you want to fuck with."

"Sure, but there's got to be some way to do this, you know."

"Number one. We gotta play the tape before the money passes."

"Agreed."

"Number two. We gotta insulate Lufkin from this." Jack knew Napoli meant that there'd be a little shrinkage before the Judge saw his cut.

"Agreed."

"Number three. I think we gotta be partners in this." "What, like equal? I don't think so."

"A third. But you gotta be straight with me."

"Deal." "So what do we tell Fred?"

"I'm pretty sure the Judge would take $200,000, push comes to shove-why not see if we can get Fred to go for the $750,000?"

Jack approached Fred the next day. As they drove to lunch Jack mentioned the 750. "I think you fellows are a bit confused, Jack. Maybe you've been reading about the salaries ballplayers are getting and mixing that up with market fundamentals. The way I see it I'm the only buyer and the value of the property is very speculative. From what I'm told the DA could decide not to indict anyway, especially if he isn't sure the tape can ever be played for a jury."

"So what kind of number did you have in mind?"

"I think you and our friend the Lieutenant have to view this as a joint venture. You contribute the tape, Napoli keeps the pressure on the DA. If I get rid of Anne for good, then I can afford to be generous. If not, what's it worth to me?"

"Listen Mr. Lufkin, there's a third party involved here who isn't going to fork over the property on spec."

"If you had trusted me Jack, that wouldn't be the case, would it?"

"But you're asking for a lot of trust Mr. Lufkin. Nothin unless it all pans out."

"I appreciate that, Jack, but you need to understand that your total return could be much, much higher my way. At this point in time I can't just come up with high six figure cash payments, certainly not without arousing suspicion."

Jack went back to the Judge with Fred's position. The Judge wasn't pleased. "That little fuck. I'd rather give it to Anne than depend on his generosity after we win the fuckin' case for him. Cash. Only cash." Jack was beginning to feel like he was a Mideast peace envoy. Ultimately Napoli came up with a plan. $300 down of which the Judge got $200 with no back end. $150 more if Anne was indicted. $750 more if she was disinherited or settled for a lump sum or payout worth less than $10,000,000 and was out of the company. Fred squawked but he had no choice. Regretfully he sold a few choice items from his collection. The next day Jack handed Napoli an envelope containing the tape.

CHAPTER XLI.

With Big John's consent, Connery decided to play the tape for the grand jury, then put Napoli on the stand to pin Anne down on lying about when she got to 314 Mountain the night her father died and read the diary entries, followed by Pendleton the dog walker. Of course at least two of those items might never be admitted at trial, but they made the indictment a lock. None of the grand jurors appeared skeptical after hearing the evidence and they voted instantaneously to indict.

Big John told Connery to give Sherman Brown a call and let Anne surrender rather than picking her up, saying "Hey Connie, if she runs, even Sherman can't keep that evidence out. You got nothin to lose." And if the shit hit the fan, the damages on the mal pros suit would be lower, Connery thought, without a public arrest.

Napoli presented Fred with a copy of the indictment. With Anne out of the office for good, Lufkin Realty retained the newly formed B/N Consultants to do market research for a $150,000 retainer.

Anne had been hanging around the house opening the Chardonnay earlier and earlier in the day since learning of the possibility that she'd be charged. She was halfway through the bottle when Sherman Brown called to tell her about the indictment. She wanted to add a count for murdering Fred, but Brown convinced her not to talk to anyone, least of all Fred and told her she'd have to surrender the next day. "You mean I'll be in jail?" Anne hadn't really focused on that disgusting possibility.

"I think we should be able to avoid that, Anne." That much Big John owed him. Brown advised her to tell her banker she might need a certified check the next day, told her not to even think about not showing up and asked if she wanted a driver to pick her up for the arraignment. That of course would save Brown the trouble of having her car stored if bail was denied. He explained the procedure and assured her it would be brief.

When she hung up the phone she chugged another glass and realized that the worst part of it was that she really had no one she could call close enough to talk to about something this awful. Certainly not her former Doctor Franca. Life hadn't been soft, at least until her father died, but Anne had never been put through anything like this. She'd had a long time to prepare for her mother's death and the gradual fade away into incoherence had made it a little less painful. The way things were going she'd be halfway there before a trial herself. Miserable as she was, it occurred to her that Terry would be ecstatic over the news, something that stupid fuck Fred hadn't even considered. She decided to call Don Morton.

As soon as Anne told him what had happened he knew that the Judge must have turned over the tape and Anne was in the soup unless it could be kept out of evidence. The indictment was bad enough. Could his dealings with Galante come out? Morton couldn't see how it would help the prosecution, since he'd never offered to pay for the tape. Of course that wouldn't stop Galante from saying he had and he couldn't deny having met with the man several times. But Anne was asking about the will contest. "I'm sure this charge will be thrown out, Mr. Morton but how will it affect our case?"

"I'd be lying if I told you the price hasn't gone up, Anne. Now that Rose character can say that you made sure to finish dad off before the ink was dry on the will."

"But if there was nothing wrong with the will, what would it matter?" Ah, but was there? A brother who could get his sister indicted for murder was capable of anything.

Anne showed up for her arraignment wearing the regulation dark glasses. Big John told Connery not to leak the arraignment, so Anne wasn't mobbed on the way into court. Brown had already agreed on acceptable bail and the plea, in an empty courtroom, was over in a moment. Brown stayed with her through the indignity of being processed and then told her to get out of town before the bloodhounds were loosed but not to leave the state. He also told her she'd have to hire a private investigator and several medical and forensic experts. "To show that even if someone were there to call an ambulance father would still have passed on?"

"Yes, Ms. Lufkin." And to deal with whatever else they might dig up.

"Oh, yes, I'm sure my brother is just waiting for a dark night to get out there with his spade Mr. Brown." Brown was surprised how tough this spoiled bitch was. Of course it also made him think maybe Big John had a case. How was he going to get her to cry on the stand?

CHAPTER XLII.

"Wait a minute, Paul, I don't have to be one of his pallbearers, do I?" Paul had come running down the hall to tell Mike what he'd learned from the sobbing and hysterical Mrs. Dolan.

To the sorrow of butchers, pastry chefs and head waiters and perhaps even Mrs. Rose, Joe Rose had died in his sleep. No more would his bellowing unsettle the stately halls of Berry & French. He hadn't exactly been a second father, but Paul was upset and he couldn't understand Mike's detachment. "I can't see how you're joking about it."

"To Joe Rose, humor would be the greatest homage, I'd say. Besides, its hardly a surprise at his size. Was that his first heart? Must have been the size of a sump pump. Besides, if you think I'm taking it well, wait til you see the stiff upper lips on his wasp partners." Paul was dreading telling his wife, who'd no doubt insist on attending the funeral and then describing the strange customs of the heathens to her parents, resulting in dredging up memories of the last twenty years of funerals the happy couple had attended. He'd also have to tell Terry, he realized. It couldn't have come at a worse time.

After many weeks of evasive maneuvers, Ritzer and Fred had finally been brought to ground by Rose and Weiss had ordered Fred to give his deposition, which had been scheduled for only two weeks from the day Rose expired. Fred had been livid, even considered firing Ritzer to get a delay.

Hearing that they'd escaped Rose, Fred and Jay exulted like Hitler and Goebbels in the bunker on learning of Roosevelt's death.

"It's a great misfortune, a great misfortune, but perhaps not for you, Mr. Lufkin."

"Well, Jay, I don't think you can take much credit, but you managed to put things off just long enough. Imagine the old rhino keeling over just as was about to charge. How did Anne get into Rose's bedroom anyway?" Fred cackled.

Ritzer, also relieved, laughed with him. Terry Stephens would now have no choice but to take a nuisance settlement. Nobody else at Berry and French would take the case and very few lawyers would consider a contingent fee on a case like that, even with such high stakes. Nevertheless, Ritzer was concerned that if anyone did take it on, Anne would be a considerable liability. "This might be the time to consider an economical resolution, Mr. Lufkin."

"Now, Jay? Without Rose they've got no chance of making a purse out of their sow's ear of a case."

"I would agree, Mr. Lufkin, I would agree, but Anne's little difficulty has its dangers. Post hoc ergo propter hoc after all."

"What are you jabbering about, Jay. We've got them on the run."

"You must understand, the timing is the problem. Terry Stephens will certainly suggest, certainly, that Anne was just waiting to get the new will signed before she murdered your father."

"Nonsense, Jay."

"You, sir are the client. But Rose's death is an opportunity, a moment of weakness. Get rid of Terry for a song. Then there's no downside if Anne goes away."

"But they've got no case. And now they have no lawyer."

"Berry and French will dump the case, I'm sure, but who's to say whether someone else might not take a shot at it." "You're not afraid of some storefront lawyer, Jay?"

"Afraid, no. But if it could be settled without any more testimony..." Maybe Ritzer was right, but Fred saw the flaw in his argument.

"But if we make an offer, Jay, then the case will look better and Terry might find a good lawyer."

"That's a risk. But just let me call the kid lawyer, Paul what's his name. Nothing in writing. We can always deny it that way."

CHAPTER XLIII.

By the end of the day of Rose's death Mike's office was full of file boxes. "What are you doing, Miller, moving into Rose's office before the Shiva?"

"No my grief stricken friend, I'm striking while the iron is hot. Without Rose there is no career path at this Presbyterian seminary for me or, for that matter, you. I've got eight or nine guilty clients that Berry and French will be happy to see the last of who will no doubt follow me to Michael Miller and Associates."

"Wow. You're starting your own firm? Where did you get the dough?"

"Trade secret. But these day's everything's financeable and you can start out in an instant office-shared secretary, reception and conference room, with very little up front." "When are you going?"

"I've already sent my tear stained resignation to the chairman of the firm, who will probably make a paper plane out of it about a week after the files and I have departed. Of course nothing was said to the clients until the resignation was duly received."

"Its like you had this planned."

"A good lawyer always has a contingency plan, Paulie. I don't suppose you've come up with one yet. Wait a minute, wait a minute, whose shoulder is Terry the tramp going to sob on?" Paul actually hadn't thought about that. He could talk to one of the partners upstairs, but he knew they thought only polyester clad lawyers took anything on the come. Now that he thought about it, there were probably a few other clients, hourly, that might follow him, for a discount of course, since no one else at B & F would be likely to pay much attention to them.

"I hate to admit it but that's a good question."

"I assume you made sure that you conveyed the news." That Paul had done, though not with any conscious design. Terry hadn't even asked about who would handle her case and Paul hadn't brought it up.

Ritzer called the next morning, hoping to take advantage of the shock factor. "I truly, truly am grief stricken, Paul, a wonderful man, a wonderful man. And quite formidable. Still, life must go on, and your client should be prepared to consider her options in the circumstances. Not an easy trial I think you'd agree, even for a Joe Rose."

"I'd probably want to defer judgment until we heard what your client has to say."

"I'll have the duty of asking Ms. Stephens what she thought when she didn't hear from Mr. Lufkin for a year despite her many efforts to contact him." Had Terry forgotten to tell him about that?

"And we'll both be going down to Whitman State to ask Anne just what she and your client knew when she watched her father die."

"That's no concern of mine, Mr. Sageman. But frankly, speaking frankly, but for the unfortunate sequence of events, with which my client had nothing to do, you have a case of gossamer suspicion and innuendo."

"We haven't quite done with the scrivener either."

"Mel Weinberg? You'll never lay a glove on him. But I certainly didn't call, certainly didn't call at an unhappy time like this to have a sparring contest with you." The emphasis on you conveyed the unworthiness of the callow Paul as an opponent. "Well it won't be necessary to adjourn Fred's deposition, Mr. Ritzer, if that's what you called for."

"No, my friend. I called to see whether you can speak for your client in connection with an expeditious resolution of this matter."

"Certainly. Is there an offer?"

"Let's say I've been exploring the concept and my concept is that you should seriously consider your obligation to advise your client that a hundred thousand a year for five years would be most generous, considering the fees she might be liable for after this case is dismissed."

"I'll get back to you."

"Please do. You might not like what comes out when your client is deposed, Mr. Sageman. When you've been at this as long as I have, you find that clients like to surprise their lawyers. And it isn't often a happy surprise."

Paul reported the conversation to Mike. "Wait a minute. Rose dies and now they make an offer? So it's the lowball special? Five hundred thousand? And that's not even the young murderess making the offer. I'd like her case. You owe me one for conflicting me out. They offer 500 So they'd for sure pay a mil. What would the fee be on that?"

"Three hundred."

"Hold the stationery order. I think the name Miller & Sageman has a certain ring to it." The idea had some appeal. Paul certainly wouldn't mind seeing the last of Berry & French. Nor they him, he knew. They wouldn't fire him, just put him on as a grunt in a mega case in some room with a million documents until he quit. Only Sandy loomed as an obstacle. She would think going out on his own far too risky.

Paul told Terry about the offer. Since it was less than Anne had offered, she wasn't too excited, but Paul said that Ritzer was clearly looking for a response. Terry asked what they should do. Paul knew that for her to seek his advice was a good sign for taking the case and was prepared.

"We can't afford to look anxious. Fred is clearly worried about how the charges against Anne will affect the case. He also never wants to be deposed. If it were me, I wouldn't respond. On the other hand, it might be an opportunity to obtain a reasonable amount of money now." Terry thanked him and called Frank. Frank thought losing Rose was a blow and wanted Terry to find a new lawyer. He didn't want to push too hard though. He figured it would be better to wait until Paul made some blunder and then use that as a lever. He also had to agree with Paul's advice that not responding to the offer was the best choice at the moment.

Fred was not happy when after a week there was no response to the offer. "Look, Jay, now you've put me in a bad position. You were sure they'd come back at a reasonable number and we haven't heard anything. You better find anther way to put off my deposition." Fred didn't want to give up Nikful yet but couldn't see how to avoid it if he had to testify.

CHAPTER XLIV.

Paul decided to avoid the fight over whether he should resign by telling Sandy after the funeral that without Joe Rose there wasn't a job for him at Berry & French anymore but that he had another opportunity. Sandy descanted on the injustice of it for some time but failed to ask whether the other opportunity had a pay check attached to it, a question to which Paul would have had no answer.

Mike, with a creative description of the certainty of an immediate million dollar recovery in the Lufkin case, had convinced a gullible bank to advance enough to allow the new partners to go further into debt by drawing against the line of credit for a few months.

So it was that within a remarkably short time the ill attended good bye lunch at Berry and French had been endured and the new partners had their names added to the sign at an instant office in the suburbs. Despite his desire to depart from the hallowed halls, the first day of Paul's descent from the glory of Berry & French mahogany to the gloom of rented formica was disheartening. Their new half a secretary, Joanne, endowed with big hair and remarkably long nails that both seemed to miraculously change color daily, immediately took to calling him Paulie but called Mike Mr. Miller. Berry and French became very bureaucratic about releasing files, so Paul had little to do for the first few days. Mike pestered him to get Terry to sign a consent to transfer the case. Paul decided that the best thing to do was to go see Terry, because he didn't think the new office would inspire confidence.

Luckily Tommy was out when Paul arrived at Mary's townhouse. Terry, who'd attended the funeral and sat with Paul, welcomed him warmly. He accepted coffee and cake and they talked about the funeral for a while. Finally he plunged ahead. "I'm afraid we have to talk about how we go forward with the case Terry."

"Yes, Paul, I've been wondering about that of course. It was all so sudden."

"I have to tell you I've changed firms, but we are happy to continue to represent you."

"Changed firms? So soon? But I thought Berry and French was the best firm in the state."

"Of course it's a very fine firm, but to be frank, they generally don't enter into contingent fee arrangements. It was a special accommodation to Joe Rose, but I don't believe they would continue on that basis." Paul hadn't asked and wasn't about to tell Terry that, but he was relatively confident that if Terry asked them they'd say no.

"What basis would they continue on?"

"I would think they'd want to be paid hourly."

"Oh." Terry thought about whether Frank would put up the money but didn't know if she could ask him.

"But we believe in the case, Terry. And my partner Mike Miller is a very experienced trial lawyer."

"Has he ever tried a case like this?"

"We feel that in essence it's a fraud case against Mr. Lufkin's children and Mike has a great deal of experience with that kind of case, yes. He was with the U.S. Attorney's office for a number of years." Mike would never know that he was the sales pitch if Paul could help it. Terry was silent.

"So the new firm is you and this Mr. Miller?"

"Well, yes."

"And if I wasn't happy with you, could I change later?" "Yes, of course, and we'd cooperate fully."

"Paul, you know I've got to consider Tommy as well."

"We wouldn't be doing this if we weren't sure we could handle it." Terry wondered whether she should talk to Frank. He'd undoubtedly know lots of lawyers she could talk to. But she really didn't want to tell the story to a lot of other lawyers, it was sort of embarrassing, and she didn't want to hurt Paul's feelings because he really did seem to care about her.

"All right. But I think I should meet your partner."

"If you could just sign this consent so I can have the file shipped over, Terry. I promise that if you don't feel comfortable we'll cooperate with whoever you choose." Terry signed.

"Wait a minute, you got her to come across on the first date? Maybe it should be Sageman & Miller. Put her there partner." Mike, who had no faith that Paul could work things out so quickly, shook Paul's hand for the third time. They were sitting in a hotel bar across the street from the new office, Joanne and her big hair in tow. "And the best part, Paulie, is Anne Lufkin is going to put us on the map. You may need a press agent." The indictment was front page news in the Ledger. There was a picture of Big John and Connery, old photos of Robert and Anne and the obligatory mansion shot.

"Looks to me like you're the one who needs a press agent, partner." Mike had talked the reporter into quoting him and adding it to part of the article referring to Terry and the will contest. "Did you think about asking the client first?"

"What did you think this was going to remain a secret? The Terry angle is hot-sex among the rich and somewhat famous. We've got to ride the wave, right Joanne?"

"I didn't think you guys were going to be so exciting to work for Mr. Miller."

"Mike." Great, was he paying for Mike to fuck her?

Paul ordered another drink. "Wait a minute, don't you want to sign the agreement? I can't have you inebriated until you sign the agreement." Joanne pulled a copy out of a briefcase and handed it to Paul.

"What agreement?"

"Our partnership of course." Mike had mentioned having an agreement but it hadn't materialized before. Now that Terry was signed up and the case was hot, they were suddenly signing an agreement?

"Do I get to read it first?"

"Don't you trust me? It's 50-50, even Steven. I have been out of school a few more years than you and I stole more of Joe Rose's doggy files than you did, although I'll admit it looks like you may have the pick of the litter. But it is a risky proposition, so all in all I'd say it's very fair." Paul couldn't disagree. Besides he couldn't possibly do the case on his own, especially after what he'd told Terry.

"I'm probably going to regret this." Marriage hadn't improved Paul's attitude towards commitment. But he knew enough partnership law to understand that it could be dissolved any time either one felt like it.

Paul, after a quick reading, signed. Mike ordered more drinks and charged them on the new firm credit card. Joanne didn't get home that night.

CHAPTER XLV.

For Connery and Sherman Brown it was going to be a battle of forensics. There wasn't enough evidence to prove that anything Anne did or didn't do caused old man Lufkin's death and Connery assumed Sherman Brown wanted to keep it that way. Of course people had been convicted of murder on less-even without a body on rare occasions, though Connery had never even tried that stunt-but as a rule you had to have some pretty solid forensic proof to get to first base, especially against a lawyer who'd tried more murder cases than any defense lawyer in Jersey.

Still, digging up the body wasn't necessarily the right thing to do. Connery didn't believe they'd find any poison. Odds were that Anne had simply been in the wrong place at the wrong time-Dad would have checked out even without her presence and her only mistake was waiting 'til he was ice cold and then lying about it after blabbing to the shrink. If the corpse was clean, Sherman Brown would only be telling the jury about that every 30 seconds or so. Of course if there was evidence that causes weren't entirely natural her goose was cooked-she'd probably have to plead and Connery could have another news conference. Connery had subpoenaed and reviewed all of Lufkin's medical records. The absence of any prior coronary history and the general good condition of the old man somewhat raised the odds that something had been administered. If it were some public defender and not Sherman, Connery might have tried to con the guy into being the one to ask for the exhume to clear his client's name by half promising to dismiss if it turned up negative but he didn't think that would work in this case.

On the other hand what if he didn't try to exhume - could Brown argue that to the jury - he could hear it now 'why haven't we seen anything about the condition of the corpse ladies and gentlemen? There ain't but one reason: the prosecutor knows the emperor don't got no clothes." If Sherman was allowed to make that argument, then Connery would have to try the case on the basis that Anne was guilty of depraved indifference because Lufkin lost the chance to live-even if she didn't spike his coffee. That was breaking new ground and it was probably what the case came down to. It wasn't an easy call-and despite Big John's presence at the news conference, Connery knew the elected prosecutor wouldn't take a position on a tricky issue like that except at gunpoint. Connery decided to at least run the question by Nappy.

Napoli had given the issue some thought because Fred was all for digging up Dad. Fred had even asked Jack if there wasn't some way to improve the results of a test by injecting the corpse before it was dug up, but Jack had convinced him that it couldn't be done without detection-Lufkin was buried in a sealed bronze coffin that JFK would have been jealous of.

Napoli personally had the cop's perspective - a fuss over an exhume would only highlight the failings of the initial investigation. Fred would never know what advice he gave Connie. As far as Napoli was concerned, the case should be tried based on unassailable logic - if the bitch had nothing to hide why was she lying her ass off? Why put the jury to sleep with three weeks of testimony from a couple of ghouls who would cancel each other out? Anne could afford a team of high priced ghouls who would swear that the arsenic leaked in from the soil, everyone in the police lab was either a moron or on the take and the corpse was so clean it was a surprise the old man didn't sit up and say hello when they popped the lid.

"Nah, Connie, leave the old man in peace. I've looked into the poison angle-we can't place her within a mile of a Poison R Us outlet- and this would have to be a pretty fast acting poison, not just some shit you could get in the hardware store. Rat poison wouldn't do the job quick enough."

"But what if he's stuffed to the gills with curare?"

"I don't buy it - she's got to go down for watching him turn blue or not at all in my opinion."

"But isn't there reasonable doubt if we can't show that she offed him?"

"Maybe, maybe but that we always knew. You and Mr. Slick each drag a bunch of stiff doctors in there to argue with each other and you're handing the shine reasonable doubt."

"But I might not get to the jury if we don't have any more."

"The press this case is getting-I got news for you Connie- its going to the jury. No judge is gonna want the heat of throwing it out and depriving the Ledger of all those great headlines."

"You're probably right, Nappy, but I've still got to make up my mind."

CHAPTER XLVI.

Paul, anxious to cement Terry's retention of the firm by creating the appearance of activity, decided to press ahead with Fred's deposition. Ritzer's opposition had evaporated with the demise of Joe Rose. He told Fred to get it over with before Terry hired a real lawyer. Mike, in between helpings of Joanne, chewed the case over with Paul and made suggestions about what to ask. He would have preferred to take the deposition himself but he didn't think Paul's ego could stand the blow. Besides, Fred wasn't likely to spill the beans even if Gerry Spence was cross examining. "I think the best we can do Paulie is to box him in to knowing nothing about the wills, old or new testament, having no communications with Weinberg or Anne about them. He's gonna want to go there anyway. Then if we manage to put Weinberg's license on the chopping block and he coughs up what he talked to Fred about, there won't be a party line any more."

"That's it?"

"Be sure to see what he knew about the stiff and the tramp, that is, our esteemed client, especially why they broke up."

"I don't even know that"

"Wait a minute. Your client never explained why she left Richie Rich for grapefruit heaven?"

"She wasn't very clear about it, I must say."

"But we gots to know that Paul. We have to."

"Why?"

"Cause Fred and Anne are certainly going to have a version of it, and probably half the people in that office will be herded into court to back them up."

"You think so? They don't need to prove that."

"Trust me. They're going to go all out."

"Do we need to know before I depose Fred? Its kind of touchy with her I think."

"Don't rock the boat until the client's sitting down? I like the way you think. But let's not forget."

CHAPTER XLVII.

Fred was ultimately served up at Ritzer's New York office. He denied all knowledge of any wills, new, old or in between, but did volunteer that his father had often said that Lufkin Realty would belong to Fred some day, neglecting to add that only the only occasion that Robert had uttered such a sentiment it was followed by the phrase 'over my dead body', which was now one of Fred's fondest memories of his dad. He also denied ever retaining Mel Weinberg to represent him personally. Contrary to Mike's thesis Fred also denied any knowledge not only of why they broke up but also of ever knowing that Terry and Dad were more than friends. Even Ritzer had to bite his tongue on that one.

Only when it came to Nikful was Fred less than icy calm. He'd taken a ride out to see the development property Nikful owned and confirmed his suspicion that it had become the jewel in the Lufkin crown. The imminent completion of the interstate was causing feverish development in the area and tracts were being sold for big money. There might be twelve million in clear profit on a flip, even more if Fred participated in subdivision, development and sale of the property. While Fred was pretty confident that Terry would eventually be disposed of he knew that Anne might well beat the rap and he hated to give up that kind of money to the little murderess

Against Weinberg's advice, Fred testified that his father had secretly given him the interest in Nikful, thereby confirming his status as the preferred child and future leader of Lufkin Realty. He denied, however, that Weinberg had anything to do with the transfer or knew that Omega was to be the vehicle for holding Nikful. Fred thought that merely incorporating Omega might not amount to enough to truly taint Weinberg and Ritzer was certainly prepared to argue that position as a last resort.

Paul, armed with the secret expert opinion asked Fred who had signed the stock power "Why my father did, of course." Nail it down, nail it down, Mike had said.

"How do you know?"

"I saw him do it."

"Where?"

"At the offices of Lufkin Realty."

"Was anyone else there?" "I don't recall anyone else being there, no."

"Who prepared this stock power, sir?"

"I believe Doris did it."

"At whose direction?"

"My father's I'm sure." Paul kicked himself for not having deposed Doris first. She might have been afraid to lie without knowing for sure what Fred would say. Now the path had been trampled for her and she couldn't very well disagree without endangering her job.

"Was your sister aware of this transfer of very valuable rights?"

"I don't know."

"Wasn't the result of this that you received a very valuable interest to the exclusion of your sister?"

"Well at the time the value was more speculative, so I can't really say that's so, Mr. Sagemen."

"Why would your father do this?"

"I was his son. The one who would carry on the family name." Which, Ritzer thought, was at least one generation old. "Now when you claim your father made this valuable transfer to you, you had only been employed at Lufkin a short time, correct?"

"My father was extremely grateful that I had decided to join the business. I didn't need to prove myself."

Pedersen, without appearing at all troubled passed a note to Morton "Will we have to cross-examine on Nikful?" Morton was afraid he'd have to, despite a strong desire to avoid breaking ranks with the rest of the defense on the will contest. He wrote back "Do we know what Nikful is worth?"

Pedersen was one step ahead, as always. "Called realtors-comparables are selling for $12,000,000+ without approvals." Shit, Morton thought, we can't give away $3,000,000 to Fred Lufkin. Now the problem was what to ask. "Any suggestions on cross?" Five minutes later Pedersen handed him a sheet with ten questions on it and the caution "I think we should stay away from anything to do with Weinberg on this."

Pedersen had also consulted with Sherman Brown as to whether Fred should be asked at the deposition if he had any reason to suspect Anne was either plotting to off Dad or had in fact done so. Brown didn't just dismiss the idea. One line of defense here was clearly that the greedy brother had put the greasy cop and the ink hungry DA on the scent and fomented the prosecution of his angelic client. But Brown wanted to be the one asking the questions and he hadn't managed to take over the civil case yet. There was some risk the prosecution wouldn't call Fred at the criminal trial, of course, and Brown wasn't likely to call him for the defense, but the jury could get the message even without Fred's testimony and this way Napoli wouldn't know whether Fred would back him up or not if he lied about how the case against Anne got started. So Brown decided to let it go.

Paul, happy with the out and out lie on Nikful, wound up his questioning. "Pass the witness." Mike had anticipated that Morton might be forced to ask some questions if Fred claimed the transfer.

"Divide and conquer, Paulie" Mike would stoop to clichés if a pun wasn't available. But having Anne question the Nikful transfer was of some value.

Before Morton could open his mouth Ritzer asked for a break and dragged Morton and Pedersen into the hall.

"Are you certain, Don, are you certain that asking questions of my client is in the best interests of the defense here? I would think we don't want, certainly don't want to give Ms. Stephens' lawyers the idea that we have any disagreements among us as to the facts."

"Mr. Ritzer, I'll make you a deal. Transfer Nikful back into the estate and my lips will be sealed." Ritzer knew Fred wouldn't do that.

"My client believes that his late father wanted him to have that property, Don and there's no reason to undo that gift."

"Crapola, Mr. Ritzer."

"But can't you see the harm, the harm this could do?"

"To your client, yes."

"To both of them, both of them Don. Perhaps if I agreed to produce Fred at a later date should it become necessary?"

"On the record."

"No, Don, I don't want to hold this deposition open for Sage boy. A gentlemen's agreement, a gentlemen's agreement."

With one of his own that might have satisfied Morton. But this was Jay Ritzer. "Just in case that agreement might slip anyone's mind, how bout if we just make a note of it."

"That's hardly necessary, but if you insist."

They went back in the conference room and Morton announced that he had no questions. "I take it, then, that the record is closed." Ritzer rejoined.

"I'd just reserve the right to reopen if further discovery merits it."

"I can't agree, Mr. Sageman. You've had a full and fair opportunity."

"Then we'll have this conversation with Judge Weiss if need be."

"Fine, Fine. And we'll be seeing Ms. Stephens next week?"

"Yes, of course."

Paul was dreading that moment. Even reasonably intelligent clients, painstakingly prepared, drilled and re-prepared had a terrible tendency to break your heart once sworn in. Terry, Paul feared was less than reasonably intelligent and more than likely to get emotional during the deposition, forget everything she'd been told not to say and recklessly volunteer the truth. It would have been bad enough back at Berry and French where, after all, it was just another case, but now his ass really was on the line. If Terry shit all over her shoes, the case was over and he suspected Miller and Sageman would be one of the shortest partnerships of all time. He hated to do it but he knew he'd have to get Mike involved with the prep.

CHAPTER XLVIII.

Terry came in the day before her deposition with Tommy to meet Mike and Paul. Mike tried to get Tommy out of the room five different ways, offering him everything except a piece of Joanne, but he wouldn't budge. Tommy wasn't happy that his mother was sticking with Sageman, who he considered a loser and he wanted ammunition for arguing for a switch. Finally Terry said it was alright if he stayed, he was going to learn all about it soon enough anyway if they went to court. Paul explained the rules of testifying and gave the usual lame examples. Mike, he said was there to conduct a mock examination.

"Can you tell me, Mrs. Stephens when you last spoke with the late Mr. Lufkin?"

"I think it was February."

"So for the last ten months of his life he had no contact with you whatsoever."

"Yes, that's true."

"But you say you were, shall we say intimate for a number of years before that, isn't that right, Ms. Stephens?"

"That's correct. Fourteen years."

"Can you explain why you ceased to communicate?"

"I didn't. Bob did." Paul began to wonder if they'd take him back at Berry & French. Mike actually thought it was the only good answer. If Terry had broke it off, the cratering of the relationship could hardly be the result of anything Fred or Anne did.

"Do you have any idea why?"

"The only thing I know is that Bob for some reason believed I was unfaithful to him. I told him it wasn't true. I swore. But he said he saw it with his own eyes. We never spoke again."

"And you have no idea what he meant by that?"

"I can't imagine. It just didn't happen."

"Did you ask him what he was referring to?"

"Of course. He just kept saying 'I saw it'. Wouldn't tell me anything else."

Tommy believed her. Mike and Paul didn't. Mike regretted asking the why question, though he'd had no reason to expect that answer-what broad in her right mind would risk so much dinero for a little on the side? But Mike tried to repair the damage.

"Couldn't Mr. Lufkin have meant heard it? From say, Fred or Anne?"

"That might be what happened, but that isn't what he said." She really was too dumb to live.

"Why do you think that might be what happened?"

"Well, I'm sure the children knew about me and they weren't happy."

"Did they know about the will?"

"I don't have any idea. I doubt Bob told them." No help. Still, what could the old bastard have seen?

"Could he have mistaken something he did see?"

"I just don't see how, Mr. Miller."

"Well did you ever just, innocently, go out to dinner with another man while you were seeing Mr. Lufkin?"

"I really don't think so."

"Did Mr. Lufkin ever come to your house?"

"Why yes."

"Did you ever stay over at his home on Mountain Avenue?"

"Yes. After Jeannine passed away. But never in their bedroom. There was a guest room. I even left some of my things there."

"And you were never with another man, even innocently, where Mr. Lufkin could have seen you?"

"Mr. Miller. I told you, I was never with another man, period."

"Don't take this the wrong way, but you have to be prepared for it. Their lawyers are going to ask if you were ever with another woman's husband - Mr. Lufkin. Then they're going to ask if you were with the executor and close friend of Mr. Lufkin, Mr. Mairone. You're going to have to answer yes. They're going to ask if you knew Mr. Mairone before Mr. Lufkin died. I assume the answer to that is yes as well."

"But Bob kept Frank as his executor, so he couldn't have thought I was seeing Frank." True enough, Mike thought But the inference of trampdom was strong and Terry was now the best witness against her case. And without her, there was no case. Even if Anne had offed her dear old dad, that didn't prove he hadn't made the new will for the best reason in the world. Maybe he'd let the headlines rush him into this partnership thing. Still at this point they had to go through with it.

Terry, flanked by Mike and Paul appeared at Ritzer's New York office for the date with destiny. Terry was fearful but determined not to show it. Fred, who had kept Ritzer in the dark, sat next to his lawyer. Anne remained in seclusion but Morton and Pedersen were there. After the usual preliminaries, Ritzer carefully approached the issue of why the affair had ended and was astonished to hear Terry admit Lufkin's seen it with his own eyes statement.

Fred wasn't entirely unprepared for that revelation but had expected Terry to come up with a less damning story. As far as he was concerned the case was over. Where was Terry's case going once she admitted that Dad changed his will based on seeing her with someone else? Her denial of the deed meant nothing. It was pure gold. Now all he had to do was send Anne up the river and he had done it. Fred had big plans for Lufkin Realty and he didn't figure he'd need to wait much longer.

Morton too figured it was over, which in a sense was bad for Anne-there was some hope that Fred could be convinced to call off the dogs if he was made to see that the suspicion of Anne's involvement in speeding Dad off on a permanent tropical vacation would help Terry's case. Now that was gonzo, Morton figured. Worse yet, it didn't look like there'd be a will contest to try.

Mike decided not to let Terry testify about her relationship with Mairone. Ritzer threatened contempt and tried to get Weiss on the phone to order Terry to testify on the spot but Weiss wasn't taking Ritzer's call for all the tea in China.

Finally they adjourned for the day and Terry nearly collapsed in the car on the way back. Paul tried to be encouraging. Mike was silent.

Ritzer couldn't help thinking it was too good to be true. Next thing they knew Anne's confession would arrive by Fedex. Fred was happier than he'd been since hearing about his father's death. "Jay, the truth serum in the coffee really worked. If you can't get rid of that tramp's case now I suggest you consider another line of work."

"Yes, Mr. Lufkin, I can't see how they can carry this on. I'll send the kid a letter about the fees we will go after if they don't dismiss, dismiss immediately, this frivolous suit."

"Do that. Now what do you hear about my poor sister's case?" As if he needed Ritzer to tell him.

"She's been arraigned I hear and is out on bail. Hired the local Johnny Cochran, but I can't imagine she'd try the case." "How can she do anything else?"

"That's just the thing-if we get rid of Terry, we have more flexibility dealing with Anne-perhaps if she knows she'll get something - a sixth, say, of the estate no matter what, I'm sure she'd plead to some lesser offense." And, Fred thought, she'd be in a poor position to fight over Nikful so in reality he'd end up with ninety percent of the estate if that deal could be made.

"Not a bad idea, but lets not look anxious, Jay, not a word to that fancy dan drunk she hired until I say so."

Pedersen had brought the concept of a similar deal up to Morton and Brown, but Morton didn't think there was a chance Anne would go for it. And Sherman Brown didn't want the prosecutor to get a whiff of fear. They discussed a plea on terms "Ms. Lufkin, I've been doing this a long, long time and its my job to tell you that you can always throw in the towel and you might even be able to throw in the towel and keep part of the estate-if your brother isn't a born gambler. But you can't be lettin' them think they can ever win a case like this by goin' to 'em hat in hand. It's bad psychology.

Someday soon this Connery is going to know what an ass kicking I'm gonna give him in front of a good Essex County jury and he be comin' to us. Then maybe we think about it." Brown figured this was the best moment to give her what might be bad news if, as he suspected, she was in fact guilty of more than depraved indifference.

"You gotta know this, too. Your brother's apparently convinced the prosecutor to dig up your daddy."

CHAPTER XLIX.

Fred was, in fact innocent of the charge. Connery after dillying and dallying over the issue for days, had decided to roll the dice and ask for the exhumation on his own. Brown needed to know whether he had to try to stop it, but he didn't want to ask a direct question so he just laid it out there and waited to see what Anne would say. "Can they just do that, Mr. Brown?"

"Well, a prosecutor can do just about anything 'til he gets to trial. You bein' kin there might be a way to oppose it but there's some definite appearance issues that arise in the situation you're in."

She was hard to read. "My concern Mr. Brown, is that if Fred can order the district attorney around, who's to say he can't influence the results of the examination?" So she wanted him to try to stop it. Not that her stated concerns were entirely groundless. For the kind of money at stake in this case Fred might just be able to buy the report he wanted.

Brown decided to test her a little further. "We could, I'm sure get access for our own expert, Ms. Lufkin, require samples to be set aside, things like that."

"But Mr. Brown, who is the jury likely to believe-not our hired gun?" She wasn't dumb.

"I've got to tell you the chances of stopping it are slim." "But we have to oppose it to keep them on the up and up-even if we lose, I want not just samples but our people watching their people perform the procedures."

"Okay, okay, I guess you're right." But Brown still didn't know if Anne had anything to be scared of. "I'd better go out and retain a pathologist then."

"Ask for a two for one special, Mr. Brown-I want Fred dissected alive when this is over."

The Lufkin publicity had actually brought in a few cases, but Terry was still looking like a loss leader to Mike. "Paulie, we got very few cards in our hand and trial is a month away. I hate to pay for expert deposition time but we've got to put the handwriting report on the table to give Fred something to think about." Ritzer would undoubtedly demand a three day deposition of the expert, then select three of his own who would declare the signature so genuine it should be in the National Archives. "Unless...wait a minute. Could we sell him the report as part of a settlement?"

"Can you do that?"

"Of course, Fred's a collector they tell me. This is a unique item. And it has multiple uses. It puts his credibility in question, it shows he's not above skullduggery and it gives Sis half of Nikful if Terry's out of the picture."

"But won't he think he can beat our expert?"

"I think we've got him cold on this one. But if you don't think so maybe I should be the one talking to Ritzer about it."

Ritzer waited a day or so before returning Mike's call, then had his secretary ring "One moment for Mr. Ritzer." Mike considered hanging up but the rent was due.

"Mr. Miller? Don't know if I've had the pleasure."

"All mine, I'm sure." "You took in young Sageman I understand."

"You could say that."

"But you I believe are a criminalist, not an estate practitioner, Mr. Miller?"

"A case is a case…and I'm not so sure there aren't criminal issues here."

"For the unfortunate Ms. Lufkin perhaps."

"No, Mr. Ritzer, we prosecuted forgery from time to time in the Office." Ritzer wasn't about to bite. "I think you know about the Nikful matter Mr. Ritzer."

"Be serious Mr. Miller." "I've got a report Jay. And its pretty conclusive."

"I can have three reports by lunch on Wednesday to the contrary Mr. Miller."

"Not from Lindsey McCormack, Jay." Ritzer had heard of him. In the top rank. Not only that but the idea of Fred as a forger was more than plausible. "You called me I believe, Mr. Miller."

"I did. We've got a special offer this week only-dismissal of the will contest and the original report thrown in. A million each. Plus a modest fee for Mr. Mairone." Mike wasn't actually authorized but he was sure he could sell it. "Don't be sitting by the phone when you should be preparing for trial Mr. Miller but of course I'm obliged to pass it on." Ritzer hung up. Mike thought he'd made an impression.

"I can't believe you'd even dignify blackmail like that by telling me about it, Jay."

"I'm ethically obligated, Mr. Lufkin, ethically obligated to convey any offer."

"Well forget it. Terry has no case and Nikful is that least of Anne's worries. But why don't we go ahead and get an expert just in case."

The experts were named and deposed. Ritzer couldn't get a top man who would vouch for the Nikful signature without reservations so he had to settle for two made as instructed reports from lesser names. Mike cut them to pieces. Even though it was Ritzer who clamored for it, Weiss set an early trial date and soon it was upon them. Terry didn't think anyone else could learn the case in time and resisted Frank and Tommy's attempts to replace Miller and Sagemen, but did get Mike to promise that he would try the case with Paul's help.

Not that there was much of a case to put on, Mike thought. Even if, as he expected, Weiss believed that Mel Weinberg was Fred's puppet, they still had to show something undue in the way of influence over a guy who was by all accounts no pushover. They pushed for Anne's deposition but Weiss wasn't about to order it and give Big John Martin anything to complain about before Anne's trial. They could make Fred look bad over Nikful but it was a real stretch to infer that the will was similarly dubious, especially after what Terry had said.

CHAPTER L.

On Monday, May 21st Paul put on his new grey striped suit, picked Terry up and went to the courthouse, more nauseous with fear than he'd ever been. Mike and Joanne arrived fifteen minutes later, she surprisingly serious and demure. Mike gave Paul the thumbs up. They'd decided to tell Terry nothing about the surprise witness. As instructed, Tommy had said he'd be looking for work in the morning and would get to court later in the day when the trial might be getting underway.

Ritzer arrived with three associates (trial was time and a half after all) and an evidence cart. Morton and Pedersen were there with a paralegal. Anne remained in seclusion. Radin appeared and dragged Mike out in the hall to see if there was any way to settle for enough to pay his fee and a sop to Frank, who'd been instructed to stay the hell out of the courtroom until called. Mike told him to sit back and watch the show.

Weiss had all the principal lawyers dragged into chambers. "Gentlemen, I have your trial briefs and I understand you're all ready for trial. While I certainly don't intend to prejudge the case, I must tell you Mr. Sageman that nothing I've seen so far would get very far with me. I don't know what kind of offers you've had. Experience will teach you, I'm sure that the certainty of some recovery is vastly superior to the slim chance of victory. Do you want me to have this case conferenced for settlement?"

Paul looked at Mike and then spoke. "Judge, there would be no point in conferencing the case right now, unless Mr. Ritzer has changed his position in the last week."

"Your honor, I must say, I really must say that Mr. Sageman exhibits the brashness of youth. The only change, the only change in the last week is the amount of time and costs the children have had to incur to get ready for this unnecessary trial, which time and costs I will certainly seek, certainly seek to have Mr. Sageman's client pay once you dismiss the matter."

"The trial was necessary Mr. Ritzer because there are serious questions about the man who wrote the will you want admitted and his relationship to the beneficiaries of that document, as I recall." Ordinarily Weiss would have been making noises along the same lines as Ritzer about frivolous to scare the shit out of Sageman and get the case settled at some reasonable number. But Weiss was not about to help out Ritzer.

They marched back out to the courtroom. Weiss appeared a few minutes later and Lisa sashayed out after him. "I assume you're ready Mr. Sageman?"

"We are your honor." Mike answered, taking control.

"I don't think I need an opening statement today."

"In that case your honor we will call our first witness, Theresa Stephens."

Terry had been thoroughly beaten and wouldn't dare to come up with any more surprises. Mike took her through the story of years of devotion, the deterioration of Jeannine, her honest love for the late Lufkin, the move to Florida and, so it wouldn't be fresh on cross, the inexplicable statement by Lufkin that he saw her with someone else. Weiss had trouble believing they were trying the case after that one.

Ritzer's cross was well done but predictable. Terry admitted the fling with Mairone after Weiss overruled the objection. Ritzer got her to concede there'd never been a promise from Lufkin as to what she would get from him or his estate and made her repeat the saw me with someone else line over and over until Weiss told him to move on.

Convinced the case was over Ritzer sat down.

"Any other witnesses, Mr. Miller?"

"We've subpoenaed a witness, your honor who should be here any minute."

"Who might that be?" Ritzer couldn't help asking.

"I suppose you'll find out when the witness shows up." Mike said. The rules didn't require you to disclose your trial witnesses. Normally that didn't matter very much because if you knew of anyone with knowledge that had to be coughed up during the pretrial discovery period or the witness could be excluded.

Paul returned from the hall and nodded yes to Mike.

"The caveatrix calls Mary Donnelly." Terry was stunned. Mary had never said she knew anything about the wills and she didn't think Mike or Paul had even talked to her about it. Fred was appalled but managed to disguise his concerns and simply lean over and tell Ritzer who she was.

"We must object your, honor we most strenuously object. This witness was not disclosed as having any knowledge. I understand she is the sister of Theresa Stephens so if she knows anything its simply inconceivable that her sister and her lawyers didn't know about this ."

"What about that Mr. Miller?"

"If we could have the witness out of the room for the moment your honor."

"Any objection Mr. Ritzer, Mr. Morton?"

"I suppose we could hear what Mr. Miller has to say." Fred was anxious to hear it as well.

"Sidebar your honor." Miller didn't want Fred hearing any sooner than he had to.

"I object to that. There's no jury here."

"Come on up Mr. Ritzer. We'll let the court reporter in on the big secret."

Mike and Paul stepped up. "Judge, I know this sounds like Perry Mason, but as god is my witness we have just recently learned some astonishing facts, facts that explain why Mr. Lufkin acted the way he did."

"And those astonishing facts would be?" Weiss asked.

"An explanation for the late Mr. Lufkin's belief our client was sleeping with someone else."

"And you expect this witness to help you out ?"

"Not if she can help it, your honor.."

"But you're calling her."

"Yes your honor. But I am confident you'll conclude that she's a hostile witness"

"Now if I find out you've cooked up some kind of Witness for the Prosecution deal, Mr. Miller I'll have your license for breakfast and Sageman's for lunch, do you understand me?"

"Of course, your honor."

"And your client's getting back on the stand if Mr. Ritzer wants her to, to testify about when she learned these facts."

"That'll be a snap your honor. She doesn't know them yet."

"Your honor, I must continue to object, to object to this mystery proceeding about evidence Mr. Miller doesn't even think his own witness will admit to."

"Your honor there is corroborating evidence. We'll put it on right afterwards. Now can I ask that no one be permitted to leave the court until after Mary Donnelly testifies?"

"On what basis?"

"To prevent the destruction of other evidence, your honor." Ritzer was beginning to get a feeling that Fred hadn't told him something pretty important. But he had to keep up appearances. "Is there to be no support for that astonishing charge, your honor? In all my years of practice I've never heard such a thing. And I don't think it should be on the record that the court even suspects that anyone would destroy evidence without a shred of support for such a claim."

"No Mr. Ritzer, I will make it clear that the condition is not and is not to be deemed any kind of determination of probable cause. Everybody can step back."

Weiss addressed the room. "Mr. Sageman, you can bring Ms. Donnelly in now. If everyone would just keep their seats until she's done." Ritzer whispered to Fred what little Mike had said about Mary. Fred asked if there was any way to stop the testimony and Ritzer shook his head.

Mary, looking shell shocked, walked to the witness stand. She couldn't bring her self to look at Terry.

"You are Terry Stephen's sister?"

"Yes."

"You knew Robert Lufkin?"

"I did."

"Did you know Anne Lufkin?"

"I met her once or twice."

"How about Fred Lufkin. Do you know him?"

"We've met."

"Have you ever been to the Lufkin's home on Mountain Avenue in Claremont?" Mary began to worry.

"I believe so."

"Have you ever been there when Theresa Stephens wasn't present?" Now Mary was sure they'd got something but wasn't sure how much they knew.

"I don't recall."

"Well, let me ask you this, Ms. Donnelly, have you ever been upstairs in the Lufkin's home on Mountain Avenue in Claremont?"

"I don't recall." Weiss thought she'd for sure remember that, even if it was just a tour. Mary Donnelly didn't look like she'd worked with Robin Leach, so she probably would remember her one and only trip to a real mansion.

"You don't recall."

"That's correct."

"Have you ever been in a bed upstairs in the Lufkin's home on Mountain Avenue in Claremont. I assume you'd recall that, Ms. Donnelly?"

"I assume I would."

"Well? Have you?" Now Mary knew what must have happened. "Must I put up with such insults your honor?" Fred just couldn't believe this was happening.

Weiss wasn't about to change channels now. This was better than Sex and the City. "I'll let you know if there's a question you don't need to answer Ms. Donnelly. Now Mr. Miller, this better not be a fishing expedition."

"Is it your testimony under oath Ms. Donnelly that you've never been in a bed upstairs in the Lufkin's home on Mountain Avenue in Claremont?"

Ritzer figured he better at least make a record. "Objection, Your honor. Mr. Miller has dragged this lady onto the stand and now he's making some irrelevant and , I must say, I must say your honor, incomprehensible accusation against his own witness. I can't see what this has to do with anything in the case. If in fact there is any point being made here, I would apply at this time for an adjournment to permit proper discovery as to what appears to be a completely undisclosed theory." Weiss had to admit that Ritzer was making some sense, and might even get an appeal out of the denial, but he didn't want to let this go. And he knew with an adjournment Mary would lawyer up and never be heard. On the other hand, she had to be warned.

"Mr. Ritzer, I overrule your objection. Should I find that there is need for an adjournment I will consider it. On the other hand, Ms. Donnelly, you appear to be here without counsel and I do not want to compel you to answer a question if you would rather assert your Fifth Amendment rights."

"Thank you, your honor. I would like the opportunity to consult with an attorney." Terry still couldn't figure out what was going on. Mike, who'd assumed Mary would either take Five or lie like a rug was unconcerned.

"Your honor, I would hope she would remain under subpoena and be required to return tomorrow morning."

"Certainly Mr. Miller."

"And at this time I would invoke the rule before calling my next witness."

"Who I trust will shed some light on this matter?" "In a manner of speaking." Mary fled the stand and drove home like a bat out of hell.

"I call Thomas Stephens." Tommy had taken a hair cut and donned a blue suit but still looked like he belonged in a pool hall. "You are Theresa Stephen's son?"

"Yes, sir."

"Where have you been living for the past three months?" "Mom and I have been living with Aunt Mary."

"That is, with Mary Donnelly?"

"Yeah."

"Now tell me what happened on Friday, the 18th of this month?"

"I got up a little late, being between jobs. Mom and Aunt Mary were out and I didn't have a car, so I decided to take a little look around the house." Tommy had been broker than the Ten Commandments and was desperate to find any cash that might be lying around. He'd remembered the little surprise in Aunt Mary's purse back home in Florida and decided to pan for gold around the townhouse. Hidden behind some towels on the top shelf of the linen closet was a loose board. Tommy went and got a chair and pulled the board aside and reached in. There was an envelope containing a videotape. No dough, but what the hell. He stuck it in the VCR and saw a blonde in bed with a guy. He didn't recognize the guy but the blonde looked a lot like either his mom or Aunt Mary. For some reason the camera didn't zoom in on the action and there wasn't a real clear face shot. The camera also focused on other stuff in the room even while the moans and sighs got louder. What the fuck was this? Due to lack of money for smoke, Tommy was more together than usual. He remembered what his mother had said about the old man thinkin she was balling someone else. Then he remembered that when he'd rifled Mary's bag in Florida, Fred had been in the address book. This had to be what the old man saw. And Mary, the cunt, had to be in on it. Tommy called Paul, who came over, watched the entire tape twice and concluded that Tommy was smarter than he looked. Tommy put the closet back together and they went to show Mike, who decided the whole thing needed to be kept under wraps as long as possible.

"And what, if any thing, did you find?"

"This tape."

"At this time Your Honor we would like to play the tape for the court, but the subject matter is, shall we say rather graphic." Weiss had a pretty good idea what was on the tape from the questions to Mary.

"I object to the court seeing this. There's no proof it has any relation whatsoever with my clients. None at all." Morton rose to join.

"Mr. Ritzer, if they can't link it up somehow, it will be excluded and, it would appear, you will prevail. If they can prove some connection to your client, or Mr. Morton's client, then we'll need to see where we are. How long is the tape Mr. Miller?"

"Very brief, your honor, barely ten minutes."

"Barely, indeed, Mr. Miller, I should imagine. Well, I will view it in chambers with counsel only for the time being." Weiss had noticed the resemblance between the sisters and wondered if it was skin deep.

"Any other questions for this witness?"

"Yes, your honor."

"Now where did you find this tape?"

"Hidden behind a loose board in the closet."

"Did you alter this tape in any way?"

"No sir."

"Do you have any reason to believe that Mary Donnelly has been in communications with either Fred or Anne Lufkin?"

"Only that I know Aunt Mary had Fred's home and cell phone numbers in her little black book."

"How do you know that?"

"I saw it one day when she was visiting us in Florida."

"Prior to the 18th, did you have any awareness of the existence of the tape?"

"No sir."

"Did your mother?"

"Not that I know"

"Did Mr. Sageman or I?"

"I'd be pretty surprised."

"No further questions."

Ritzer crossed Tommy on what a loser he was and how ungrateful a bastard he was for tossing his Aunt Mary's house when he was a guest living there for free, but he really got nowhere. Tommy thought it was a trip. Wait til he told fuckin Al DeLucia.

Weiss called counsel into chambers for the feature attraction.

"Now how do we know who this is and where it was filmed, Mr. Miller?"

Mike did a freeze frame on the best shot of Mary, which was not totally clear but certainly a ninety percenter. "As to the where, Judge, frankly at this point I'm guessing based on the attention paid to the furnishings that someone wanted it to be pretty clear where this was going down. But I imagine we can get someone to identify the locale. I'm sure my client can, but we can probably get one of the help from the Lufkins to do it as well."

"I see. But perhaps you have a bigger problem."

Ritzer jumped in "Exactly, exactly your honor. They can't prove Robert Lufkin ever set eyes on this tape." And Fred, he was certain, wasn't about to admit it.

"I am constrained to agree with Mr. Ritzer, that I have that problem with it. Now if Ms. Donnelly cops to this and says it was put in the hands of one of the children or their agents before the father changed his will, I might be willing to consider the probabilities. I do agree with Mr. Miller that even without any credits it clearly appears to be Ms. Donnelly and an as yet unidentified male whose face is never seen but, I gather, is not the deceased. Any idea who it is?"

"Not at this time, your honor."

"Well, I think we're adjourned for the day. I won't be ruling on admissibility until you come up with some more evidence to link this up. Is there much more to the case?"

"Frankly your honor, I may be going along with Mr. Ritzer on his adjournment request. I think we need to look into Mary Donnelly's finances and phone records. But we could recall our client tomorrow to identify the setting."

"Come back in the morning and we'll at least do that and talk about scheduling."

Ritzer ran out to talk to Fred, who wouldn't say a word 'til they were sitting in his car. "So what you're telling me Jay, is that the tape doesn't come in unless they link it to Anne or me?"

"That's exactly correct, I convinced the court of that in chambers, you understand, and without it, Weiss recognized that we would prevail."

"I think that can be taken care of."

As soon as Ritzer left Fred found a pay phone and called Jack. "Jack. I need a little favor."

Jack called him back with Weiss's home address.

CHAPTER LI.

Fred had limited confidence that Mary, even with the promise of a million, wouldn't sell him out now that the tape had surfaced. She could come clean and make a deal with her sister and avoid a long vacation at Whitman State. He also didn't trust Ritzer's version of whatever had gone on in chambers. He waited until everyone had left the courtroom, then slipped into Weiss's chambers and knocked at the door to his office. This show had to be shut down. Weiss answered the door himself. "Mr. Lufkin, I'm sure you know you shouldn't be here."

Fred stepped inside "Judge Weiss, I'm sure you know you shouldn't have been at the Morristown Hilton with Miss LeMieux on April the 14th while Mrs. Weiss was visiting her dying mother in Miami." Fred pulled out one of the better pictures. "Would you care to autograph it, your honor? Or should I send it to 14 Edgewood Road as is?" Weiss didn't respond. "I think we understand each other." Fred walked away leaving Weiss in shock. Lisa LeMieux, sitting in the next office heard the whole thing. Weiss left the courthouse without a word to her.

Fred called Mary but she wouldn't answer the phone. Her lawyer had warned her not to talk to anyone until he could decide what to do, especially Fred. Fred didn't think it would be a good idea to leave a message.

Mary arrived in court the next day with Burt Kane, Esq., a second tier criminal defense lawyer who probably wasn't averse to taking some of his fee in kind. Burt certainly had nothing against the possibility of a little news coverage and saw the possibility for a win-win. Burt pulled Mike out into the hall. "Of course, Mike, I can't tell you what my girl told me, but I have a feeling that it would make you very happy to hear it. Only its my professional obligation to keep her trap sewn shut, even if I can't see that anything she did was criminal—but of course I haven't seen the tape."

"So wait a minute, Burt, what you're telling me is we can't get hitched without a preacher?"

"Exactly, exactly. I gotta have a walk. Now of course I know plenty of guys in Big John's office, but, frankly I think I'm sitting pretty here takin five-cause nobody else is about to admit to holdin the camera and long dong silver is long gone." Mike knew where this was going and would be happy to make a deal with the devil-so long as it didn't hurt the fee too much-but Mary wasn't exactly trustworthy and if she sold them a sack of shit – gave a story that could in any part be taken apart by Fred-who might still be in the bidding-they'd be fucked. It also might not be too easy to get a prosecutor to look at this deal-especially while Anne was still out there-they'd be afraid it would tarnish that case. Still, Mike couldn't see an avenue other than Mary for getting the goods on Fred.

CHAPTER LII.

Lisa LeMieux knew she had a problem. She found Weiss attractive, she enjoyed the older man thing but she wasn't in love. She had no interest in breaking up his marriage or becoming the next Mrs. Weiss. She'd hoped he could help with her career. But she was troubled over keeping silent and pretending she hadn't overheard Fred and Weiss in chambers that afternoon. She knew that if Weiss thought she hadn't heard, he'd never mention it to her. She believed that to avoid a scandal and a divorce he might well throw the case. But if the truth some how came out, she feared the collateral damage. If she told Weiss she'd heard Fred she was only getting in deeper.

Sherman Brown was beginning to worry that Anne's case was snake bit. The Judge hearing the application to exhume and examine Robert Lufkin, Robert Coughlin, was an ex prosecutor and drinking buddy of Connery who wasn't likely to be swayed by arguments about the sanctity of eternal rest, the lack of probable cause or, at least in this case, the burden on the defense. More important, he might not cotton to any suggestion that the police lab was hardly a combination of the Mayo Clinic and the College of Vestal Virgins and that Anne's hired gun should ride shotgun on the autopsy and toxicology to make sure everything was according to Hoyle. But a man can only try.

Since this was not a routine legal issue and the request to monitor was veritably novel, Brown accepted Pedersen's offer to brief the issues. Ferguson & Mather had a slightly bigger library than Sherman Brown, who admitted that paper wasn't his finest product. The brief was a jewel - short, clear, hard hitting and backed with a summary of past flubs by the police lab and an article on the uncertainty of tox results after the corpus delecti had been fermented like a thousand year egg. The real question was whether Brown should show any cards about the case – let the Judge know it was a private prosecution – in the hope that would make Coughlin think twice about putting the taxpayers to the expense of the exhume.

When the time came to argue the request to exhume Connery anticipated Brown's attack. "Judge, we're here today for what is for me a new experience – not a challenge to admissibility of evidence – Mr. Brown knows he can't keep that out – but a challenge to the search for truth. In every murder case it's central to that search to know how the victim met his end and his condition at the time. But Anne Lufkin really, really doesn't want this to happen. So much so that even Sherman Brown wasn't enough of a defense. Ferguson & Mather was brought in from New York City to fight this. That brief, and I admit it's a thing of beauty, probably cost more than my house Judge. Judge, a grand jury has decided there's enough evidence to bring this case to trial. I've never heard of a case where evidence of the state of the corpse was excluded. Mr. Brown knows that. He more or less concedes it by proposing conditions – and if this was the only murder case we were even going to have in Essex County, maybe I'd agree to let the defense experts watch the autopsy and the tox, but if you let Anne Lufkin do this, I guarantee you every murder suspect will ask for it and if they can't pay for it, as Anne

Lufkin certainly can, they will say the taxpayers should. Before you know it, we'll have to ask the Freeholders to set up a defense lab."

Coughlin, Connery knew too well, had a great poker face, but Connery thought he had done well. Coughlin asked no questions but merely asked Sherman Brown to respond.

"Your Honor, I've been know to quote the good book from time to time. I guess Mr. Connery's in trouble – nothing in law and nothing in the bible supports this venal prosecution of my client, so Mr. Connery has to turn to that old standby of Greek mythology, Pandora's Box. Mr. Connery doesn't want to talk about this case, oh no, he wants the Court to think about all the other cases. But how many other cases you gonna see where no one thinks there been a murder til the body's been in the ground for six months. Not the police, not even the relatives I guess. How many other cases you gonna see where the result of a conviction is a thirty million dollar benefit to the very man who's been the cheerleader from the beginnin' of the game? So lets not worry bout other cases – this is a case so flimsy they can't get to first base on what they got – I don't need to tell Your Honor how little an indictment proves – they can't get to first base if there's a team in the field with what they got – so they need to dig something up. I've handled a few murder cases Your Honor."

"You beat me in a few murder cases Sherman, don't be modest," Coughlin chuckled.

"Well maybe more than a few, and I've never seen one as flimsy as this. If it wasn't for the treasure hunt going on in the Probate Court you know we wouldn't be here neither. But let's say you give Mr. Connery and his new friends the benefit of the doubt and let them dig up Mr. Lufkin, Judge I only need to give you two letters."

"O.J. Mr. Brown."

"Yes Judge. I don't want to put the medical examiners' office on trial here but honestly Judge I'm gonna. There's just too much temptation floating around in this case. There's only one way to avoid it. An open process. Give me split samples, let my experts observe the procedures. And to be honest Judge, you know I'm givin' up a pretty high card askin' for this rather than just letting the jury know all the ways things could go wrong in the dark."

"Such generosity Mr. Brown. It is Christmas?"

"Not yet. I wouldn't mind a trial date the week before though."

"Well I understand your argument and I don't 100% buy that you're giving anything up – it's more like a trade – you have someone watching every minute they're gonna be able to, shall we say dissect the technique of the lab with a much sharper scalpel. But I do agree this is a unique case and unless Mr. Connery decides in his infinite wisdom to appeal I don't think it sets a dangerous precedent. So I'm allowing the dig, I'm ordering split samples and I'm permitting you to monitor the autopsy and the testing protocol – provided you let the State monitor yours."

The monitoring of Brown's expert was no problem. Brown recognized it as a sop to Connery, who was now wondering if Napoli wasn't right. Brown was surprised Coughlin had succumbed to the dread big case fever but figured that had to be the reason – if the stiff wasn't clean the case could go national. After five years sentencing pushers to the revolving door Coughlin could hardly be blamed for making a ruling that would attract some attention. Coughlin's next move convinced Brown he was star struck. "While we're here gentlemen, can we set a trial date. I have an opening on October 13th." Connery and Brown now had to think fast – was this enough time and was Coughlin the right Judge? Brown was happy to have a jury of Essex County's finest think the Judge and the prosecutor were a team. That way when he exposed the puppet strings the Judge couldn't do much to salvage the case in the eyes of the jury. Connery recognized the problem but also saw Coughlin as more likely to let the case go to a jury than some other Judges. Both agreed to the trial date. Anne hadn't showed but Brown was pretty sure she didn't have anything more important that week.

CHAPTER LIII.

Connery called Napoli to give him the news. "Gee'z Connie, I never knew Coughlin was a Jap name, who'da thought he'd be lookin' for fame in all the wrong places."

"Well look Nappy, you got me into this mess, so I expect you to help my guys vet all the witnesses. And you better start working on your own story about how you were sleepwalking at the crime scene and didn't wake up until four months later."

"It's a medical miracle Connie."

Weiss felt better about himself because he had stated the flaw in Terry's case before Fred's visit – there was no proof old Lufkin ever saw the hot loop. Of course the star of the show might be able to fill in the blank, but Weiss didn't think so. The young Lufkins would never admit it. Mel Weinberg might know but Weiss was sure his lips were sealed. Of course Weiss knew what had happened. Terry's statement about Lufkin saying he'd seen her with another man now made sense and she'd apparently said it before the tape was discovered. Unless the whole thing was a put up job – which Weiss found farfetched, Weiss had no doubt that the blackmailer was behind it all – which didn't make his job any easier – he had to find a way to throw Terry's case out that would stick.

Weiss usually discussed all of the cases that came before them with Lisa. She tried not to show that she noticed he hadn't mentioned anything about the Lufkin case to her. She decided that she had to be in the courtroom to see if Weiss was affected by his chat with Fred.

Mary was recalled to the stand and took five as to everything but her shoe size. Ritzer didn't cross examine but reserved the right to call her later. Since Mel Weinberg was beyond the subpoena power of the Court, Mike introduced his deposition. Ritzer argued that it proved nothing. Morton joined the objection.

Terry went back on the stand to disavow knowledge of the tape. She identified the setting of the tape as the room she stayed in on Mountain Avenue. Morton got up to ask whether Terry knew whether his client had anything to do with the tape, knowing the answer had to be no. Morton also asked whether Terry knew if his client was aware of the content of any of Lufkin's wills, again knowing the answer would be no. Pedersen had figured that no time should be wasted distancing Anne from whatever Fred had cooked up, so that even if it all came out they could argue that the new will should be invalidated only as to Fred's share. Ritzer saw what Morton was up to but told Fred there was nothing to do about it. The real issue was whether to renew the request to adjourn. Fred had not let Ritzer in on his little chat with Weiss. Once Mary took five Ritzer was sure Miller would have to ask for a delay so a deal could be made to allow her to testify or to get information as to her finances. Ritzer decided to let Miller ask.

"If the caveatrix has no more witnesses Your Honor, at this time I would move to dismiss the caveat, to dismiss the caveat with prejudice."

Mike rose. "If I understand the application, Your Honor, Mr. Ritzer wants you to dismiss this case while the stonewalling by a witness who we can only assume was part of a sordid conspiracy to defraud is keeping us from getting to the facts. In any event, Your Honor, we have another witness, Mr. McCormack, who will testify to a forgery of a document transferring property worth $12,000,000 out of the estate to Mr. Frederick Lufkin."

"I must object, Your Honor, to this witness. Mr. Miller's client has absolutely no interest, no interest in the estate, or any claim it may have to the property. That would be a matter for the executor to deal with in any event."

"If I may be heard, Your Honor, that would perhaps be a legitimate objection if recovery of the asset was the sole purpose for the evidence. We offer it in addition as evidence of an ongoing scheme by Fred Lufkin to obtain for himself as big a piece of the pie as he could, by hook or by crook, culminating in the will before you."

Mike's speech put Weiss in a spot - he didn't want to make any ruling that could get in the way of the later dismissal he was contemplating. On the other hand, ruling against Fred on this preliminary issue might make him look less like Fred's bitch.

"I can't say that it comes in for that purpose Mr. Miller, but I needn't decide that. Mr. Radin, will the executor be assenting a position regarding the transfer?"

"We will of course investigate the facts Your Honor and proceed in accordance with our obligations." Frank pulled on Radin's sleeve. "Just a moment, your honor." "Judge we join in offering this witness, which I think disposes of Mr. Ritzer's objection."

"Call your witness Mr. Miller."

McCormack took the stand as Fred tore Ritzer a new one in the ear. Mike thought his only problem was that Joe Rose had died in blissful ignorance of bank secrecy laws. McCormack recited his examination of the documents, and his conclusion that the Nikful stock power was a phony.

Ritzer rose and made it clear that McCormack was not questioning the signature or the will and had no clue who owned Omega at the time of the transfer. "So Mr. McCormack, for all you know, Robert Lufkin may have owned Omega."

"Perhaps, Mr. Ritzer, but I've been doing this since you were a little boy and never seen anyone forge a transfer of his own property to themselves."

"So what were you paid for such objectivity, Mr. McCormack?"

"Only my standard rate."

"Now how did you happen to get to look at these private documents Mr. McCormack?"

Paul knew what was coming.

"Mr. Sageman and I examined them at the Offices of Union Trust."

"Mr. Sageman or his clients have an account there?"

"I couldn't tell you."

"Was there a legal authorization from Lufkin Realty or the estate?"

"I don't know."

"Your Honor. Your Honor, I move at this time to exclude the testimony of this witness. I cannot fathom, I cannot imagine the recognition of evidence obtained in violation, in gross violation of rights guaranteed under the law of our state and the United States of America."

"Denied. Any more questions?"

"Only this. Mr. McCormack I suppose not even you could presume to tell me who committed this supposed forgery?"

"No, Mr. Ritzer, but I think Deep Throat said it best – follow the money."

"I move, I move to strike at once."

"Denied."

"Any further witnesses Mr. Miller?"

"At this time, we move for an adjournment to permit discovery on the newly revealed issues arising from the very demonstrative evidence presented earlier Your Honor."

"Mr. Ritzer?"

"Your honor, this has gone on long enough, really, long enough. No matter what anyone says, there is no proof and will be no proof that Mr. Lufkin saw this videotape and if so that he reached any conclusion from it and took any testamentary action as a result. Even if the daisy chain Mr. Miller is trying to weave is assumed, nothing ties my client or, for that matter, Mr. Morton's to it." Paul thought about calling Fred but realized that not even Mike Tyson could beat the truth out of him. Mike and Paul had already decided that calling Anne was likewise a waste. She didn't need to take the Fifth on the essential question of whether she knew what was in any of her father's wills. And if, like Fred, she denied all knowledge, they were no where.

Ritzer droned on. "We should recognize your honor, we should recognize the facts – the caveatrix didn't even visit Mr. Lufkin for over a year before he passed away – no one challenges the authenticity of the will, the competence of the testator. There simply isn't a case to sustain.

"If I may be heard Your Honor." Weiss let Miller speak but he wasn't heard. The Judge wanted to get it over with. "I will be sending my opinion within the week. Good day gentlemen."

Weiss was fairly certain Fred wouldn't stand for any discovery. And he had no doubt why. Mary McTramp had clearly been put up to it by Fred. It would look bad to pull the trigger, but if the Appellate Division reversed, so be it. Fred would hold off and Weiss would find another way to thwart blind justice. There was no choice.

Tommy practically tackled Mike as they left the courtroom. "That Judge is going to fuck us, Mr. Miller. What are you going to do about it?" Mike knew the little stoner was right. Something was bent. "Wait a minute, Tommy, we can't have that discussion right here."

Terry caught up with Tommy. "Tommy, let Mr. Miller be, I'm sure we can talk soon." Fred overheard the exchange and agreed with the little bastard but said not a word to Ritzer.

CHAPTER LIV.

Weiss who'd taken good notes and knew how to spin the facts with the best of them, wrote a very careful opinion that subtly stressed the sordid nature of Terry's claim, the undoubted competency of the testator and the absence of proof of causation. To read it one would hardly have known that Mary took the Fifth, someone had gone to a great deal of trouble to make it appear that Terry was shitting where she ate, Mel Weinberg was a three dollar whore, and Fred was apparently a shameless forger. Weiss larded the opinion with quotes from venerable cases spouting irrelevant presumptions of the validity of wills. It was a masterpiece of injustice.

"Well Jay, what chance do they have on appeal?" Ritzer had some suspicion that Fred had somehow managed to pull strings with Weiss. He'd been shocked that the Judge closed down the show before permitting discovery regarding Mary. But the Appeals Court wouldn't have any idea that strings had been pulled. Weiss was well respected and Terry's claim was not one calculated to elicit tremendous sympathy. On the other hand Mary had taken the Fifth and Miller had managed to get the tape at least offered into evidence and described. The potent potion of criminality and sex might cause the appeal judges to look more closely than they would at a less titillating case. Of course for Ritzer the essence of any answer to Fred's question was that it continue the representation.

Fred was smart enough to appreciate that the chance of affirmance might be enhanced by retaining respected or connected New Jersey counsel. Any lack of confidence could be fatal. "Very little, very little chance Indeed, the opinion is very strong, very strong."

"So you wouldn't recommend some token payment to get rid of Terry and her motley crew?"

"Certainty has value. But what the price of certainty is I couldn't say. Sageman and Miller would be fools not to recommend any reasonable number. And I don't know if they can finance an appeal and endure the delay without any assurance that they'll get a dime later."

Mike was thinking the same thing but didn't want to let on to Terry or Paul who were both convinced that Fred had not merely caused the new will through Mary but somehow gotten to the Judge. Mike gave away no points for cynicism to anyone but believed that proving the latter was veritably impossible. And the merits of a cause of action were not in his experience any barrier to its dismissal, especially if the other side was well heeled.

He and Paul were sitting Shiva over their case the evening after receiving the opinion. The only cheer Mike could manufacture was: "At least the transcript is short." At a thousand dollars a day that was important. But they had a few weeks before they had to put up the money and Mike was still hoping Fred would see some value in sealing the crypt with a settlement that would at least pay for their time. After that Sageman and Miller could be disbanded.

Mike didn't think it was necessary to tell Paul he was going to call Ritzer. "I'm sure, Mr. Miller, I'm sure I could convince my client to forego seeking costs and fees from your client if she is willing to accept the result. Otherwise...." That was the position to start from and Mike had expected it. "Very magnanimous of your client considering Weiss saved you the cost of further discovery about the tape, Jay." This was the strong point of the appeal, of course, and the area of Fred's vulnerability.

"But my client is set on the appeal, unless your client sees the value of putting this to bed. Perhaps he could talk to Mary about that."

"Nothing to talk about, Mr. Miller. I will of course pass on the message, but I wouldn't hold my breath if I were you. We feel very strongly, very strongly indeed that the decision will stand up. Of course if I had an idea of what you had in mind." "There's still $40,000,000 in issue Jay." "I see no issue, but I might recommend $50,000 to save the cost of the appeal." "Three hundred fifty."

"Have you done a lot of civil appeals Mr. Miller?" The percentage of affirmance is quite gratifying."

"But normally all the evidence is in before the decision."

"Let's not debate it, Mr. Miller."

CHAPTER LV.

A few days later Ritzer came back with a hundred. Mike tried to convince Paul they should cut their losses. Paul wouldn't consider it. "You might be right but once we file the appeal the price might go up and Anne might see some value in settling as well then."

"We have an obligation to pass the offer on. And we're going to be out of pocket for the transcript. Not to mention they could tag Terry for the fees. I wouldn't be counting on mercy from Weiss." Paul promised to relay the offer but refused to recommend it.

Terry talked to Frank about it. "We can't let Fred get away with this Terry. I can't believe any judge would make you pay the fees. If he does, I'll make sure it goes away. And if you need anything for the appeal let me know." He really was in love, though perhaps hatred for Fred helped a bit.

Ritzer was told that the offer was declined.

The day of judgment for Anne was meanwhile creeping up on Sherman Brown. Pedersen was becoming an integral part of the defense team, against the better judgment of Ferguson & Mather, which shunned odious publicity and blamed Morton. Pedersen, the careerist that he was, saw the value of trial experience and exposure especially if, as he feared, being associated with Morton wasn't the path to glory and partnership at Ferguson & Mather. Brown, facing the possibility of forensic complexity over the exhumed remains and the unique legal issues of Anne's failure to act, was glad of the help, though he made it clear to Pedersen who would be the one speaking for the defense in court and to the press. But he couldn't help being impressed with the kid's sharpness.

Connery's case, they agreed, was a non starter unless the tape came in or the post mortem came back positive for some poison that would have caused almost immediate cardiac arrest. The tape was in Pedersen's view completely fatal if the jury heard it. Pedersen, like Morton, had no doubt Anne was capable of spiking Lufkin's coffee but he didn't think the prosecution would need to show it. If they could, of course, even Sherman Brown couldn't save her.

Assuming the body was clean, which they would know in a day or two, and the tape could be kept out, Connery would need to make a lot of mileage over whether Anne lied about when she got to Mountain Avenue. That would be no case at all except they probably couldn't let Anne open her mouth. She didn't have an alibi, she came across like a young Leona Helmsley and she wasn't near good looking enough to win over the male jurors. Brown and Pedersen were in agreement on that much. They sat down in Brown's office with two weeks to go. Anne was scheduled to come in in an hour for a progress report. "So what's the prosecution line up?" Brown asked.

"First they put on Napoli as the investigating officer." "He's got to be carryin' at least four pails of water, or more likely champagne from Fred Lufkin's well, for the State." "That's right. It's basically him and the dog walker." Connery had been forced to turn over everything on Pendleton the dog walker.

"You're forgetting the best supporting actor, brought in special for the jury of my peers – Clarence Mayes."

"So they'll have Mayes testify to the shakedown at the police station, not Napoli."

"Unless they get the Pizza connection jury, which ain't happenin' unless I be dead and you're pickin'."

"I'm sure you'll be there – unless you eat some of our client's cooking."

"Innocent until proven guilty or the retainer check bounces."

"But if Mayes carries the load on the shakedown how do we ask Napoli why he just happened to show up...." Pedersen realized the problem. "That's a dangerous question isn't it?" Brown was impressed that Mr. Wonder Bread picked up the point. "It could open the door...." You never ask a question that might make the inadmissible tape admissible .

"Well maybe unlock the door. I can't see it bein' admitted, but I think it might hurt us if that grease ball blurted it out in response to our question. And baby he's bein' paid to blurt."

"So we have to put on our own case against Fred?"

"I don't like it but it just might be the only way. It's tough cause I've got to show the jury two things – hopin' they remember one."

"Two?"

"Yeah – no one ever brings a case like this – which is what I plan to shove up my brother Big John's rear end for playin' Uncle Tom. And two – Fred is the smelliest, lowest, shiftiest needle dick sister fucker on this side of the planet. So how we gonna do that?"

"On the defense case?"

"If, as I'm beginning to fear, Judge Front Page, doesn't throw the case out before we need to put on a case."

"And we're not calling Fred."

"Not likely. When you gonna get the transcript from that treasure hunt before Judge Weiss"?

"Terry's lawyer should have ordered it, but I'm told it could take a month."

"So how we gonna show how Brother Fred tried to set Terry up for ho'in around in the very same mansion where he says we were offin' daddy? We need a neutral witness to relate what went down."

Pedersen thought about it. "What about the law clerk? A very healthy specimen. And she saw the whole trial."

"Let's send her an official invitation."

"A subpoena?"

"You did go to Harvard, after all."

"Then I just have to figure out how to get that story in evidence."

"I have the greatest confidence."

CHAPTER LVI.

So it was that Paul came to hear the astonishing words "Mr. Sageman, this is Lisa LeMieux. We need to talk." From the background clatter Paul could tell she was calling from a pay phone, so whatever they needed to talk about was on a subject Weiss couldn't be permitted to overhear. Shocked as he was, Paul wasn't about to ask why they needed to talk. If she wanted to talk about dominoes or interior decorating he was ready to listen, so if as appeared to be the case she had something important to say he wasn't about to discourage her. Nor was he going to say anything to Mike about it until he had to.

Lisa LeMieux. Her presence at the trial hadn't gone unnoticed even though Paul had a lot of other things to think about. She'd been there with her slightly pouty look and laser eyes and killer clothes. Could he even think about what she smelled like, how smooth her perfect skin must be.... Lisa LeMieux. "Mr. Sageman." Lisa's breathy voice was hypnotic. "Oh. Yes."

"Could we meet today?"

"Sure."

"I'm leaving work early. But I'm not sure I should come to your office."

"No, no..."

"How would Claremont Park at 3:30 be?" It sounded good to Paul. "I'll park by field 4. I have a silver Beemer." Paul thought about renting a car so he wouldn't have to show up in his vintage yellow Corolla.

"That should work out." He wasn't even going to pretend to be busy. Even if he weren't fully prepared to eat the peanuts out of her shit, this would have been pretty fucking exciting, but he thought he managed to maintain pretty well. "See you then." Paul was useless for the rest of the day. Fortunately Mike was out at a deposition and Joanne, Mike's bimbo, paid no attention to Paul or his moods. What could it be? Paul felt it had to be good for Terry. This wasn't prohibited ex parte contact was it? Not that it mattered. To be alone with Lisa for a half hour Paul would have burned his law license if he had to rub two sticks together to start the fire. And why was she calling now? Weiss had given them the heave ho weeks ago.

3:30 finally arrived. Paul had parked where he could see if Lisa was really going to show up. At 3:45 she rolled into the lot by field 4. There was no one around. Paul drove in and parked a few spaces away, jumped out of his car and walked as nonchalantly as he could to the driver's side of Lisa's prep mobile. She lowered the window. "Why don't you get in? We'll go for a ride." Oh baby. Paul got in, with crazy thoughts of what Sandy could get in a divorce. Lisa started to drive like a mad woman around the park, checking her rearview mirror while Paul ogled silently. "Maybe you know Anne Lufkin's trial is October 13." Paul knew but he still didn't make any connections – it wasn't intuitively obvious that Lisa could be a witness. "I heard something like that." Lisa was nervous which apparently caused her to drive even faster. Why was she doing this? The rational reaction to the subpoena should have been silence, the hope that she would never actually be called, and the further hope that she wouldn't be asked a question that would require her to perjure herself about Fred's little chat with Weiss, and why would anybody ask?

The oath, of course, called for the whole truth but that was asking too much. The average witness instinctively avoided volunteering. Lawyers were taught that they didn't want an answer broader than the question. At bottom it was anger and disappointment over Weiss that got to her. Lisa knew he would never have tossed the case on his own until Mary had been turned inside out. If she let it go she'd be as bad as him. And the hot potato routine hadn't helped. Weiss barely spoke to her now, the stream of superlatives over her mind, her beauty and her passion had ceased.

That the affair would come out would hurt him far worse than it would her – thought if she kept quiet she was sure he'd make certain she had a position with a good firm. At the same time she wasn't a hundred percent committed to spilling the beans, which was why Paul rather than Mike had been called. Mike, who she found very compelling, would have for sure gotten the whole story. With Paul she could still back off if she felt a need to. But she had to say something – God knows she hadn't set this up for the chance to ride around with Paul.

"Can you tell me whether anything that went on in my courtroom has relevance to Anne's trial?" Paul wasn't quite thinking straight but the question was clearly carrying heavy freight and the answer might be important to Terry's case. "Well, the prosecution would like the jury to believe that once the will was changed it was the right time for Robert Lufkin to die."

"And the defense?" Anne's lawyers must have talked to her. Paul was thinking straight now. He sensed there was something here that could resurrect Terry's case. After all for enough money you could buy a woman who looked like Lisa and have something left over for alimony.

"The defense would want to show that Fred Lufkin is the puppet master. That there wouldn't be a prosecution for murder without Fred – and that he plays dirty – he had to be behind the camera on the videotape."

"What if there was more to it than that?" More? What did she know? Was she going to make him guess? "Mr. Sageman, I guess I'm asking your legal advice here."

"Yes?"

"What if I know why Judge Weiss had to dismiss your client's case. And what if that really did relate to your puppet master theory?" Had to? Weiss had to dismiss the case. Why? Fred must have something on him.

"Have you spoken to the defense about this?"

"No. Not yet." If Anne's lawyers knew they might never call Lisa – there were other ways for the defense to prove Fred was a manipulator without risking the whole estate. Anne was after all on the other side. Of course Paul could try to get her to make a statement, but he had not way to compel her. At the moment they had no case to issue a subpoena in. Plus, if it came out for the first time in the criminal trial it would be a surprise and also infinitely more convincing.

"My legal advice, such as it is, is not to talk to anyone about this. You might never be called to testify." Paul felt he wouldn't get to the bottom of this if looked too eager.

"But I can't just let this go."

"Well, you still should keep your own counsel til then. There's a lot of money at stake and a lot of people desperate to keep the truth from coming out. Give anyone a heads up and they might find a way to keep you from telling the truth." Anne was on trial for murder after all. Paul hoped it would work. There was no better scenario for busting things wide open. Of course Weiss and Fred could deny it, but they'd for sure get a new trial before a new judge. Of course it meant holding your cards for a long time. Lisa could get cold feet, she might not be called anyway and Paul wouldn't have any way to prove what he just heard. But the alternatives – getting a statement or urging her to go to the Judicial Conduct Commission – had their problems too.

"Well, considering what it means to your client's case, if you are telling me to wait, I guess that must be the best thing. I promise I'll call you if anyone tries to talk to me."

"Ok. I know you'll do the right thing." She dropped Paul off. He went back to the office to think things over. It had to be that Fred had something on Weiss, probably something to do with Lisa, though he'd deliberately avoided asking. He wouldn't tell Mike but he did call Terry to say there'd been a development and she definitely shouldn't settle. Terry was happy to hear it and luckily didn't press him. She decided not to tell Tommy.

Frank, though secretly thinking it was bullshit, encouraged Terry. Radin had told him that his friends in the Appellate Division probably would reverse, if only so they could later hear the whole story of Mary Fucked a Little Lamb and the settlement Fred was talking about was an insult, so there was basically nothing to lose.

CHAPTER LVII.

Fred thought things were looking good, though he would have to deal with Mary eventually. He was already considering how to solve that problem. If she kept her mouth shut she's still expect the million bucks he'd promised her. But leaving the tape around where Terry's little punk could find it put an end to that. Now the risk wasn't that she'd decide to talk but rather that someone could make her. Why should he pay her? Better to spend the money making sure she couldn't talk – though that couldn't happen for a while and it would have to look like an accident. Fred had spent years daydreaming about getting his father out of the way 'accidentally' and concluded it wasn't easy. The other alternative was to make sure no one would believe her. It wasn't nearly as good of course. Why would she make that tape on her own in Robert Lufkin's guestroom? It would have to be some kinky revenge on Terry thing, which was improbable. No doubt the snuff out was the way to go. Of course if Mary had a tape someone else might as well. Fred was fairly certain Jack didn't have a copy, though he too knew too much. Fred thought briefly of the blood the roman emperors had to shed to live long enough to adorn one of his coins.

The key was to keep the lid on until Anne was in the can. Terry's appeal, Fred realized could actually be turned to his advantage – He'd get a message to Mary that the deal was still on if she kept the faith but payday had to await final rejection of Terry's claims. If Ritzer, mediocre as he was, could stretch out the process for a while, Fred could arrange to get Mary out of the way quietly.

Now in control of the business Fred was looking into burnishing his image by donating a collection of art and coins to the Claremont Museum in his father's memory and buying some political cover by promising a stream of donations. Let that soak in for a while and who would believe he'd robbed Terry, railroaded Anne and snuffed out Mary? If you could buy a prosecution like he had for Anne, you could certainly quash an investigation. Fred favored the bungled robbery shooting setup. Not that the bitch deserved such a quick death. Napoli could probably handle the job and he doubted the greedy bastard would go moral on him. But Napoli had to be handled carefully. Fred didn't want a partner for life. There was no rush if Mary could be kept on the Reservation. So Fred went to an Internet Café and sent a message to Mary forgiving her for the tape incident and promising to pay, with interest, once the appeal was decided. You could promise a high rate of return if you never intend to pay. Mischief was best done in the dark. The whole ruckus over the big dig was a true shame – otherwise it might have been possible to needle dad just one more time.

Napoli wasn't surprised by the results of the exhume. "Not even a little Drano? I told you Connie, digging the guy up was a mistake. If you'd left him in the ground you could have had the doc say any result after that long a dirt nap would be uncertain and the jury might believe Anne had spiked the coffee." The lab test had come back clean. Connery wasn't surprised. The case was now back to depraved indifference.

Big John wasn't discouraged. While a plea would have been nice, a groundbreaking trial was probably better. If Connery won Big John could elbow him out of the way at the news conference. If not, Big John would find another horse to ride. But he told Connery "You'll be needin' a medicine man to say the old slum lord could of pulled through if Anne made the call. Best find a doctor who's got rhythm, cause Sherman's gonna be doin' his Central Ward shuffle for the brothers and sisters."

"Already on order. And don't forget we got Clarence on the team."

"And don't you forget that he best remember it was you and not Napoli who decided that Anne should be talked to out in West Ridge." Big John hadn't picked up a law book in years but he still knew what a trial was about. He'd toyed with taking the ball on this one – it had already been mentioned in the New York Times after all, but a conviction was a little too much of an outside shot. Besides Sherman could be counted on to make a positive for the defense out of the DA's extraordinary presence on behalf of the memory of some rich honky. Mayes and Dr. James Brown would be sufficient melanin to counter that part of Sherman's game plan.

Fred was more anxious than Big John to give Connery advice but any suggestions had to be filtered through Napoli. He beat a drum for the use of the diary. Napoli agreed to advocate its use knowing the true charm of the piece was that it gave Anne a motive unrelated to the new will – and thus to Fred – for dispatching dad. Connery, without evidence of poison, was coming around to the idea. There was nothing else strong in his case, so the motive might as well be.

CHAPTER LVIII.

Anne was now confident of victory. When Sherman told her about the test results she said "Surely you're not surprised Mr. Brown? What I want you to be thinking about now is making sure we win the malicious prosecution case against my brother and the county. If you keep that in mind, I'll own Lufkin Realty and a mortgage on the court house." This crazy bitch gonna be running for President next, Brown thought. Or maybe it was just the liquor talking. She'd obviously had a few with lunch. He was gonna have to make sure she dried out. The truth was they still had a murder case to win.

"Ms. Lufkin, its great news, but I'm gonna worry about winning this case not the next one."

"But they don't have a case and you told me it would never have been brought if Fred wasn't behind it."

"And that's so. But I take every murder case very seriously."

No one took it more seriously than Fred. With less than a week to go he was calling Napoli three times a day with suggestions. Fred had been scouring the internet. "Isn't the time of death the key here, Lieutenant? I've read that it can be quite precisely determined if your medical examiner was on the scene quickly enough."

"Mr. Lufkin we've been over that. Connery can get the doc to say 8:30 give or take fifteen minutes."

"I think he should be able to do better than that."
"I'll ask again. But give me the name of the study

you're relying on." Fred didn't need to be told not to email it.

Napoli told Jack. "If I'd known what it was worth I would'a shoved a thermometer up the old man's dead asshole at the crime scene."

"Without a rubber glove."

"Anyway it ain't time of death its time of arrival." Distrust made Butler and Napoli almost inseparable whenever Napoli could get out of the station. "So whadda we got on that?"

"The dog walker."

"Didn't the maid say she set up dinner for two and the old man said Anne was comin' over."

"That's what's in the report."

"Didn't you talk to her?"

"Let me see." Napoli pulled the murder book which should never have left the station off the backseat. "That's what she said way back when. Gladys Minosa, age 63, worked for Lufkin twelve years. Set out tea for two if Lufkin told her to. Did so that night. Were you planning to call her to the stand?" "Just for that fact."

"That was before."

"Before what?"

"When you talked to her."

"Yeah." They were at a red light. Jack grabbed the murder book. "148 Grant Avenue, Broomefield, Apartment 4G." Napoli grabbed the book back. "This is an official police investigation."

"They've done wonderful things with memory enhancement the last few years, you know."

CHAPTER LIX.

Mike was not happy with the case or what it would cost to play it out. "Can't Terry at least advance the cost of the transcript? I mean we put a lot of time and effort into this, Paul, the client turned down some fairly reasonable offers and I'm not sure we're even legally obligated to do this on the come. If it's even worth doing."

"Well we filed the notice of appeal."

"Wait a minute, you filed it without asking me?"

"We had to, Mike."

"It would have been a lot smarter to get Terry to agree to pay before filing. If you want to have a partner you've got to act like one." Sure, Paul thought, like paying half the bimbo's salary so Mike could get blown for lunch every day and Paul didn't even get sloppys. Apart from Terry, Mike did have a lot more business. Paul suspected the partnership wouldn't last long. But he knew he couldn't make it on his own. "Besides," Mike continued, "I don't think we have a prayer."

"Let's just wait for Anne's trial. If the appellate division knows she offed him after the new will they might take it more seriously."

"Wait a minute, do you know something I don't know? Who's gonna beat Sherman Brown in front of a jury like he'll get here on a case like that?"

"I looked at the law."

"The law's got nothing to do with a trial Paul, I'd think even Terry knows that now."

"But listen, I think if it isn't dismissed after the prosecution case they have to plead. And depraved indifference is enough, which might be if the judge thinks there's evidence that she watched him die."

"Maybe, maybe. In the meantime ask Terry about the transcript." Paul agreed, happy he didn't have to disclose his parking lot adventure to keep Mike on board. Actually he had looked at the law. And he didn't need a conviction, just the defense having to put on a case.

CHAPTER LX.

Sherman Brown had explained the importance of demeanor in front of the jury to Anne but he'd feared it fell on deaf ears. They'd pick a jury in two days, pretty fast for a murder trial. Anne sat stone-faced between Pedersen and Sherman, not deigning to participate actively but managing to look the prospective jurors in the eye. Connery sat alone. Generally he had the officer in charge at counsel table but in this case he'd opted for the Lone Ranger look, knowing that the less Napoli sauce the better and concluding that Clarence Mayes as Tonto would be seen as pandering. Connery made no attempt to bleach the jury panel. It wouldn't work anyway and they had found Dr. James Brown to sing a rap duet with Sergeant Mayes:

"The Bitch is White.
Her Daddy's Dead.
It's just as bad as if she shot him in the head.
How long she was watchin' she won't say.
So let's get together and put her away."

Sherman Brown was halfway happy with the jury. He'd wanted smart – because they might grasp reasonable doubt - and no healthcare workers – because they'd be sure Lufkin could have been saved if Anne had dialed 911 that night instead of Bergdorf Goodman and could convince the rest of the jury better than any paid expert. But one out of two was ok – he could sell the conspiracy theory easier to the down home folks.

Sherman's big worry right now was the witness list. Connery had handed him a list the first morning and Sherman Brown and Pedersen had gone over it. They had all the investigative reports and lab work but one name on the list – Lucy Gomes – didn't show up in the file. "If there's one thing I hate more than an enema from an ugly nurse it's a surprise witness," he said to Pedersen. Anne didn't know who she was. From the ethnicity Pedersen deduced that she was somehow related to Gladys Minosa. The rules didn't require Connery to disclose what Lucy was going to say and he beat back every attempt by Sherman to get a preview. Sherman hated to look weak but he'd asked Coughlin to make Connery cough up something. Coughlin wouldn't help either, merely stating that if it turned out that the investigating officer or the prosecutor's office had something they should have disclosed, Coughlin would deal with it.

Connery's opening didn't make Sherman Brown any happier.

"We will prove beyond a shadow of a doubt that Robert Lufkin, age 63, died no earlier than eight thirty p.m. We will prove beyond a shadow of a doubt that Anne Lufkin's BMW was a Mr. Lufkin's home no later than eight in the evening. We will prove that Anne Lufkin under a will of Robert Lufkin, signed just months before his death, stood to inherit some thirty million dollars. Thirty million dollars. Most important we will prove that Anne Lufkin told the Claremont Police that she arrived at Robert Lufkin's home no earlier than nine o'clock, but that she has no witnesses to her location and no evidence proving she was elsewhere at any time after she left her office at 6:00 p.m. that evening. You will hear the testimony of our medical expert, Dr. Arthur Perkins, Chief of the Department of Cardiac Surgery at University Hospital, that Robert Lufkin died of a myocardial infarction and that prompt medical attention would have given Robert Lufkin an excellent chance at survival."

Eight o'clock? Sherman Brown thought, where did that come from? And 'at' is different from pulling into the long driveway. Pederson was already pulling out Pendleton's statement. Sherman Brown looked at it and whispered "Have you heard from the investigator?" They'd sent an investigator to talk to all the witnesses and added Lucy Gomes to his list even before Connery and Coughlin had fucked them over. Gladys had refused to talk to the guy, thanks no doubt to Anne's general cuntiness.

"Not yet." Sherman thought maybe Pedersen should try again after court. He most probably spoke fluent Portuguese and a few other languages.

Sherman Brown listened to the rest of Connery's opening. The boy was smart – he didn't promise the jury what he might not be able to deliver – the tape or the deceased's notebook. He didn't bore the jury. Sherman had notes for a few different versions of his own opening depending on what Connery said and what he thought the jury was buying. By the time Connery was done he thought the jury was buying a lot so he decided to go with an aggressive approach. After the standard bullshit he said.

"Anne's father Robert Lufkin died of a heart attack. No gun, no knife, no poison, no karate chop. Anne called the police. She didn't run away. The police came. They saw a man dead from a heart attack. They didn't think there was anything suspicious. Looked just like what it was – a heart attack. The Claremont Police closed the file. Mr. Lufkin was buried. That would be the end of the story except for one thing.

Money. Who really started this witch hunt? Anne's brother Frederick Lufkin. He ain't here today in court. And I'm not a bettin' man, but I don't think you'll see him during this trial. Why? Well Frederick Lufkin figured out if Anne could be convicted he'd get her thirty million. That's right. You can't inherit from someone if you are responsible for their death.

So months later Fred Lufkin went to the police and started this whole thing. Fred Lufkin has been seen not less than five times, five times, with the officer he got to bring these charges – Lieutenant Napoli.

Let me tell you something else Mr. Connery didn't happen to mention, they know how weak this charge is so they tried to find evidence. They actually dug up Robert Lufkin. Well I'm glad they did cause not only does it show how hot they were to find something – they didn't. Robert Lufkin died of natural causes. A heart attack. No knife, no gun, no poison, no karate chop.

Now they say Anne was there and watched Robert Lufkin die. They got no witnesses to that. Maybe they have a witness who months later says he thinks he saw Anne's car there. Maybe he saw a car drive in there – he didn't see Anne. Maybe a witness thinks he saw the same kinda car Anne drove – a BMW. Do you know how many BMWs of the same model Anne drove were registered in the State of New Jersey as of last year? Well we found out. Over two thousand – two thousand." Pedersen had thought of this yesterday – it was great cross material – who on the jury would believe anyone remembered a license plate months later? Brown had wavered over saving it for cross but he was it as important not to have to turn the jury around halfway through the trial.

"So they can't prove Anne was even there. They sure can't prove she gave her father a heart attack or that she or anyone else coulda saved him. I've been doin' this for a long time and I've never not once seen a charge of murder in a case like this. I'm sure you never have either. Thank you."

Paul slipped out of the courtroom as Sherman wound up, sensing, like Anne's lawyer, that the prosecution had something pretty convincing that put her at the scene, assuming it wasn't Lisa's BMW. If he was right, Coughlin probably wouldn't toss the case. Paul would love to have chewed it over with Mike, or even Terry. But he'd told Terry to stay away and having kept a secret for two weeks he wasn't going to let Mike in on it.

CHAPTER LXI.

Over lunch Connery called Napoli to tell him that everyone knew he was going steady with Fred Lufkin. "Don't worry Connie – the best thing that could have happened was for Mr. Bojangles to spill the beans on that one. I'll have an explanation for every single meeting and you'll make the jury think Anne was pretty darn worried to hire an investigator to follow me around. If I were them I'd be a lot more worried about Lucy Gomes." But Napoli didn't mention it to Fred or Jack. For all he knew Jack was playing both sides of the fence. Maybe hitting up Anne's team for an extra fifty.

Connery didn't ordinarily worry over niceties like the order of witnesses – his usual murder trial was rarely a minuet. The ordinary problem wasn't lack of eye witnesses, it was finding people who weren't too scared to remember who was pulling the trigger. Now he was in the game and very anxious to beat Sherman Brown on the front page of the Star Ledger. Big John was taking it pretty seriously too. The case was getting more press than anything in years. Big John told Connery "Warm them up with motive and opportunity then let my brother Dr. Perkins bring it on home."

So Napoli got called first, described the crime scene, recited Anne's statement that she wasn't around til her dad was chillin' and put in the old and new wills. Pedersen argued against the diary while the jury was outside the courtroom and lost and Napoli finished up by reading from it. Sherman would have liked to cross Napoli on how he just happened to show up in West

Ridge but figured he'd call him back after Sergeant Mayes if he had to, so he made it short and sweet.

"You had no suspicion that this was a homicide when you first investigated correct?"

"No sir, because Anne Lufkin told me she wasn't there and her father was alone when he died." Motherfucker.

"And you had no reason to disbelieve her?" Pedersen cringed, hearing the hinges on the door squeak.

"Not at that time, no."

"And you closed the file?"

"Yes, based on what I knew then."

"And you didn't ask for a post mortem?"

"Not at that time."

"And you didn't do anything with the case until you met Mr. Frederick Lufkin some six months later?"

"No, because I didn't have any facts that cast doubt on the defendant's story."

"And you only reopened the file after you met with Mr. Lufkin at his office?"

"That's correct."

"And that was your second meeting with Mr. Lufkin?"

"Yes."

"And you've met with Fred Lufkin on a number of occasions since."

"He was able to provide information about his father and the Defendant that assisted the investigation."

"And you yourself brought this case to the attention of Mr. Connery?"

"Yes."

"And you had the body of Robert Lufkin exhumed?"

"Yes."

"Ever done that before?"

"No."

"Ever work on the homicide of a man with sixty million dollars before?"

"No."

"Your Honor, I may need to recall this witness at a later time."

"I'm sure that won't be a problem." Coughlin wondered why Sherman would leave so much hanging.

Pendleton was called, did the dog show on direct and managed to look fairly relaxed when Sherman Brown stood up.

"So it was Lieutenant Napoli came looking for you, right, you didn't report anything suspicious at the time?"

"No."

"And you don't know who was driving that car you say you saw?"

"No, as I told Mr. Connery, I think it was Anne."

"But you can't swear to it?"

"That's correct."

"And it was dark?"

"Yes."

"And someone drove by who you had no reason to pay attention to?"

"That's correct."

"And you didn't think about it until Lieutenant Napoli came callin' months later?"

"Not that I recall."

"Just one more question Mr. Pendleton, you're on Wall Street right?"

"Yes."

"Tradin' stocks and bonds?"

"Bonds."

"But your company they trade commodities too?"

"Objection, relevance, scope of direct."

"Overruled."

"I believe we do."

"And Fred Lufkin, the reason we're all here today, he was a commodity trader."

"Objection."

"Overruled."

"I think I heard that, yes."

"I think so too. No further questions, Mr. Pendleton."

Connery toyed with redirect – it was probably a bluff by Sherman to suggest that Pendleton and Fred had a business connection. But he'd never asked if Pendleton had ever done business with Fred. And Nappy wouldn't have put that in any report. Best to leave that alone. But leave the jury with a positive.

"Mr. Pendleton, we appreciate your patience. You are sure and you can swear you saw a female driving a BMW turning into Robert Lufkin's driveway on the night he died?"

"Yes, that's right."

CHAPTER LXII.

Connery called Gladys Minosa the housekeeper. She was indeed addled brained and had to be handled with care – but he thought her story could be turned into a perfect trap.

"Where were you working last year?"

"For Mr. Lufkin at the house."

"And were you at work on the night of November 3rd?"

"Last year?"

"Last year."

"Yes, 'til six."

"Six in the evening?"

"And you left then?"

"Yes."

"And what did you do before you left?"

"I cooked dinner."

"For who did you cook?"

"Mr. Lufkin and Ms. Anne. She come for dinner almost every other Friday."

"How did you know Anne was coming to dinner?"

"If she wasn't, Mr. Lufkin would have told me." This wasn't the answer she'd been coached to give but Connery didn't want to break the rhythm.

"So you left at six and Anne Lufkin wasn't there?"

"Yes, Lucy picked me up. Mostly my husband picks me up but sometimes he busy. Mr. Lufkin was there though."

"So you couldn't say whether Ms. Anne showed up?"

"Yes, she did."

Connery stopped, as did Anne's heart. "How do you know that, Mrs. Minosa?"

"Well when I got home and went to look at the TV Guide I realized I left my glasses and I couldn't be without them all weekend, so after dinner I asked Lucy to take me back."

"And what time was that?"

"About 8:30 and I saw Anne's car in the driveway."

"No further questions."

Pedersen swore silently to give up trial work. Sherman Brown pretended it was no big deal but he knew the courtroom was quieter than a wooden Indian and the jury was startin' to look at Anne like a goose comin' out of the oven.

"Ms. Minosa, I've just got a few questions for you." And they better be good.

"So you went back to Mr. Lufkin's house?"

"Yes, sir."

"To get your glasses?"

"Yes."

"Cause you don't see so well without them?"

"I see okay - just to read."

"And what time did you get there?"

"I think it was a little before eight thirty."

"Well did you go inside?"

"No."

"Well you went all the way there why didn't you go inside?"

"Cause when I was looking for my keys I found my glasses in the bottom of my handbag." Connery wished he could use Gladys in all his cases. Sherman thought the jury would for sure believe her now.

"What kind of car did Ms. Lufkin drive?"

"I don't know much about cars, but I've seen it before."

"What was the license plate?"

"I don't know."

"What color was it?"

"Grey, silver, gold."

"But it was eight thirty at night and it was dark out."

"Oh I saw it once during the daytime."

"But at night you couldn't see the color so well, right?"

"No."

"And you never told the police you saw her car?"

"Yes, I tell them. Last week."

"Last week? But when you spoke to them both last November you didn't."

"I don't think they ask me then."

"And last week you spoke to Lieutenant Napoli?"

"Yes, yes, Lieutenant Napoli."

"And he asked you if you knew Anne was there that night?"

"And I remember seeing the car."

"Who are you working for now Mrs. Minosa?"

"A very nice family, the Randells."

"When did you last speak to Frederick Lufkin?"

"Oh it must be at the funeral."

Well it wasn't any textbook cross-examination but at least she hadn't seen Anne smothering Lufkin through the window. He was about to sit down when it hit him. Lufkin was quite an old goat. He probably didn't eat alone six nights a week. "Ms. Minosa, Mrs.

Lufkin, that is Robert Lufkin's wife, had passed some years ago."

"Yes, poor Ms. Jeannine."

"And Anne Lufkin wasn't the only person who ever came to the house the last few years."

"No."

"In fact Mr. Lufkin had lady visitors from time to time?"

"Yes."

"And business associates came to visit?"

"It was mostly ladies."

That brought down the house. Even Coughlin chuckled and made eye contact with Sherman. Sherman wanted to laugh but couldn't.

"So it could have been one of their cars you saw?"

"I just don't know."

"No further questions."

Connery called Lucy Gomes, a very attractive little number. She confirmed the story.

"Now you remember bringing your Aunt back to 314 Mountain Avenue?"

"Yes, cause that was the last time."

"So you'd been there before?"

"Yes. A few times."

"Have you ever met Anne Lufkin?"

"No."

"Did you see a car?"

"Yeah in the big circle thing behind the house, a two door BMW. I want to get one when I finish school so I noticed."

"No further questions."

Sherman could strangle Coughlin for not givin' up anything on this girl. How was he gonna shake her with nothin' to work with? Those lawyers who said never ask a question on cross-examination you don't know the answer to must not have defended many murder cases. This one was tough. There was just one fact, the ID of a model of a car. She had no axe to grind, least none he was gonna find out about while she was on the stand.

"Good afternoon Ms. Gomes, I'm sorry we didn't get a chance to meet earlier. I'm Sherman Brown and I represent Anne Lufkin. You testified you never met Anne, correct?"

"Yes sir."

"And you didn't see her that night?"

"No."

"And you don't know if it was her car that you saw?"

"No."

"When you met with Lieutenant Napoli seven months later did he ask you if you saw a two door BMW that night?"

"I think he said BMW, I don't remember him saying how many doors."

Whew. Sherman didn't dare look at Coughlin, who knew that was a bluff with a nine card high. Goddamn honest witnesses Connery thought. Of course Nappy had been overly anxious.

"So Lieutenant Napoli suggested that you had seen a BMW?"

"I guess."

"Now an old man like me I drive a Buick, all those little foreign cars look alike."

"Is there a question?" Connery objected.

"Overruled. You sold the Bentley Sherman?"

A judge can't make a bad joke even during a murder trial. Everybody guffawed on cue.

"It was pretty dark, right, Ms. Gomes?"

"Yes. I mean there was some light, but…."

"You didn't think they'd skimp on 'lectricity like that up in Claremont?"

"I could see."

"But Lieutenant Napoli couldn't get you to remember the license plate?"

"Objection."

"Withdrawn."

"Did Lieutenant Napoli take any notes when he met with you?"

"I'm trying to remember. I don't think so."

"Did Lieutenant Napoli show you any pictures?"

"Just of your client."

"But you couldn't recognize her?"

"No. But I'm too busy to read the papers."

"Maybe tomorrow you will Ms. Gomes. I thank you." Connery couldn't save Napoli, but maybe the ID could be resurrected.

"Apart from anything Lieutenant Napoli said, you didn't normally hang around Claremont?"

"No."

"And the Lufkin place was pretty impressive."

"Oh yes."

"And you weren't there all the time?"

"Only when my Uncle couldn't pick up Aunt Gladys."

"And you wouldn't testify you saw a BMW if you weren't sure?"

Sherman Brown stood up.

"Sustained."

Coughlin had to keep it on the up and up.

"What did I ask you to do when we met this morning?"

"Tell the truth."

"And that's what you've done today?"

"Of course."

Connery wasn't happy but he figured they believed her and he had her phone number for after the trial, so it wasn't a complete loss.

Anne was disappointed. She thought Gladys could have been tied up in knots and this little tramp should have been stomped. Coughlin recessed for the day and she stayed under control until the jury filed out. Then she hissed at Pedersen. "Is that the best you people could do? It's obvious Fred put those women up to this." Sherman heard but didn't respond.

"We'll talk at the office Ms. Lufkin." Clarence Mayes was on his mind. Sherman figured he'd be called next mornin' while the jury was fresh.

Coughlin was enjoying the show. If he wasn't sure the Chief Justice would have his ass he would have given an interview. The trial had staked out the front page of the Ledger and gotten some TV news time.

CHAPTER LXIII.

Lisa was appalled by the publicity. If she told what she knew it would be a media event. There would be no going back. She could be an instant celebrity but she might never practice in New Jersey or maybe anywhere. Weiss would be ruined, not that he didn't deserve it. Terry would get a new trial. Anne would probably get off and might be getting away with murder. But she couldn't let Weiss walk.

Clarence Mayes didn't like to rock the boat, but he didn't really care for the smell of this case, especially with Sherman Brown sniffin' around. Of course saying no to Big John was a career decision. He'd been minding his own business having lunch at Momma Greene's when Big John sat down next to him. "Keepin' the world safe for democracy brother?"

"Least for Democrats." Big John laughed.

"Let's hope it stays that way. Mind if I join you?" Momma herself ran over. Big John waved away the menu. "You know what I like Momma."

"Yes I do. But what you want for lunch?"

"This a stand up comedy club or a restaurant?" Momma went back to the kitchen. "You haven't testified yet sergeant?" Like he'd be having lunch with me if I had already, Mayes thought.

"No. Tomorrow morning Connery says, it's moving right along."

"I'm sure you took good notes like always Clarence." "They're not gonna get any better now, we had to give Sherman a copy."

"Of course, and I'm sure he been sleepin' with them under the pillow. But those notes don't say how you happened to be out to West Ridge." Clarence wasn't about to say how that was. "Connie tells me he was the one wanted you to interview Miss Anne for this office and it just happened to be the case that Napoli mentioned he heard she'd been picked up and you wanted him to come with you cause he'd taken her statement back when." "Well Anne don't know otherwise." But could Sherman figure it out? At least Big John wasn't asking him to say some Italian cop he never heard of from West Ridge called him in the middle of the night.

Clarence stuck with the program the next morning. Sherman knew Mayes had to be Robin and Napoli Batman that night. But Mayes didn't say anything about Napoli asking Anne if she told her father he didn't have a heart, so Sherman wasn't going to touch anything Mayes said happened during the interview. If someone was gonna blurt it out it would have to be Napoli. When Connery finished, Sherman asked. "Sergeant, you turned over your entire file, correct?"

"Yes Sir."

"And the earliest entry in that file is your notes of this interrogation of Anne?"

"Well, they were made after she signed the Miranda form Mr. Brown."

Mayes wanted Connery to tell Big John that Mayes was a team player. Sherman appreciated the job, but Pedersen had given him the counterpunch by looking very closely at the Miranda form their fool client had signed.

"Um hum, that's right, but that's on a Claremont Police Department form isn't it Sergeant?"

"Yes Sir."

"You're not with the Claremont Police Department, Sergeant"

"No."

"And this midnight call, it wasn't in Claremont?"

"No."

"So I guess you didn't exactly prepare for this interview?"

"Like I said, I had discussed the case with Mr. Connery."

"You know Mr. Connery pretty well?"

"Been workin' with him about four years."

"Four years? So I guess you know he used to be a policeman himself?"

"Objection." Goddamn if Sherman wasn't tryin' to pick up a first down, just when you think he's just going to sit on the ball, Connery thought. "My brilliant career has nothing to do with this case."

"May we approach?"

"Certainly Mr. Brown." Brown and Connery went up to whisper to Coughlin. "Where are you goin' with this Sherman?" "Judge, I think the jury is entitled to know that Lieutenant Napoli and Mr. Connery used to be partners. Just take me one or two questions."

"Judge this is a slippery slope. Next Mr. Brown'll be putting me on the stand for one or two questions."

"Not in this trial he won't. Overruled. But just that one question Sherman. The objection is overruled."

"You knew Mr. Connery used to be a policeman?"

"Yes Sir."

"And Lieutenant Napoli was his partner, isn't that right?"

"I believe I heard that, yes."

"Okay, so now let's go back to my original question, Sergeant. You wrote nothin' on this case before you went with Lieutenant Napoli to meet with Sergeant Tucci at the West Ridge Police Department the same night my client was interrogated?"

"Well, I went to question Anne Lufkin and Lieutenant Napoli came with me."

"Um hum." Sherman let him sweat a little while the jury thought about how defensive that answer was.

"But you wrote nothin' on this case that got put in the file before that night?"

"That's correct, except if I wrote it, it went in the file."

"I wouldn't doubt it Sergeant. No further questions."

Now the tough call was whether to call Napoli if they ended up having to put on a defense case. Sherman Brown didn't think anything he asked Napoli would make the tape admissible and if the cop volunteered it even Coughlin would have to grant a mistrial and if that happened he had some confidence he could persuade Big John to drop the charges. Pedersen had a lower opinion of Jersey justice. One thing they agreed on was Anne would have to make the decision and that would have to happen with both of them present so they could later confirm telling her all the risks.

Connery closed his case with the medical and forensic witnesses. Sherman Brown's cross-examinations were brief. Pedersen had wanted to get technical until Brown explained life to him. "Ain't no point in fightin' with 'em when we don't disagree 'bout anything 'cept whether our client should have let her fingers do the walking and called 911." So he just asked if without an autopsy they could testify to a medical or scientific certainty that Robert Lufkin would be walking among us if EMS had been called and whether there were any signs of gunshots, knife wounds, poison or karate chops. It wasn't the kind of defense you wanted to rely on but if the jury believed Anne was there when daddy keeled over, it was all they had.

As soon as the jury retired for the day Sherman moved to dismiss. "How could any juror except Fred Lufkin conclude beyond a reasonable doubt that Anne Lufkin was responsible? No witness placed her at the scene at the time of death, there's no evidence of any action that caused his heart attack. They couldn't even find anyone who would testify that the late Robert Lufkin would have survived a massive coronary infarction even if EMS had been called immediately. I will not belabor this Your Honor, but this charge should never have been brought and I'm very troubled about why it was. It would only compound the injustice to prolong this trial when you know a conviction could not stand or even sit. Now I will."

Connery was ready. "Well Your Honor, I won't let Mr. Brown sit too long because we have a trial to finish. If Mr. Brown chooses not to put on a case, because he thinks I don't have one, the trial won't be prolonged." Once in a great while a criminal defense lawyer took that route, and Sherman had actually considered it here. "But let's remember what the

State's witnesses have shown. First, Anne Lufkin was there that night; it's only a question of when. Second, Anne Lufkin had no explanation of her whereabouts at the time the States' witnesses say Robert Lufkin was suffering a heart attack and the State has presented three disinterested witnesses who provided evidence that Anne Lufkin was there, her denial is uncorroborated and she has not served notice of an alibi. Third, there was plenty of motive to go with the opportunity. Her father was apparently very critical of her performance at the time and she wouldn't have wanted that to translate into a change in the will that had so recently been made in her favor. Fourth, the State's medical witnesses testified to the overwhelming likelihood that prompt medical attention would have saved Robert Lufkin, a man previously in good health. We've all seen it Your Honor. There are millions of people walking around after heart attacks because someone performed CPR or other lifesaving treatment. Robert Lufkin didn't get that chance. No, my witnesses did not say it was a medical certainty that this man would have lived. But, Mr. Brown hasn't given you a case under the depraved indifference statute saying that medical certainty is an element. So you may allow this case to go to the jury based on the record."

Coughlin listened but he already made up his mind. Sherman Brown had prepared Anne for the worst because he expected it. He'd said to Pedersen, "The ringmaster ain't strikin' the Big Top before they shoot the lady out of the cannon."

"Mr. Connery, Mr. Brown, I appreciate your arguments. The State has presented evidence from which a jury could conclude that the Defendant is guilty of depraved indifference. Accordingly, the motion is denied. Should the defense choose to present a case, it may do so starting Monday at 9:00."

Pedersen began to wonder whether they ever let you remain free on bail pending appeal. Anne could not improve her case by taking the stand because they'd hate her and if she didn't testify the jury would assume she was guilty. Pedersen had little faith in the conspiracy theory, if only because by a stroke of genius, Napoli had Mayes as a witness to Anne's moronic statement and Sherman really hadn't done any more than show that Napoli was working the case hard, with maybe a push from an interested party. Maybe the complexion of the jury inclined them to be skeptical of the motives of the police, but people like Anne Lufkin weren't the kind that got railroaded, the pigs protected the farmer who filled the trough. Then there was the minor detail of Anne's actual guilt, kept from the jury by a privilege. Coughlin, knowing about the tape's contents may have been meting out a little rough justice by letting the case go to the jury, even if he couldn't let Connery roll the tape.

CHAPTER LXIV.

Napoli gave Fred the good news that night outside a diner in Broomefield. He'd been thinking about how to incentivize Fred to make the final payment if a conviction was upheld without putting his own ass in a sling. Fred would only pay if Napoli had a way to make it happen. Thirty million extra bucks wouldn't convert him into a loose fisted philanthropist or even a stand up guy, and it would buy a lot of protection even if Napoli decided he'd been handled and came after Fred. Jack and Judge Galante, who would no doubt attempt a comeback as one of the many fathers of success, were another problem.

Fred refused to play Napoli's game, "Well Lieutenant, I've really gotten nothing out of this until all her appeals are rejected." "I'm not sure that's so Mr. Lufkin."

"If she's convicted, she will go all the way to the World Court. It could take years. It seems to me that we'll all just have to sit tight until that happens." Napoli thought Fred could figure out how to steal a sack full of Justinians from Lufkin Realty with Anne out of the way even temporarily, but he didn't think Fred would appreciate the compliment.

"Of course, if we could get her to plead, maybe with the promise of a recommendation."

"Have you raised that with Connery? What could he offer her?" A plea would short-circuit everything. But it wasn't going to happen. Napoli didn't plan to wait for years. "I was wondering, Mr. Lufkin, if you couldn't see a way to maybe advance something against what we talked about."

"I thought I already had, Lieutenant. I really see no reason to change our understanding, but I see this ruling as a moment of opportunity for both of us. If you can arrange for a plea, I would certainly have to consider a kicker for you."

Napoli sat on Connery pretty hard to get him to offer a plea to a lesser offense. Connery knew Big John would call a plea to jay walking a victory over Sherman, but he hated to give up the splash a guilty verdict would cause. And he didn't see how Anne could plead even for a suspended sentence and be disinherited. On the other hand, if Sherman thought he was losing, he'd recommend a deal.

Pederson and Sherman were in the middle of explaining to Anne why she shouldn't testify when Connery called. When he got off the phone he was hesitant to relay the offer immediately – it would look like a setup to bring up a plea at the same time they were explaining why her act wasn't going to sell. But Anne insisted. "Well Ms. Lufkin, they're offering you a recommendation of only serving two and a half . . . now if the jury were...."

"Mr. Brown, this just proves that Fred is behind the whole charade. I'll bet he's counting my money already. You tell them to forget it."

"Yes, but you gotta know what a conviction by the jury could mean...."

"Mr. Brown, I might just as well take the risk, because I'd have nothing to live on once I pled anyway. Not another word. And I'll decide whether I testify." If this bitch breaks out of jail, I wouldn't want to be Fred, Brown thought.

CHAPTER LXV.

Paul read every word and watched all the TV coverage. Sandy, without knowing how important it was, shared his fascination. "I just can't imagine how a daughter could watch her father die no matter what he'd said to her. It just can't be the case. Mom was saying the other day that Mrs. O'Neill, her daughter's a nurse at St. Val's, said that a woman just isn't capable of not helping. Now a man, that would be something else..."

Paul had to agree. He could easily watch his mother-in-law writhe in agony. But he was more worried about Lisa. She'd been subpoenaed, but would she come through? There was nothing he could do about it if she chickened out, or if they didn't ask the right question. He would love to have called her, but her home number was unlisted and it probably wouldn't be a great idea to ask Judge Weiss. He also had no way to know when, if at all, the defense would call her unless she called. The uncertainty was almost intolerable and Sandy's running commentary was nearly unbearable. Could Lisa keep her own counsel til she took the stand? Would she change her whole life rather than lie?

On Monday, the rest of the world was concerned with the far less interesting question of whether Anne would take the stand. Mike even managed to get fifteen seconds of fame with a brief appearance as a talking head on the local morning news. Paul noticed that he didn't bother to use the firm name but got himself billed as "a former federal prosecutor now in private practice." What a cock. Paul couldn't wait to see his face when Paul told him he'd known about Lisa all along – if she came through.

Pedersen was having second thoughts about calling Lisa, but Sherman Brown was convinced that they needed to push the conspiracy theory for all it was worth. "Cause right now my mother doesn't even have reasonable doubts." Lisa was in any event a safe witness. Nothing she could say would increase the evidence of Anne's guilt and she had no allegiance to Anne so no one would think she was hypin' the story. Anne said she knew ten worse things about Fred than Lisa LeMieux ever would but Sherman Brown said "They won't be cross-examining this witness about where she was between 6:00 and 9:00, Ms. Lufkin."

Connery thought he had a pretty good idea of why they were calling her and he rolled out every objection he could, demanded a voir dire outside the hearing of the jury, and threatened to ask for a mistrial if such irrelevant nonsense was permitted. Connery knew the newly star struck Coughlin would allow Lisa to testify; he just didn't want Sherman Brown to suspect the forward pass he was planning. Coughlin, who had a pretty good idea why she was clerking for Weiss, couldn't resist and Lisa took the stand.

Paul had made up an appointment and slipped out of the office. He was lucky to get a seat in back. Lisa hadn't called him but he knew the defense was up. Lisa was pale and somber but still magnetic. He had never been so nervous.

"Ms. LeMieux, my name is Sherman Brown. We've never met. Now could you tell the jury what brings you here?"

"I was served with a subpoena."

"You're an attorney at law of the State of New Jersey?"

"Yes."

"Well, I won't hold that against you. Where do you work?"

"I am a law secretary in the Probate Division."

"Right here in Essex County?"

"Yes."

"And who is the Judge?"

"Harold T. Weiss."

"Were you present for a trial called In Re the Last Will and Testament of Robert Lufkin?"

"I was."

"In an official capacity?"

"Yes, as part of my job as law secretary I attend court so as to be familiar with the legal issues."

"The Judge don't do his own research?"

"I assist the Court."

Coughlin bit his lip and avoided looking at Sherman.

"What was the nature of the Lufkin proceeding?"

"Objection."

"Overruled."

"A caveat had been lodged by one Theresa Stephens."

"You want to tell us people who didn't grow up with Julius Caesar what that means?"

"Oh, yes. Theresa Stephens was challenging Mr. Lufkin's will, which she wasn't in, because she was in an earlier will."

"And who was in the will she was challenging?"

"Anne and Fred Lufkin."

"And what was the basis of the challenge?"

"Two things. First, that the lawyer who drafted the new will had also done work for the children. Second, and I think this came out almost by accident, that someone had gone out of their way to convince Robert Lufkin that Theresa Stephens was cheating on him."

Paul thought she was doing great, but she wasn't raising her hand, volunteering. And it dawned on him that Sherman Brown probably had no interest in asking about how the probate case had ended – just wanted to get the video on the record. Which was exactly right.

"Do tell. What had someone done?"

Connery restrained himself from objecting because he knew Coughlin would slap him down.

"Someone smuggled Teresa Stephen's sister, Mary Donnelly, who looks a whole lot like her, I saw them both in court, into Robert Lufkin's house and took footage of her in bed with a man."

"And why would anyone think Robert Lufkin had seen the tape?"

"By inference, because Theresa Stephens testified the last thing Robert Lufkin ever said to her was that he had seen her with another man."

"But she said it wasn't her."

"Yes."

"Thank you Miss LeMieux"

Lisa didn't volunteer. Connery considered not cross-examining. But first he moved to strike. He asked the witness to step down and approached.

"Your Honor, this testimony simply must be stricken and the jury instructed. There's no evidence who was behind the tape and even if there was it's got no bearing. Aside from that, it's all hearsay." Pederson had actually dug up a response to that which Sherman was prepared to use, but figured he wouldn't need to.

Coughlin took care of it.

"Mr. Connery, I think the defense is entitled to pursue the theory that what's going on here isn't just the natural course of events, that it's a setup. But if you don't want to dignify Sherman, Mr. Brown's theory, just let her go. Much as we'll all miss her." The court reporter omitted the last sentence. Lisa was called back up. Paul was down to his last chance.

"Ms. LeMieux, Anne Lufkin got just as much out of her father's new will as Frederick Lufkin, correct."

"That's right."

"And you have no way to know whether Anne, or Fred were aware of that new will before Mr. Lufkin's death."

"No, I don't."

'And if someone did try to convince Robert Lufkin to disinherit Theresa Stephens you have no way of knowing that it wasn't Anne?"

"That's correct."

Paul was losing all hope of a divorce and a new Jaguar.

"And Mary Donnelly never said why she was on that tape or who put her up to it, if anyone did."

"That's correct."

"And you don't know if Robert Lufkin ever saw that tape?"

"No. Of course he didn't have a chance to say."

Everyone except Paul had a good laugh.

"And Judge Weiss dismissed Theresa Stephen's challenge to the lost will."

"That's correct."

"So there's no reason to believe Frederick Lufkin had anything to do with any plot to get his father to change his will?"

It's now or never babe. Paul could almost hear the buzzer.

"I couldn't really say that Mr. Connery."

Shit, Connery thought. One question too many.

"You see Mr. Connery, the case wasn't decided on the merits."

Stop talking like a fucking lawyer, Paul wanted to scream.

Connery was going to try to change the subject but Coughlin put his foot in.

"What do you mean, Ms. LeMieux?"

"Judge Weiss didn't have any choice, Fred Lufkin blackmailed him."

Coughlin had never heard anything like it. He actually had to use his gavel to get the place under control. Anne was smiling like a Jack O'Lantern. Several jurors began to think about book deals.

Coughlin called a time out, cleared the courtroom of everyone except Lisa and the lawyers. Paul agonized in the corridor. Could they get her to swallow her words? It would be tough now. Reporters were chattering into cell phones like it was a wireless version of The Front Page. Terry would get a new trial. Terry. Paul had to be the one to tell her. She'd had to move out of Mary's house and gone back to Florida. Tommy, shiftless as ever answered the phone. Paul, feeling that Tommy had done more than anyone else to break the case, told him the news.

"Out fucking rageous, man."

"But listen Tommy, the cat is out of the bag but they're in there trying to stuff it back in."

"Where the fuck are you?" "At Anne's trial." "So you knew something was up. Maybe I underestimated you guys." "Well, we got lucky."

"So did that Judge Weiss, huh. With that babe from the court."

"Don't worry, I think we get a different judge next time." "And that one will be sure to keep it in his pants."

Coughlin was now in chambers with Lisa, Connery and Sherman Brown, who left Pedersen to deal with Anne. "Put me on trial, that cock sucking Dracula freak asshole. I fucking told you this was a setup. I'm suing him for a billion dollars. I'd rather see Terry Stephens as fucking queen for a day than let him get away with this. Call Don Morton and tell him I want my fucking brother out of the company."

Coughlin made Lisa tell him the whole story twice while he tried to figure out what to do. He had no desire to protect Weiss, but didn't want to be a pariah among his fellow judges, especially if this turned out to be jilted bitch uncorroborated bullshit. That Weiss had been boning her he had no doubt, but he was equally sure Weiss would deny it if he could.

Could this girl be a psycho who identified with Terry as a fellow jiltee and figured this was the way to bring down Weiss and get Terry a new trial? It was a total Joan of Arc kamikaze thing – unless she had an understanding with Terry or her lawyers for a hard earned contingency fee. That kind of money made anything possible.

And the really fucked up thing was that it was going to get Anne, who was almost certainly guilty of watching her father croak when he might have been saved, off the hot seat. So he couldn't even rule Anne out as the source of this story, though that seemed way out there. Which just showed how crazy this whole thing had gotten to be.

He needed to get to the bottom of whether Lisa was on the level, but he didn't want to do that in front of anyone, and he was pretty sure that it wouldn't be kosher to interrogate her alone. Look at the mess the last judge who'd been alone with this broad was now in. This had turned into the most incredible cluster fuck he'd ever seen. Plus he would have liked to protect Connery who now looked like he'd been set up to bring this case big time or was flat out pimping for Fred. Time was what he needed and it was a Goddamned Monday – he couldn't just send the jury home for the weekend. And people thought this job was easy.

"Miss LeMieux, I'm sure you know how serious this is. I'd like you to step out, but I'd strongly advise you not to talk to anyone, especially not any reporters. And get yourself a lawyer."

"Thank you Your Honor." Lisa was calm now. She'd done the right thing, she thought. As soon as she left, Coughlin told Connery he better get Big John down here right away.

Sherman thought things were looking up for Ms. Anne. "Well Judge, this gives new meaning to that old expression outta the mouths of babes."

Connery didn't think it was funny. How could the jury believe this whole trial was anything but a bought and paid for witch hunt? And losing was the least of his problems. He knew Big John would rather be trying to get votes in Alaska than anywhere near this shit storm and would blame Connery for talking him into it.

There'd be an investigation and a malicious prosecution suit and he and Napoli would be lucky to be working as night watchman at the sewerage authority when this was over. Connery had no doubt Lisa had spoken the Gospel, Fred had fixed the will contest and Napoli was in it up to his eyeballs and was more than a little concerned that he had put on perjured witnesses.

Big John wouldn't pick up the phone but Connery, calling in Coughlin's presence, left the message. Big John would show, Connery believed, but would be sure he knew what the fuck was up and had his story straight first.

While they were waiting Coughlin set the jury free for the day after telling them how ugly it would get if he heard that any of them had talked to a reporter, then went into a private room and called the Chief Justice to give him a heads up and get a little guidance.

The Chief wasn't happy to have this hot potato heaved in his direction, but it came with the job. Even Don Morton, who was now two for two on Jersey judges who made felony a hobby, would have been amazed by the hijinks the Chief had seen among his unruly charges over the years. Drunk drivers, wife beaters, bribe takers, drug addicts, sexual harassers. The Chief secretly believed it was a matter of a process of adverse selection from a bad gene pool – politically active power hungry lawyers. He'd heard Weiss had a siliconed zipper, a not uncommon affliction, but that problem was usually handled quietly. But now Lisa had literally blown two big cases sky high and the institution would need to take swift and public action to preserve such honor as it had left.

"The Clerk, does her story have any corroboration, Judge Coughlin?"

"I did not get a chance to ask those questions, Chief, and didn't want to ask any questions while she was unrepresented and in the presence of counsel."

"You were wise not to do so. Of course technically your case could proceed without resolving the charge against Judge Weiss."

"Well, I've got a skunk in the jury box. I've called John Martin down here to see what the State's position is."

"I wouldn't expect much of a position. And I can't tell you whether I believe there are grounds for a mistrial, though why Sherman Brown would ask for one I don't know." Coughlin and the Chief both knew the only way out was for the charges to be withdrawn in exchange for a release by Anne Lufkin of all claims against the State and the Prosecutor's Office.

CHAPTER LXVI.

Big John came in with his first assistant, Parker Holmes, and a strategy. First his decision to prosecute was not based on anything but the unassailable evidence of the tape and the untainted police work of Sergeant Mayes. Second, the decision on where this would go was going to be kicked upstairs to the Attorney General who was, fortunately, a good democrat. Third, he, John Martin, was shocked to learn that Napoli had met so frequently with Mr. Lufkin. Not that there was necessarily anything wrong with it and, of course, he'd had to leave the details in Connery's experienced hands being busy running an entire office, as Parker Holmes would gladly attest.

The Attorney General was rousted from the fourteenth hole at the Breakers and told Big John to let Coughlin know that he better instruct the jury to disregard the last answer and terminate the cross examination. Weiss was a bigger fish than Anne Lufkin and cross-examination of what might be the AG's star witness was to be avoided at all costs. If the jury could not forget the answer, so be it. The AG told Martin to tell Connery to object to any redirect on the subject from Sherman Brown.

The story reached Weiss via the most unpleasant of means – a call from the Chief Justice recommending immediate medical leave and a good divorce lawyer. By the time the Courts closed for the day it was widely assumed that Weiss was history and ambitious judges and lawyers were beginning to campaign for his prestigious perch.

Napoli knew there were was no way to save Fred without getting rid of a lot of witnesses in a hurry. Jack, Mary, maybe even Weiss. Since none of the dough was banked in his name he could probably hold onto his pension and eventually get his hands on the money they'd squeezed out of Fred. On the other hand, Fred was now a desperate man and might be forced to make a partner out of anyone who could save him.

Sherman's conspiracy theory was now gaining traction. If Fred had fooled Robert Lufkin and blackmailed a Judge to steal two-thirds of the empire from Terry, it was reasonable to think he'd orchestrated a murder prosecution to steal half the estate from Anne. But of course the jury and the world didn't know that Anne had in fact done the deed and admitted it. Napoli and Fred spoke payphone to payphone and agreed to meet at a place Fred had chosen, a turnout off a parkway at the other end of the county. Napoli knew Fred was spooked, though he'd sounded under control, and would suspect Napoli was wearing a wire, which also meant Fred wasn't going to order up a killing spree. Napoli had what he thought was a better plan and no fear that Fred would try to avoid prosecution by burning Napoli. Of course it wasn't going to come cheap.

CHAPTER LXVII.

Coughlin rose early the next morning and retrieved the Ledger from the front porch, expecting an article about Lisa's bombshell but the headline was nuclear "Millionaire's Daughter Brags She Watched Him Die" the article quoted the tape and synopsized the trial testimony. There was even a sidebar with pontification from some insomniac ex-prosecutor on whether what Anne did amounted to depraved indifference. But the Ledger didn't say how it got the tape. Coughlin knew Connery and Big John weren't mad enough to do it. He suspected Connery's former partner the greasy cop, but that would be someone else's problem. That the jurors all knew he had no doubt and that was his problem.

Jack Butler and Mary were already on their way to extended vacations outside the country courtesy of Fred Lufkin and Napoli had a new retirement account. The tape had been delivered to a dead drop with a short fuse. It if wasn't in the morning edition, the note warned, Channel 9 would have the tape at noon. The reporter who'd been following the trial had his most exciting moment as a journalist and the editors hesitated only briefly. So impervious had the Fourth Estate become that there was no hand wringing, Deep Throat, Washington Post, All The President's Men concern and the ass covering temporizing of the Ledger's house counsel was ignored. This was a scoop, an exclusive, a banner headline hit opportunity rarely experienced at a rag like the Ledger. That it would turn the trial upside down was even a further attraction. The Ledger would both break the news and make the news.

With Jack and Mary out of the way, all Weiss had to do was deny the shakedown and the decision dismissing Terry's case might even stand up. Fred hated to spend the money but Napoli's logic was compelling. Anne's apparent guilt, even without a conviction might even take the wind out of the sails of an investigation of the whole plot. Even so, Fred moved as much money as he could get his hands on offshore and had Doris empty several safe deposit boxes of his collection in case he needed to go flying down to Rio.

The largest mob of reporters to besiege the Courthouse in anyone's memory greeted Sherman, Pedersen and the heavily sedated Anne. She hadn't seen the Ledger, but when Sherman and Pedersen, rather than usual driver and bodyguard appeared at her hotel, she scented the shit on the fan and became hysterical and refused to budge. Sherman eventually coaxed her into swallowing a couple of pills with promises of a mistrial – Pedersen had a crew of Ferguson & Mather associates researching the mistrial motion.

To Sherman it was a no-brainer, if you got a confession suppressed then copies were handed to the jury, the case had to be thrown out. The bigger issue was whether the leak could be pinned on the cops or the prosecutor so he could argue double jeopardy – assuming he couldn't convince Big John that the case should be dropped. But he shook his head at how quickly yesterday's momentum had dissipated. To Pedersen he said "That's trial work son, you're gettin' a blow job one day and givin' one the next."

Coughlin was prepared to toss the case if any juror admitted the truth and acknowledged hearing of the tape – no instruction could overcome it and he wasn't anxious to be reversed on appeal. Not to mention the brownie points he could score with the AG by keeping Lisa off the stand. He hauled Connery into chambers and told him that if the prosecutor's office had anything to do with the leak, they'd better hope the misconduct trial wasn't in his courtroom. Everyone knew it had to be Napoli, but how to prove it – the tape could easily have been copied before it got into police custody, and even if the Ledger knew where the tape came from they'd make a stink over the sanctity of the newsroom and throw a whole rack of lawyers at it to keep the pot boiling.

They'd never even finished hashing out whether Lisa would be back on the stand and now Coughlin had to deal with this. He began to long for a nice, quiet crack dealer icing.

Sherman marched into the courtroom and asked the judge to examine the jurors one by one on the record, hoping to get some good sound bites showing how much the verboten tape had tainted their thinking.

Connery objected and Coughlin took pity on him. "Sherman I don't have to tell you the general practice is to examine the jurors behind the curtain in cases like this."

"Well I don't know about yourself Judge but I never had a case like this."

"Be that as it may, I'll see juror number one in chambers and you gentlemen are welcome to be present."

Juror one copped to it. The Ledger was sold at busy intersections by people who ran out in the middle of the street at traffic lights. What was he supposed to do? Just to be sure they checked two more jurors who also confessed to peeking.

"Well, I only had two alternates gentlemen. Is there a motion?"

They went back out to the courtroom. Connery tried to argue against it but the party was over. "I have no choice gentlemen but to declare a mistrial." Sherman took a stab at getting Coughlin to say Anne couldn't be retried, if only so Anne wouldn't ask why he hadn't, but Coughlin didn't have to decide that messy question on the spot and refused to.

CHAPTER LXVIII.

Paul was numb. Yesterday it looked so easy - an automatic reversal of the dismissal of Terry's case followed by a quick settlement. He'd thought about demanding that Ritzer personally deliver the check while leashed to an organ grinder, then dreamed of spending the money in ways that would mortify Sandy. His big regret was the necessity of splitting it with Mike.

Today it looked harder. Lisa's accusation of Weiss was yesterday's news and the system might well be less concerned about a little genteel blackmail than a passive patricide. Paul couldn't even be sure there would be an investigation of Weiss and he had the sense that Lisa's accusation, now irrelevant to the issue of Anne's guilt, might yet be smothered, leaving him nowhere. If Weiss strategically retired there might be no clamor for an inquisition and the fraternity might protect him.

Nor did Paul underestimate the pressure that would be put on Lisa to recant. It was beyond him, he knew, to press the right buttons in the prosecutorial apparatus. The hideous inevitability of it was oppressive so he got it over with. "Wait a minute, you knew that French piece had the goods all along? That's why you were there. How could you not have said anything?"

Paul had bit the bullet and confessed as soon as Mike got to the office. "And now the show is over. We've got no facts. You didn't get a statement or anything?"

"I thought it best not to push too hard." "Isn't that what Marilyn Monroe's first husband said? Look where it got him."

"I thought it would come out at the trial."

"With no practice, no vetting, no fact checking? You are a born optimist. Well, its one line. At least we can afford the transcript."

The world may have moved on but Judge, for the moment, Harry Weiss knew the Chief, the Attorney General and the 40 lawyers who wanted his job hadn't forgotten. What was that cunt thinking, going girl scout on him? Well, if he got away with this, his next law clerk was definitely going to make Rosie O'Donnell look like Audrey Hepburn and be stone deaf. Weiss wasn't planning to admit he'd been blackmailed, though he certainly wanted to know if there was anything to back up Lisa's story. He doubted it was taped – the conversation with Fred has been unexpected and too short, unless she'd been thinking ahead, which Weiss doubted. No one else had been around. The affair Weiss might have to admit. They could probably prove that. Besides without it, Lisa's motive for fabricating the shakedown would be unfathomable. For the affair alone he probably could escape removal, though it would be a fight.

Anne's testimonial to the benefits of psychiatry had given him some breathing room, but he had to choose a course of action. He'd deny the blackmail and fight removal, maybe settle for a private reprimand. But the creation of a story was tough without more facts. Number one being when Lisa claimed the shakedown occurred. If it was after the meeting where he'd told the lawyers that without proof Lufkin had seen the tape there probably wasn't a case, he was halfway home.

There was still the discovery problem – the mistress should have been given time to dig up a link between the porn star and the children, but that could probably be finessed. Weiss was inclined to say he'd ended the relationship and Lisa had been distraught and started to identify with Terry, argued with him about dismissing the case and imagined or invented the shakedown. Weiss was confident Fred had covered his tracks. With a good lawyer to point out the skimpiness of the case against Weiss and the plausibility of the jilted avenger story the criminal investigation would probably go nowhere. He'd arrange for Lisa to be put on paid leave for the few months remaining in her term and eventually things would settle down.

Mike's instinct was that Weiss would stonewall and unless Lisa could back up her story he'd probably get away with it. Paul, being a mere civil lawyer, had failed to appreciate the consequences of not getting a detailed statement from Lisa before she let the catting around out of the bag on the stand. Assuming the Attorney General was going after Weiss, the first thing they would do was threaten her with female circumcision if she talked to anyone. Unless, of course...

CHAPTER LXIX.

Paul couldn't believe it when Mike told him. "Whadd'ya mean you're Lisa's lawyer? Did you forget we have a client? We could be conflicted out. Isn't she a material witness in Terry's case?" Paul was steamed.

"Wait a minute. Why do you think I'm doing this? It's our only way to be inside the huddle to get the goods on Fred." Of course neither Terry nor professional ethics has been uppermost in Mike's mind when he got an FBI buddy to filch Lisa's unlisted number. The chance for free publicity and testosterone were the sources of inspiration. Paul was unconvinced and suspected Mike was out to screw his new client in every sense of the word.

"So Lisa came in and Joanne brought her a cup of coffee?" He knew Mike wouldn't risk letting his steady hump get a whiff of the competition but couldn't resist taking the shot. Mike had of course rendezvoused with Lisa at a safe remove from the office.

"Jealous? Remember, you're a happily married man." "Fuck you very much. But this better not cause a problem for Terry."

"Worry not partner, I got waivers from both clients. Now we can advertise. Miller & Sageman, ho's a specialty."

"You talked to Terry already?" "She thought it was brilliant."

"Motherfucker. Anyway, in those brief periods when you have your clothes on, think about how we keep the case away from Weiss on remand." He hated to admit it but Mike probably had made a good move. "I don't suppose you got a retainer?"

"I'm working on it."

"I mean money."

"The lady is rich in more ways than one."

Anne, in limbo while waiting to hear if she would be re-tried before a jury that knew she said she had fiddled while dad burned, was now in the strange position of Terry's bedfellow. Both needed to show Fred had successfully poisoned justice. Paul thought Sherman Brown might play ball and wasn't surprised when the old man returned his call. "Mr. Sageman you and your partner are turning this case into a growth industry. Who else you plannin' on representing?"

"With the miracle of TV hopefully many more damsels in distress, Mr. Brown."

"What can I do for you?"

"You've already done wonders, but I was hoping you'd looked into how Fred made your client public enemy number one." "And what's in it for her 'cept losing most of the estate so you can retire at 35?"

"Maybe her share of 15 million Fred tried to run off with. Maybe a chance to stink things up so bad for Big John that she never has to look another jury in the eye."

"So what are you lookin' for?"

"Just a little cooperation, information sharing."

"Well, we will take it under advisement – my girl might have her own ideas 'bout that."

"Do you mean when I'm your age I'm still gonna have to care what the client wants?"

"Ain't no 13th Amendment for us folks." They agreed to meet if Anne approved.

Paul was feeling like it was all getting away from him. He read Lisa's testimony alone in the office when it came over from the court reporter, half surprised the envelope hadn't been addressed to his partner. The fuck. Snaking Lisa, talking to Terry behind his back. If they did get Terry a bundle Mike would hog all the glory for sure and maybe figure out a way to grab the fees as well. But did they have a case? At the moment, no.

They needed to question Mary, and she wasn't likely to talk. They needed to get at her bank records but without a case there was no way to issue a subpoena. There was now a lot more questions to be asked of Fred, but again no way to compel him to talk, unless the appeals court found Lisa's charge sufficient to reopen the case. But that would take months, and maybe more patience than Terry had. The problem was that Terry's case, hopeless as it appeared, might start looking like an attractive loss leader to other lawyers.

Joe Rose would never had sat around waiting. Paul decided to file a motion to vacate the judgment based on Lisa's testimony, coupled with a motion that Weiss recuse himself. The big advantage was even if it was denied, Lisa's testimony would be right in the Appellate Division's face as part of the record.

CHAPTER LXX.

The courts in Essex County were run by the Honorable Nicholas Cittone, the assignment judge recently imported from Trenton by the Chief to get cases moving. As luck would have it he was friendly with Frank Mairone's family and had taken an immediate dislike to Weiss, who looked down on lawyers who went to State schools and became judges by way of the legislature. Radin had actually called Paul to suggest the motion to vacate and Paul was happy to say he was already working on it. Radin then advised him to send Cittone a copy of the motion.

Before Mike heard anything about it, Cittone had called the Chief and obtained permission to pull the case from Weiss, signed an order transferring the case to Cittone's courtroom and made Paul's day when he told Mike. Mike managed to upset him a bit though: "Good move partner. But we may want to ask the client who should argue this." That fuck. Was he slipping it to Terry on the side? First the waiver, now this.

Sherman Brown agreed to let Paul talk with Anne "Course you gotta sign in blood you won't be tryin to add her to your client list, Mr. Sageman."

Paul was forced to defend Mike's double barreled solicitation of Lisa. "No Mr. Brown, unlike Ms. LeMieux, Anne and my client have substantial adversity. But the enemy of my enemy is my friend." Paul, Pedersen and Sherman met for breakfast and Paul took Anne through everything she could remember that Fred had done since ... well, Paul tiptoed around that subject. He remembered how lucky they'd been that the Lufkins had changed banks so Joe Rose could get Lynton Childs to sneak them into the bowels of Union Trust and asked Anne how that had come about.

Anne told him the story about Mary's letter and realized the truth as she talked. "Oh my God, Fred must have set that up too!"

"But why this Suburban Trust?" Sherman wondered aloud.

"I don't know, Mr. Brown."

"Gotta be a reason, huh, Paul? Fred got more moves than a scared snake." Sherman was regretting not having gone over this background. 'Course mostly you didn't want to ask a client too many questions, especially once you had the story down.

"Who was the person Lufkin Realty dealt with at Suburban?"

"I only spoke to him a few times. Martin ... what was it ... Weiss."

" Martin Weiss?" It couldn't be could it? "Are you sure?"

"You thinking what I'm thinking?"

"Yeah, this is most likely nothing, but I'll make a few calls."

"Now I take it Fred was more involved than you were with this Mr. Weiss."

"I suppose. Are you saying you think he's related to the judge?"

Paul was sure of it "Coincidences are not the stuff of life for people like your brother. But let's keep this quiet."

"Amen."

It took only a few calls to confirm that Martin was the proud younger brother of Judge Harry Weiss and Lufkin Realty had become one of Suburban's best customers. Paul decided Mike didn't need to know about this latest development.

The theory of civil litigation was that everyone had to play all their cards face up. It made it harder to bluff and that of course encouraged the ultimate judicial nirvana of the system – settlement. The presence of the criminal issues and the Fifth gave people a chance to play their cards face down. Up to now the other side had played the game solitaire. Paul wanted to force Weiss and maybe Fred to declare without knowing what cards Lisa and their new bridge partner Anne Lufkin held. Curiously the dismissed state of Terry's case gave more cover.

But how to put Fred on the hot seat? Paul's hearing before Cittone might be their shot. Mike asked him about the procedure. "Do they call witnesses at hearings like that?" Live witnesses were discouraged. After all, a judge might miss a lunch date if stuck listening to a droning witness.

"Generally not" Paul didn't want Mike to know too much. Mike persisted "Who were you thinking of subpoenaing Paul?"

"How about your girlfriend?"

"Which one."

"Lisa, asshole."

Mike was against it. "We keep her under wraps. The whole idea is to get Weiss's whole story before they get hers." This bothered Paul. Wouldn't her testimony be the most compelling?

There was one big problem with the story, which Mike pointed out " Wait a minute, what if the shakedown was after Weiss told us we had no case if we couldn't prove the old geezer ever saw the tape?" Paul had tried to forget that and didn't like that Mike was thinking of it.

"It hurts, but we still have the discovery angle."

Mike came up with another problem. "We just became witnesses." Weiss's conference in chambers where he said he agreed with Ritzer that Terry had no case if she couldn't prove Lufkin ever saw the tape. "Of course" Mike continued "we don't both need to be witnesses." This fucking weasel, Paul thought, not doubting who Mike would try arrange to be served up as the witness. And now he couldn't even murder Mike because as the only witness and surviving partner he'd be disqualified as Terry's lawyer.

CHAPTER LXXI.

Laying in bed in a cheap Atlantic City motel, too strung out to change the channel, Jack Butler's brother Jeff heard the magic words "Up next the incredible story unfolding in New Jersey, where the fight over the Lufkin family real estate empire has taken yet another turn as it was revealed that lawyers for the mistress of late real estate magnate are moving to reopen her case based on bombshell testimony in the murder trial of Anne Lufkin"... Lufkin, Lufkin. A few synapses fired. Weren't those the people where Jack got him the crazy gig? But the story was on. He heard the name of Terry's lawyers something and Sageman and rolled over to grab the phone.

Everyone was saying the case might be reopened, but Paul didn't appreciate how the tide had turned until he picked up the phone to hear "Mr. Sageman, can you hold for Mr. French?" Paul, in five years at Berry & French, had never been so honored. Now, his most Christian majesty, Roland French, a WASP with a capital P who thought fiberglass yachts were vulgar and sniffed over the demise of catgut strings and tennis whites, sat down to dinner in his own house in a coat and tie and if he knew one word of Yiddish would fain let it pass his pursed gentile lips, was calling Paul. There had never been any agreement as to the rights of Berry & French in the fees for the simple reason that the Firm hadn't considered it worthy of discussion. Mike had said let sleeping foxhounds lie, but now the publicity had awoken the Firm's interest.

There was a considerable body of jurisprudence over fee disputes in these circumstances and Paul knew

Berry & French would have a case for a share. Roland had drawn the short straw at the executive committee and been compelled to abase himself by calling this inconsequential ex-associate. It was the sense of the committee that the call should be made before the case settled or was retried for appearances sake.

"How are you Paul?"

Paul was tempted to respond "Jim Dandy" an expression associated with the anachronistic Mr. French, but settled for "Well enough, Mr. French."

"And how is Mr. Miller?"

"Quite well I believe."

Paul, you fellows have been very much in the limelight lately over my late friend Joe Rose's case, I must say." Not a bad segue, Paul had to admit, but he decided that it required no response. Roland continued "It would not appear that we had any understanding when you took the client with you, correct?"

"The client made her own decision, I believe." "Certainly, certainly but there had been a considerable amount done before that time, I believe. Complaint filed, depositions taken and so on."

"Some."

"And the case was still pending at that point? As I understand it as a result of Joe Rose defeating a motion." This stiff had done his homework, or more likely apologetically assigned an eager flunky to reconstruct the record with typical Berry & French thoroughness.

Paul wondered if Roland had a proposal in hand. "We wouldn't dispute the facts, Mr. French, just the spin."

"Well, I trust at the end of the day there will be no dispute. Of course we're familiar with some of the fellows on the fee committee."

"Naturally."

"But we'd like you and Mr. Miller to know, I'm authorized to compose this file for fifty percent plus the firm's costs, provided we don't need to waste any time tussling with you." "Appreciate the call Mr. French. Good day." Paul slammed down the phone. Between Mike and the voracious pilgrims he might be stuck with Sandy for a long time. At the moment nothing to be done about the pilgrims. Luckily Mike was out of the office and he was able to give the surprised Joanne the afternoon off so the coast was clear.

CHAPTER LXXII.

Ritzer had represented some desperadoes in his day but Fred Lufkin was now in a league of his own. Cinema falsité to fool the old man into changing his will, no doubt bribing Mel Weinberg to be sure it got put through, blackmailing a judge and almost railroading his sister. And now it could all blow up in his face with Ritzer lucky if he only got his beard singed. The potential for an unpaid bill loomed large. And publicity like this he didn't need. It would be a relief if Fred decided to bring in local talent.

Criminal counsel, he knew had been consulted over the blackmail but Jay was careful not to go there. Weinberg had suddenly decided a month in Florida was a good idea when he heard about the law clerk's testimony, and Ritzer had little doubt as to what had occurred and was only surprised that he hadn't been questioned yet. His only leverage with Fred was as a witness to the chambers conversation where Weiss had said there was no case without proof that Lufkin had ever seen the tape. The upcoming hearing could make that status very valuable or render it meaningless.

Roland reported the rebuff to the executive committee. Matthew Armstrong, a member of the committee, had pulled out a calculator and the contingent fee agreement and figured out that if their client prevailed the fee would be almost five, so even a reasonable settlement would likely result in two, and half, an amount that was worth pursuing. "What if we offered to help?" Armstrong, the genius with the calculator asked

"Help whom?" Roland responded

"Our client."

"Not Miller and Sageman?"

"Well they'd refuse based on your report, Roland."

"But she's their client. How can we approach her?" "Find out how Rose got the client in the first place." Roland reluctantly had his secretary interrogate the late Rose's former secretary who Paul had foolishly failed to keep in touch with.

Radin wasn't particularly anxious to help Roland French, but Berry & French had a bigger future as a referral source and would if refused be a more formidable enemy than Miller and Sageman, so he passed on to Frank Mairone the message that Berry & French were generously volunteering to assist Terry.

Mike was appalled when he heard that Berry and French were trying to stick their nose under the tent wall. "Wait a minute, isn't this like Treasure of the Sierra Madre, where the bandits laid around waiting for the donkeys to come down the mountain laden with gold dust? Of course that assumes there is any gold dust."

"Gold dust. What are you talking about?"

"It's like that story about the naked Emperor. Our case all depends on whether you look at it carefully."

"How so?"

"Look Paulie, our whole case is based on the videotape. But we have no way to prove when it was made. Couldn't it have been made after Terry testified that the old man said he saw her with someone. As a manufactured explanation?" Paul got the feeling Mike was still pushing the cheap settlement, but couldn't figure out exactly why. Of course Paul hadn't exactly kept Mike up to date on the recent positive developments.

"But what about Mary taking five?"

"They could say it was all an act."

"But it wasn't."

"And how could the tape have been made afterwards in the house?"

"A purloined key, a bribed butler."

"Good thing you're on our side."

"All I'm saying is there's no certainty the case will be reopened." Mike was surprisingly philosophical, perhaps because he'd spent a weekend in close consultation with his new client Lisa LeMieux in Bermuda.

"What are we going to do about Roland French?"

"You know the old saying, Paulie, the big dog does the fucking. I don't see any good alternatives. We could file an ethics complaint, but you don't file ethics complaints against Roland French and live to tell the tale. We could tell Terry we'll resign if she lets them back in, but she just might think that's okay. Or, we could call their bluff and put them to work."

Paul didn't like any of those alternatives and he was worried that Mike was looking ahead to a referral relationship with Roland bought with Paul's money. He'd better figure out how to keep the wasps from stinging on his own. He needed something to convince Terry and Mairone that it was a bad idea. As soon as Mike left for a long lunch with Joanne, who thought Mike had gone to visit his parents in Miami Beach for the weekend, Paul called Hal Myers a law school friend who spent a lot of his time in the county courthouse.

Paul remembered that there were a number of state court judges who didn't particularly care for the Berry & French style. Maybe Cittone was one of them. "Paul Sageman, almost famous. Do you do Miller's makeup for TV these days or just carry his bags?" He'd complained to Hal about Mike hogging all the face time.

"Nah, I just schedule the interviews, he does the rest." "So what's cookin' besides that Lisa LeMieux?"

"I was wondering what you know about our new judge." "Probably doesn't take a lot of bribes, but I'm sure it can be arranged."

"Only if I really need it. That's the other side's specialty. Got any idea how he feels about my alma mater?" "B&F?

"..."Right."

"Well they dinged his last two law clerks when they applied." That was good but probably not enough. "Let me see what I can find out. But it'll cost you."

"I'll see what Mike left in the expense accounts." "Later."

CHAPTER LXXIII.

Weiss, who had no use for Ritzer or his unspeakable client and knew how dangerous it would be to communicate with them reluctantly concluded that they had the same interests. Defeating the motion to reopen would deflate the Impeach Weiss balloon at least a little but how could he help Ritzer prove that the conference occurred before the shakedown without admitting the shakedown? It was possible to make the argument but only once they knew when Lisa would say Fred had made his visit.

If that wasn't possible, the only alternative was to admit the affair and say that Lisa's hallucinations began after he broke it off. The problem with that story was that if the Attorney General got Fred to flip, Weiss could go down for perjury because then Fred and Lisa would be telling the same story.

So it was also important to know whether Fred was talking to the Attorney General. Weiss's lawyer, he knew, would get none of that dope from the Attorney General. The AG might posture that Fred was cooperating even if it wasn't so. Weiss tended to believe that Fred would see no percentage in cooperating unless they had something else on him. Of course if, in response to the motion to reopen the case, Fred denied the shakedown it was just his word against Lisa's.

Weiss called his secretary Suzanne and asked her to give Cittone's secretary a ring to see if Weiss could get a look at what had been filed on the QT. Suzanne came back with the bad news. Cittone had sealed the file at the request of the Attorney General. The next day Weiss got a subpoena to testify at the hearing. He simply had to know whether Fred denied the shakedown. It was simply too dangerous to contact Ritzer. There was only one way to open the file without fingerprints - as easy as it would to bribe a clerk, the danger was too great.

Weiss instructed his lawyer to call outside counsel for the Ledger to suggest that the Attorney General was trampling on the First Amendment and a free press wouldn't stand for it. The lawyer for the Ledger unselfishly suggested to the publisher that to maintain control of the story it was imperative that he be instructed to move to oppose this oppressive sealing of the file,at five hundred an hour plus, hopefully, some TV time.

The smart thing to do, Ritzer urged Fred, was to settle with Terry, file no papers and cancel the hearing. But Fred was told by his criminal lawyer that a settlement might not derail the blackmail investigation and could even encourage it. If Fred said nothing in opposition to the move to reopen, it would look bad, of course, and increase the odds that he'd have to fight the case all over again. If he denied the blackmail Weiss could hang him. That, however, Fred regarded as remote. How could Weiss admit it happened, he failed to report it and he threw the case in favor of the blackmailer? No, Ritzer was wrong. Jack was in Rio, Weiss would deny it and he had reason to believe the big earred law clerk slut could be bought off or impeached.

Paul wasn't just worried about the effect on the fee if Berry & French muscled back into the case. There was the lingering distrust of Fred. Could he pay them to throw the case? Even without that he had doubts about their ability to change their stripes. Berry & French was a defense firm, insurance companies, merchants of death, from the purveyors of asbestos causing old men to cough their lungs out to the makers of baby paralyzing vaccines were the firm's stock in trade. Most of all, if they got back in, Paul would be shunted aside. Mike was doing a good enough job of that on his own. Paul was discouraged.

Then Hal Myers called with great news. Seven years ago, before Paul had started at B&F, Cittone had sanctioned a B&F partner for failing to produce evidence in a case and the firm had countered by moving to disqualify him, something a judge rarely forgot and never forgave. It had all been settled and B&F had kept the sanctions out of the law journal, so Paul had never heard of the incident. "So how did you find it, Hal?"

"I was in Trenton yesterday so I chatted it up." "Got the name of the case?"

"I've got copies of the papers." Hal was working overtime. Paul figured the price was going to be high. Fortunately he had something to give. "Have you got the time to represent a witness in the case?"

"Does the witness have any money?"

"No, but if we win, Terry will pay and I can guarantee she won't look too closely at the bill. And we can advance a grand."

"That's a deal." Paul went to Mike's office looking for the checkbook. No one home but Mike had surprisingly detached his stylishly small cell from his ear and left it in the charger where it was now ringing. After checking to make sure Joanne wasn't around, Paul picked it up. "Mr. Miller? Mr. Miller?" Paul didn't answer and the line went dead. But he'd know that voice anywhere. Paul couldn't believe it. He hit the menu button and selected recently dialed calls, grabbed a post it and copied down the numbers. Three of the last twenty to the same number. Paul put the phone back, went into his office and called 411. "Yes, may I have the number for Lufkin Realty?" He didn't need to write it down, it was already on the post it.

Paul wasn't about to let Mike in on the Cittone dope or Hal Myers' new client, but he overnighted copies of the papers Hal had found to Terry and told her letting B&F back in might not be a great idea. It worked like a charm. Then he called the firm's wireless carrier to see if he could get print outs of all the calls, claiming that the charges seemed too high.

CHAPTER LXXIV.

Cittone let the attorney for the Ledger put on the freedom of the press show but he wasn't about to disagree with the Attorney General and the file remained sealed.

Paul arranged for subpoenas to be served on Weiss and Fred. The return date of the Motion arrived. Mike, at Paul's insistence, had Lisa on call.

The day of the hearing Paul arrived at Cittone's only to find the biggest crowd he'd ever seen in a courtroom. There were more lawyers than chairs and more reporters than lawyers.

Ritzer had been replaced as Fred's counsel by Richard Winter, a lawyer from a big Jersey firm in case Ritzer had to testify, though Ritzer's affidavit about the meeting in chambers was on file. Paul had spotted what it left out. Ritzer correctly recited the statement by Weiss that there was no case unless Terry could prove the old man had seen the tape, but somehow failed to mention that Weiss indicated he might take a different view if the children could be linked to the tape – making the dismissal while that was hanging inconsistent. Paul didn't even ask Mike to put in the answering affidavit that filled in the blank.

Cittone called the case and took appearances. Fred was not present, but Weiss and his lawyers were. Don Morton and Pedersen were there but it had been decided that they would take no position until they heard the evidence. Anne couldn't take the chance of looking like the hit woman in the conspiracy to take Terry out of the will and then take her father out of the world before he found another mistress worthy of testamentary regard.

Cittone had his game face on as he asked for appearances. “It’s your motion I believe, Mr. Miller.” Paul wasn’t too comfortable leaving it in Mike’s hands but he was still playing his knowledge of Mike’s contact with Fred close to the vest.

Mike gave the spiel, winding up with the Lisa revelation. “But where is this woman, who I have not, I assure you, seen on the tape you say she appears on, Ms. Donnelly?”

“I believe Mr. Sageman’s affidavit addresses that Your Honor. Our investigator found that she’s in the wind, hasn’t been at her job, her home.”

“And not, I take it visiting with your client.”

“No Your Honor.”

But Cittone’s question could be read to mean he wasn’t convinced. “Will you be calling any witnesses to supplement what you filed?” “We have asked Judge Weiss and Mr. Lufkin to join us.”

“Well, let me hear from Mr. Lufkin’s counsel first.”

Richard Winter, the picture of a lawyer, down to the navy blue suspenders, rose with practiced confidence. “Thank you Your Honor and I particularly appreciate your mentioning Ms. Donnelly, because that’s just the point, Your Honor.

We have been given nothing to even suggest that, assuming it is she on the tape, my client, or even Mr. Morton’s client, had anything to do with whatever happened there. All speculation, all assumptions, all conjecture. Not just as to what happened but why. We have no idea why that tape was made. Not evidence, not proof. And Ms. Stephen's lawyer, Mr. Sageman, does not deny that Judge Weiss pointed out its just a theory.

The missing link is still missing, Your honor. There isn't any reason whatsoever to think Robert Lufkin ever saw the tape, let alone changed his will because of it.

In fact the videotape itself is highly questionable for another reason Your Honor. There is no proof as to when it was made. For all we know it was made to help Ms. Stephens' case - not to hurt it – and made after Ms. Stephens was forced to testify that Robert Lufkin told Ms. Stephens he had seen her with another man."

Interesting, thought Paul, that this was just the weakness in Terry's case that Ritzer had never come up with but Mike had mentioned the other day.

Winter continued and Cittone looked like he was buying it. "Perhaps, indeed the refusal of Mary to testify was calculated, as was her disappearance." Winter paused and to Paul's horror, Cittone nodded.

"Remember also what they are trying to do with this dubious evidence. We shouldn't forget this was unquestionably Robert Lufkin's will, he was of sound mind when he made it. And there are very strong presumptions in favor of enforcing a will. Presumptions they haven't overcome. What Ms. Stephens can't deny is a fact – she moved a thousand miles away and didn't see or talk to Robert Lufkin for many months before he made that will. He could have decided for any number of reasons to change his testamentary arrangements. We don't lightly overturn a will; there needs to be evidence. We don't lightly reopen a case after a judgment is entered. There needs to be evidence clearly establishing each and every element justifying such an unusual action.

As to witnesses being called, that would I submit, be irregular and in this case uncalled for – no witness can say Robert Lufkin saw the tape. No witness can say it made him change his will. I respectfully ask the court to deny this motion."

"What about you Mr. Miller? Would you call any witness who will address those questions if I deem it proper?"

Paul was nauseous. Maybe they wouldn't get a chance to put on witnesses. Had he blown it by not getting an affidavit? Mike, who didn't know what Paul had waiting out in the corridor, made the only points he could. "Mr. Winter wasn't at the trial Your Honor, or I'm sure he'd remember a few things he didn't mention. First, we only found out about the tape practically on the way to court and we asked Judge Weiss to give us the opportunity to investigate. Second, Mary Donnelly refused to testify. Third, Judge Weiss said, at the time, that if was could show any connection between the tape or Mary Donnelly and the living Lufkins, he might feel differently. That's uncontradicted. Fourth, refusing to let us investigate was inexplicable until we were presented with the missing link.

The missing link isn't the inability to know what Robert was thinking. It's testimony of a disinterested witness that Frederick Lufkin obstructed justice, blackmailed Judge Weiss to prevent us from getting the truth. Now Mary is mysteriously missing and it appears that Fred Lufkin may not have stopped there. With all due respect, I can't imagine a clearer case for reopening."

"But, Mr. Miller, Mr. Winter raised a very good point – how can I conclude that this tape even existed while Robert Lufkin was alive?"

"Without reopening the case, I guess you can't." Despite the argument he'd made, was Mike going in the tank on purpose?

"Mr. Winter, anything else?"

"This claim of blackmail Your Honor, troublesome because without it we wouldn't be here. It's uncorroborated, undocumented, denied by Judge Weiss and Mr. Lufkin. This is not a clear case. It's a single line uttered in another case under peculiar circumstances by someone who apparently had her own ax to grind against Judge Weiss. Certainly if they say their case shouldn't have been thrown out without the opportunity to explore, you shouldn't reopen this case without more.

And here is the most astonishing fact - I tried to contact this witness only to be told that her lawyer is none other than Mr. Miller."

Paul now knew it wasn't a good idea to let Mike get involved with Lisa. Could that have been the real reason Mike insisted on representing Lisa? To tarnish her evidence?

Cittone looked surprised for the first time.

"Perhaps that" Winter continued, "is the missing link." That was the problem with analogies and catchy phrases, Paul thought Once someone put them in play they tended to get volleyed back and forth over the net.

Winter was now making his best point."No one stood to gain more than Mr. Miller's client, Ms. Stephens, from Mr. Miller's client Ms. LeMieux's revelation." Winters wound up. "Given that entanglement, it's hardly a clear case. We submit that Ms. Stephens hasn't made a case to reopen this matter. If they believe Judge Weiss erred by failing to give them time to investigate this tape and how it came about, they have recourse to the Appellate Division. But in the absence of any evidence that my client, or Mr. Morton's client, Anne Lufkin, had anything to do with it, or any evidence that Robert Lufkin ever saw the tape or, as Your Honor noted, that the tape even existed at the time, we trust the Appellate Division will affirm."

"Mr. Miller, is Mr. Winter correct? Do you represent this witness, whose testimony appears to be the basis for this motion?"

"Yes Your Honor, but only after Anne Lufkin's trial."

"Well, I do agree with Mr. Winter, that raises some troubling questions." This mess had already gotten enough Judges in trouble. Cittone wasn't anxious to be added to the list for reopening the case on what might be tainted evidence. And he was hesitant to let them put Weiss on the stand. "And am I correct that you really have nothing new tending to prove Anne Lufkin or Fred Lufkin procured the making of this tape?"

"If I may be heard." Paul stood up as he spoke.

"Mr. Sageman?"

Mike whispered "What do you think you're doing?"

Paul ignored him. "We do in fact have a witness who may be able to shed some light on that."

Winter was on his feet: "We would object to Mr. Sageman calling some mystery witness Your Honor. A party seeking to reopen should give fair notice of the grounds relied on."

"Mr. Sageman, can you let us in on the identity of this witness and what he or she might have to say?" Cittone was at least giving them the chance.

Mike and everyone else in the court were for once paying attention to Paul.

"Your Honor, his name is Jeff Butler, an aspiring actor, and he will testify he was hired by his brother, Jack Butler, a private investigator, who was working for Fred Lufkin, to be videotaped making love to Mary Donnelly in Robert Lufkin's home."

Winter rose again:"We object to this witness, Your Honor. We should have been given notice of this. Perhaps Mr. Miller represents this man as well." Winters had to raise his voice to be heard over the din of reporters.

"If I may be heard," Paul responded. "The witness has his own counsel and is available at this time."

"So, Mr. Sageman, the testimony of this witness has nothing to do with Judge Weiss allegedly being blackmailed, but goes to the connection between the video and Fred Lufkin."

"And when the tape was made." Paul added.

Winter tried to save the day. "Your Honor, we need not hear from this witness to know any such connection would be hearsay."

"Perhaps not as to timing Mr. Winter. I want to hear what he has to say. Call the witness."

Paul went out in the hall. Hal Myers, Jeff and an assistant lugging a TV/VCR marched into the courtroom.

"If I may, Your Honor, we will need to show you a moment from the video, just to authenticate a blow-up of Mr. Butler's face that appears momentarily on the tape, so you can confirm that Mr. Butler here is the man who appears on the tape. Perhaps in chambers Your Honor?"

"Your application is granted, and for the record, the court will not be viewing the balance of the tape."

The blow-up had been Hal's idea after viewing considerably more of the tape than Cittone was telling the press he had any interest in seeing.

Ritzer slipped out of the courtroom to call Fred, though he wondered how he would collect his receivable from a client in Brazil. Morton called Anne while Pedersen joined the crowd in chambers. "Well Ms. Lufkin, the good news is the whole world will now believe Fred was behind the prosecution. The bad news is if Terry's case isn't reopened the papers will be saying Weiss wasn't the only judge who was blackmailed."

Cittone kept it short in chambers. Paul had Jeff get on the stand.

"You are the person who appears on the tape we just saw a moment of?"

"Yes." The tape image was indistinct but the blow-up helped.

"How did you come to be on the tape?"

"My brother Jack offered me a thousand dollars."

"Why?"

"He said he needed an actor to, uh, make love to a woman on tape for a client of his."

"Objection."

"Overruled."

"And who was that client?"

"Objection."

"It was a man named Fred."

"Where was this taped?"

"We went to a big house in Claremont one afternoon. We were there about an hour."

"Who was the cameraman."

"Jack."

"And the actress?"

"I never met her before. She was introduced as Mary."

"And were you paid?"

"Yes."

"Now what brought you to talk about this?"

"I was watching the news about two weeks ago."

"When was the tape made?"

"About fifteen months ago."

"Never met me before the news story a few weeks ago?"

"No."

"Or Teresa Stephens?"

"No."

"Not even Mr. Miller?"

"Never."

"So, before you saw this news story did you have any idea this tape was mixed up in a court case?"

"No. Jack never mentioned it. And he wouldn't give me Mary's phone number either."

"When did you last speak to Jack?"

"He gave me some money, said he was moving away. Oh, about six weeks ago."

"Did he say why?"

"Just that things were getting a little hot around here."

"I'll pass the witness."

Winters couldn't very well say he needed time to investigate, so he had to wing it. Lawyers hate that.

"Sir, just so it's clear, Mr. Sageman has known what you had to say for how long?"

"I called him two weeks ago and we met the next day."

"Did he ask you questions?"

"Yeah that's what you guys do."

"Did he ask you to sign an affidavit or anything?"

"No."

"He introduced you to Mr. Myers here?"

"Yes."

"So you don't know any reason that we couldn't have been told what you have to say before today?"

"No."

"Your Honor, I move to strike all of the testimony."

"Mr. Sageman, why all the drama?" Cittone had been impressed with the testimony but he had to give Paul the chance to justify his conduct.

"Your Honor, I believe Mr. Butler here was entitled to discuss this with counsel before giving an affidavit."

"Well, I'm not too happy about it. But for the moment I'll take the motion to strike under advisement." Cittone knew where he wanted to go with this whole mess. "Do you have any further questions Mr. Winters?"

"Mr. Butler do you regularly, uh, perform on tape?"

"No sir. I'm an actor, but not that kind of actor." That explained Jeff coming forward, Cittone thought. Fifteen minutes of fame could make him more marketable.

"Do you have any basis for saying a man named Fred asked your brother to make this tape beyond what your brother said in that one conversation."

"No."

"Got paid in cash?"

"Right."

"So you can't prove that even happened?"

"Never met Frederick Lufkin?"

"Nope."

"No idea why this tape was made at the time?"

"No. But Jack didn't give me a grand to spend an hour in bed with Mary just for grins."

"But for all we know it could have been Mary's idea or Theresa Stephens idea?"

"I couldn't tell you. I don't know who Theresa Stephens is."

"Exactly. What is your address sir?"

"I've been kind of moving around."

"So how could we get in touch with you?"

"Call Mr. Myer, I guess."

"Your Honor, if you're going to consider this witnesses' testimony, and we don't think you should, we'd ask you to order him to appear for further testimony at my office two weeks from today. But since the witness has just admitted he doesn't have any firsthand knowledge as to who in fact was behind this, you should not consider it."

"Mr. Sageman?"

"What the witness did say, and I haven't heard Mr. Winter deny, is that Jeff's brother was working for Frederick Lufkin. I haven't heard Mr. Winter deny that, because he can't. What we all know is that Frederick Lufkin had the strongest possible motive to convince his father that Theresa Stephens was disloyal.

We're not asking you to decide the case today, just the chance to prove what this testimony and all the circumstances so strongly suggest – that Robert Lufkin was defrauded into changing his will, a chance Judge Weiss didn't give Theresa Stephens, for reasons that circumstances suggest had nothing to do with the merits. What Judge Weiss did prevented us from asking Mary any questions. Had we been given the chance it would have led us to Jack Butler and his brother. Now both Jack and Mary have mysteriously disappeared. We're entitled to know why, to see if we can prove what I think we all believe – that Fred Lufkin is responsible for that remarkable coincidence as well. Jeff Butler's testimony is the best available evidence until we get a look at Fred Lufkin's bank accounts. You'll note that he isn't here today despite being subpoenaed, or we could ask whether he had anything to do with the disappearance of Mary and Jack. You need no more evidence to reopen this case."

"Mr. Winter, I will order Mr. Butler to appear at your offices. Any other witnesses, Mr. Sageman?"

"Yes Your Honor. We subpoenaed Martin Weiss, Judge Weiss's brother."

"Wait a minute, what does he know?" Mike whispered.

"Listen and you'll find out."

Winters again objected in vain and Martin trudged to the stand.

"You are a Vice President at Suburban First Bank?"

"Yes."

"And is Lufkin Realty a customer of Suburban First?"

"Yes."

"And how did that come about?"

"Fred Lufkin called and made an appointment."

"And Lufkin Realty is a large customer of Suburban First?"

"Fairly large."

"And when did Fred come to see you?"

"I believe about a month after his father passed away."

"Or shortly after the case was assigned to your brother?"

"That I wouldn't know."

"Now you got a subpoena that asked that you bring checks drawn on the account of Omega Corporation?"

"Yes, I brought them." Martin reached into a brief case and produced a bundle. Cittone nodded and Paul took the bundle and pulled two checks out.

"Sir, is this a check drawn on the account of Omega Corporation to JB Investigations?"

"It appears to be a copy of such a check."

"And this one as well?"

"Yes."

"Who is the drawer signing for Omega?"

"Fred Lufkin."

"No further questions." Winter did his best to create confusion.

"So if these checks represent payment to JB Investigations, they were months after Mr. Lufkin died?"

"By the dates I would guess so."

"And Omega had no account with you before Mr. Lufkin died?"

"No."

"And you don't know what they were in payment of."

"Absolutely not." Winter decided to wing it a little.

"Did Fred mention that the case was before your brother at any time?"

"Not at all."

"Did your brother mention the case to you?"

"We never discuss his cases, no."

"So you couldn't say if Judge Weiss even knew Lufkin or Omega were customers of Suburban First?"

"No, I couldn't say because if he knew it wasn't from me."

"Your Honor, I move to strike this testimony as irrelevant, incompetent and meaningless."

"Denied."

"Anything else Mr. Sageman?"

"Not at this time."

Paul, who thought he'd put his best foot forward waited for Cittone to continue.

"I've now heard enough to convince me, Mr. Sageman, that the case should be reopened, basically for the reasons you stated. I am, however, making it clear that I make no findings as to Judge Weiss, nor as to any ultimate conclusion that the last will was the result of undue influence nor that anyone in fact attempted to mislead Robert Lufkin. I will tell Mr. Winter, Mr. Morton and all here that no documents or records are to be destroyed or removed or altered. I will, however, stay any discovery or further proceedings for one month, with the exception of financial information regarding the date of death values of the estate, which I order Anne and Frederick Lufkin to provide and I trust this month will be used to good effect. Mr. Sageman will submit an order."

CHAPTER LXXV.

Success has many fathers and Mike Miller was suddenly the proudest of papas. He slapped Paul on the back, shook his hand and acted as if he hadn't practically fucked his way out of millions in fees or as Paul was now convinced, sold his soul, at a very inflated value, to Fred. Paul was too stunned by the results to be angry. "Great job Paulie, I gotta say pulling that rabbit out of your hat."

Don Morton even came over to shake Paul's hand. "Never know what's going to happen in court in this state Sageman – you just better hope Jeff Butler only fakes it with his clothes off." Morton didn't want Terry's lawyers thinking Anne was going to throw in the towel, but everyone figured the price of settlement had gone up.

Paul was besieged by reporters, with only the stragglers paying attention to Mike. It had all worked out. Now the key was keeping Terry from getting a swelled head. Ignoring Mike, as soon as the crowd thinned he found Radin, who despite swallowing for Berry & French would still come in handy for controlling Terry.

"Joe would have been proud of you Paul." Fuck him, he's dead Paul thought. Radin moved to his real agenda:"I'd say its high time Frank gets his ass in the chair up at Lufkin Realty." Radin was co-opting victory. Paul was all for that. Fred's failure to appear had him worried he would disappear with everything that wasn't nailed down.

"We better move quick." That would put more pressure on the Lufkins to settle.

"Agreed." Cittone was likely to go along.

Radin tried to get a little bit of a feel for the stakes "So what do you think the number is?" Paul wasn't sure he wanted Radin to know the answer to that question, even if they were talking about Frank's dowry.

"I'd have to run the numbers after they cough up some information. Real estate's looking up they tell me."

Radin wanted to be the peacemaker. "I've got a pretty good idea what the operation's worth. Equity of about forty, ten in cash on top of that. But take it from me, there's always a discount if you force a sale."

That was all bullshit. Who knows who Radin's really working for? The question was whether Fred had any fight left in him.

CHAPTER LXXVI.

Up on Mountain Avenue, Fred was digesting Ritzer's report. Miller had let him down, despite the promise of a million five wired offshore. Fred should have tried to bribe both of them while he had the chance. Now the tape was hanging around Fred's neck and this new judge was threatening to become a believer. Why Jack had never told him who the actor was he couldn't understand. Unless Jack didn't want to chance having to share any of the shakedown money with his brother. Could it all fall apart over this loose end?

Fred had just about run out of cards. He recalled his existence before Anne's one useful act in life; before he'd managed to get Terry out of the will. Fred was sort of proud of what he'd managed to accomplish and hated to throw in his hand, but he'd also planned for that eventuality. He remembered what he'd done. Subverting Mary, not that it had been difficult. Making the tape. Convincing his father of the value of video surveillance at the shopping centers so he Fred could have a video setup in the office, sending the tape anonymously and his father would watch it.

Dad had never mentioned the tape to him. Fred had worried that he would see through the scam until Weinberg called. Those had been great days. If Anne hadn't beat him to it, he would certainly have been studying the more exotic poisons. untraceable and discreet, for when a respectable amount of time had passed after the will was changed.

Now all that was left to do was pack. He'd wired as much Lufkin Realty money as he could get his hands on down to Rio as soon as he heard Ritzer's report.

Paul could now almost taste the money. All they needed was any proof that Fred has been working with Mary and the new will would be shredded. What Paul didn't want to do was share the fees with Mike, the fucking traitor. The phone bills came in big. Twelve calls to Lufkin Realty. Apparently they'd been haggling over the present value of twenty pieces of silver.

A partnership could be dissolved just like a Muslim marriage. Paul could just say "I divorce thee, I divorce thee, I divorce thee." If only Sandy could be dispensed with so readily. But killing off Miller and Sageman wouldn't terminate Mike's claim to the fees and the timing would look bad. He would like to have talked to Hal about it but didn't want to encourage Hal to try and figure out a way to cut a slice for himself. This was Paul's score. Life wouldn't give him another shot like this and he wasn't in a generous mood. If he played it right, got rid of Mike and kept B&F to a minimum, there'd be enough to dump Sandy, buy a Jag and live pretty well without killing himself.

Radin had gone into overdrive and quickly found that Fred and most of the ten million in cash had disappeared. Cittone gave him an order barring any other transfers, authorizing Frank Mairone to take over the office and allowing him to investigate.

The loss didn't bother Paul too much – that much would have been Fred's in a settlement – provided Fred hadn't gotten the chance to whack other assets. Fred's disappearance was a boon for Terry – now who would ever believe he hadn't fooled the old man, fixed the case and railroaded Anne? The only problem was, if Mike put up a fight over the fee. Fred wasn't around to confirm the treachery in exchange for a deal. And Mike would know the fee was now a lock.

CHAPTER LXXVII.

Paul said nothing until the transcript came back, but drafted a dissolution agreement leaving a blank for the division of fees for Theresa Stephens. When the transcript came in he underlined the parts of Winter's argument that he believed Mike had supplied and highlighted the entries on the phone bill for Mike's cell for calls to Lufkin Realty, then asked Mike to lunch to talk about their next steps in the case.

Mike was only too happy to strategize. "I think we now go after Anne. She's not out of the woods yet with the DA. I could probably get them to leave it hanging for a while. Maybe we could get her to take a haircut and get out of the business. Then we're Terry's partners helping her run the business once Radin's paid off."

You had to give Mike that, he was creative, figuring out how to get a lifetime income from a case he'd tried to give away for a quick buck, and the hint that Mike was better equipped than Paul to get the DA to stall on the decision on retrying Anne. If you could trust Mike as far as you could throw him it might be worth considering, but for all he knew, Mike was already sleeping with Anne. And Paul didn't like the pull Mike seemed to have with Terry.

"I've been going over the transcript from last week Mike. That Winter's a pretty good lawyer."

"Without a client I hear."

"Well I was struck by some of the arguments he made, because the only place I ever heard them before was from you." Paul paused. "Wait a minute, Paulie, what are you saying?"

"I'm saying when Winter pointed out that we couldn't prove when the tape was made and that Mary's act could just as well have been on Terry's behalf as anyone else's, it had a very familiar ring to it."

"Great minds think alike, unconscious parallelism. Anyway Jeff took care of that for us didn't he?"

"Here's what I think, Mike. You sold Terry out to Fred." "You're crazy." Paul took out the phone bills and shoved them across the table. Mike was, for once silent.

"Now you can keep whatever Fred gave you, but we're done. Terry is my client. And you're going to agree that your entitlement on the fee is limited to $200,000. Or else we're going to be in court. With the phone bills. "

"Wait a minute, Paulie, I was just trying to settle the case."

"One time offer, you sign it before we get up, or the figure is zero." Paul handed Mike a copy of the agreement. "Where did this tough guy thing come from? Maybe you made those calls on my phone."

"We could ask someone at Lufkin Realty. Now in the custody of Frank Mairone."

Mike looked down at the bills. "500 and no hard feelings, Paulie."

"300."

"And I keep all fees on my clients."

Paul filled in the blank. "I think we better have a couple of witnesses for your signature, Mike."

CHAPTER LXXVIII.

With Mike out of the way, Paul considered letting Radin play peacemaker and set up a conference at Lufkin Realty. You'd think it would be simple now, but everyone had their own angle and negotiations went nowhere.

Anne was still in a delicate situation and didn't trust Terry not to take over for Fred and seek to use the still unresolved murder charge to disinherit her, even in a civil case.

Sherman Brown, despite the shrink tape, figured Big John would be open to some kind of deal to salvage whatever integrity remained in his office, but wasn't about to make the first move. Without resolution of the criminal charges, Anne couldn't settle the estate.

Anne would need some convincing to make a deal, Paul knew, while everything was still up in the air.

Radin was the big problem. Fred's disappearance with all the cash meant Lufkin Realty would need to refinance quickly to avoid bankruptcy, which meant Radin couldn't be trusted not to sabotage a deal with the prospect of endless fees in a Chapter 11 and lots of work to give out to his accountants and lawyer buddies in the undertaking business.

Only Paul and Terry really needed a quick deal, but Paul had learned that the worst thing you could ever do was look desperate by making a second offer. Mike's constant attempts to settle had no doubt emboldened Fred.

The other mistake was to be reasonable in a negotiation. The reasonable party always got eaten alive. Paul offered to give Anne only the same amount Fred had stolen, which Morton, who was also in no hurry to settle, said was a non-starter.

Frank Mairone, already counting Terry's money, was anxious to settle but afraid Anne would use too partisan an attitude on his part to argue for his removal in favor of a more neutral executor, and was in any event now busy trying to repair the damage Fred had done.

The stalemate dragged on for weeks.

It was the old sharpie Mel Weinberg who solved Paul's problem. With Fred gone, he was left in the odd position, unique in his experience, of trying to figure out how to profit from the truth.

Paul was surprised to hear from him. "Mr. Weinberg, we shouldn't be talking. You're still a witness and we never finished your deposition."

"And you never will."

"So you called to say what?"

"I can win the case for you."

"Aren't you kind of locked in already?" Paul was wondering what the price was and assumed the call was being recorded.

"Well, maybe I had a brain cramp the day I testified. Or maybe Fred had one of his goons threaten me."

"Why would anybody believe it if you loosened up that cramp now?"

"Didn't say it would be me, Mr. Sageman."

"So there's another witness?"

"Forgot to ask that question, huh? It just so happens that I'm going to be in Claremont tomorrow. I'll meet you at the diner on Claremont Boulevard at

11:00." Weinberg hung up. If Weinberg had the goods Anne could be forced to settle out, but Weinberg had a price. The question was how to pay it without having to spend the contingent fee in the prison canteen. Mike would probably visit often.

Paul wished he could bring a witness but figured it would scare Mel off. Mel was fashionably late. They shook hands. "I imagine you're curious, Paul. That's a good trait and a bad trait. Play it smart here. Don't ask any questions, don't tell me what I testified to. Just listen."

Paul had spent his whole life listening. "Nother piece of advice – keep everyone on a need to know basis. Here's what you need to know. Your client and Mairone have gotta agree not to challenge the retainer agreement Fred signed for the company. Don't worry, Mairone agreed already. Love is a beautiful thing, don't cha think?" Paul who'd never been in love was prepared to agree. "Anyway, I'll give you a free sample. Bob absolutely believed Terry was two timing him and that's why he changed his will."

"And you…"

"No questions, remember? There's a witness heard him say it. Lovely lady, goes to church every Sunday, believes in heaven and hell, so she wouldn't lie if her life depended on it." Well at least it couldn't be a relative of Mel's for two very good reasons. "But she wouldn't say a word except on my say so." So it had to be someone in Mel's office. Mairone must have promised he would get Terry's agreement or Mel wouldn't be giving away so much. But why should this witness be believed? Still, it could be enough to get Anne to the table. "You got only one problem now.

Getting the DA to cut Anne loose." Did Weinberg have a plan for that too? "There's a man named Simon Thomas runs a PAC called AACC, out of Washington. Big John wants to run for Congress, they tell me. Course we want Anne to know she can't win the case first, then let her know what a good cause AACC is. So do we understand each other?"

Paul thought he understood. Anne would pay Big John off through AACC to get out from under the prosecution. Terry would pay Mel off by keeping him on retainer in exchange for the evidence that would force Anne to conclude that there was no possibility of winning the will contest and that ten million was a lot better deal than tin license plates.

Paul was sure Terry would go for it if Mairone said to. Maybe this was just the way things were done when that much money was involved. "Well I'll have to talk to my client." "Sure, sonny. Thanks for the coffee. Seems to me you must have learned enough about our legal system by now to see the value in the solution I'm offering you." Weinberg got up and left. Paul was still in a daze, calculating the fee on forty million dollars and wondering how much danger there was as he followed Weinberg out of the diner.

Right across the street was a Jaguar dealership. Paul decided to go in and ask for a test drive in a Vaanden Plas.

Six weeks later Big John let it be known that Anne Lufkin, regrettably could not be re-tried. The release of the tape, which a thorough investigation proved had not come from his office, simply made it impossible for Ms. Lufkin to get a fair trial. Within the month he had formed an exploratory committee for a Congressional campaign.

Days later Anne settled for ten million plus 33 percent of the net proceeds from the sale of Nikful's land in West Jersey after hearing Weinberg's secretary testify to the reasons her father changed his will.

Divorce lawyers were soon busy representing Frank Mairone and Paul. Paul was also being sued by Berry & French. He decided he was now a good enough lawyer to represent himself.

We all make mistakes.

Made in United States
North Haven, CT
14 March 2023

34093460R00200